THE DREAM-DETECTIVE

By Sax Rohmer

DOVER PUBLICATIONS, INC.
NEW YORK

CONTENTS

This Dover edition, first published in 1977, is an unabridged republication of the work as published by Jarrolds, Publishers, London, in 1926.

International Standard Book Number: 0-486-23504-1
Library of Congress Catalog Card Number: 77-077454

Manufactured in the United States of America
Dover Publications, Inc.
180 Varick Street, New York, N.Y. 10014

CASE OF THE TRAGEDIES IN THE GREEK ROOM

I

When did Moris Klaw first appear in London? It is a question which I am asked sometimes and to which I reply: To the best of my knowledge, shortly before the commencement of the strange happenings at the Menzies Museum.

What I know of him I have gathered from various sources; and in these papers, which represent an attempt to justify the methods of one frequently accused of being an insane theorist, I propose to recount all the facts which have come to my knowledge. In some few of the cases I was personally though slightly concerned; but regard me merely as the historian and on no account as the principal or even minor character in the story. My friendship with Martin Coram led, then, to my first meeting with Moris Klaw—a meeting which resulted in my becoming his biographer, inadequate though my information unfortunately remains.

It was some three months after the appointment of Coram to the curatorship of the Menzies Museum that the first of a series of singular occurrences took place there.

This occurrence befell one night in August, and the matter was brought to my ears by Coram himself on the following morning. I had, in fact, just taken my seat at the breakfast table, when he walked in unexpectedly and sank into an armchair. His dark, clean-shaven face looked more gaunt than usual and I saw, as he lighted the cigarette which I proffered, that his hand shook nervously.

"There's trouble at the Museum!" he said abruptly. "I want you to run around."

I looked at him for a moment without replying, and, knowing the responsibility of his position, feared that he referred to a theft from the collection.

"Something gone?" I asked.

"No; worse!" was his reply.

"What do you mean, Coram?"

He threw the cigarette, unsmoked, into the hearth. "You know

1

Conway?'' he said; "Conway, the night attendant. Well—he's dead!''

I stood up from the table, my breakfast forgotten, and stared incredulously. "Do you mean that he died in the night?'' I inquired.

"Yes. Done for, poor devil!''

"What! murdered?''

"Without a doubt, Searles! He's had his neck broken!''

I waited for no further explanations, but, hastily dressing, accompanied Coram to the Museum. It consists, I should mention, of four long, rectangular rooms, the windows of two overlooking South Grafton Square, those of the third giving upon the court that leads to the curator's private entrance, and the fourth adjoining an enclosed garden attached to the building. This fourth room is on the ground floor and is entered through the hall from the Square, the other three, containing the principal and more valuable exhibits, are upon the first floor and are reached by a flight of stairs from the hall. The remainder of the building is occupied by an office and the curator's private apartments, and is completely shut off from that portion open to the public, the only communicating door—an iron one—being kept locked.

The room described in the catalogue as the "Greek Room" proved to be the scene of the tragedy. This room is one of the two overlooking the Square and contains some of the finest items of the collection. The Museum is not open to the public until ten o'clock, and I found, upon arriving there, that the only occupants of the Greek Room were the commissionaire on duty, two constables, a plain-clothes officer and an inspector—that is, if I except the body of poor Conway.

He had not been touched, but lay as he was found by Beale, the commissionaire who took charge of the upper rooms during the day, and, indeed, it was patent that he was beyond medical aid. In fact, the position of his body was so extraordinary as almost to defy description.

There are three windows in the Greek Room, with wall-cases between, and, in the gap corresponding to the east window and just by the door opening into the next room, is a chair for the attendant. Conway lay downward on the polished floor with his limbs partly under this chair and his clenched fists thrust straight out before him. His head, turned partially to one side, was doubled underneath his breast in a most dreadful manner, indisputably pointing to a broken neck, and his commissionaire's cap lay some distance away, under a table supporting a heavy case of vases.

So much was revealed at a glance, and I immediately turned blankly to Coram.

"What do you make of it?" he said.

I shook my head in silence. I could scarce grasp the reality of the thing; indeed, I was still staring at the huddled figure when the doctor arrived. At his request we laid the dead man flat upon the floor, to facilitate an examination, and we then saw that he was greatly cut and bruised about the head and face, and that his features were distorted in a most extraordinary manner, almost as though he had been suffocated.

The doctor did not fail to notice this expression. "Made a hard fight of it!" he said. "He must have been in the last stages of exhaustion when his neck was broken!"

"My dear fellow!" cried Coram, somewhat irritably, "what do you mean when you say that he made a hard fight? There could not possibly have been any one else in these rooms last night!"

"Excuse me, sir!" said the inspector, "but there certainly was something going on here. Have you seen the glass case in the next room?"

"Glass case?" muttered Coram, running his hand distractedly through his thick black hair. "No; what of a glass case?"

"In here, sir," explained the inspector, leading the way into the adjoining apartment.

At his words, we all followed, and found that he referred to the glass front of a wall-case containing statuettes and images of Egyptian deities. The centre pane of this was smashed into fragments, the broken glass strewing the floor and the shelves inside the case.

"That looks like a struggle, sir, doesn't it?" said the inspector.

"Heaven help us! What does it mean?" groaned poor Coram. "Who could possibly have gained access to the building in the night, or, having done so, have quitted it again, when all the doors remained locked?"

"That we must try and find out!" replied the inspector. "Meanwhile, here are his keys. They lay on the floor in a corner of the Greek Room."

Coram took them, mechanically. "Beale," he said to the commissionaire, "see if any of the cases are unlocked."

The man proceeded to go around the rooms. He had progressed no further than the Greek Room when he made a discovery. "Here's the top of this unfastened, sir!" he suddenly cried excitedly.

We hurriedly joined him, to find that he stood before a marble pedestal surmounted by a thick glass case containing what Coram had frequently assured me was the gem of the collection—the Athenean Harp.

It was alleged to be of very ancient Greek workmanship and was constructed of fine gold, inlaid with jewels. It represented two reclining female figures—their arms thrown above their heads, their hands meeting; and several of the strings which were still intact were of incredibly fine gold wire. The instrument was said to have belonged to a Temple of Pallas in an extremely remote age, and at the time it was brought to light, much controversy had waged concerning its claims to authenticity, several connoisseurs proclaiming it the work of a famous goldsmith of medieval Florence, and nothing but a clever forgery. However, Greek or Florentine, amazingly ancient or comparatively modern, it was a beautiful piece of workmanship and of very great intrinsic value, apart from its artistic worth and unique character.

"I thought so!" said the plain-clothes man. "A clever museum thief!"

Coram sighed wearily. "My good fellow," he replied, "can you explain, by any earthly hypothesis, how a man could get into these apartments and leave them again, during the night?"

"Regarding that, sir," remarked the detective, "there are a few questions I should like to ask you. In the first place, at what time does the Museum close?"

"At six o'clock in the summer."

"What do you do when the last visitor has gone?"

"Having locked the outside door, Beale, here, thoroughly examines every room to make certain that no one remains concealed. He next locks the communicating doors and comes down into the hall. It was then his custom to hand me the keys. I gave them into poor Conway's keeping when he came on duty at half-past six, and every hour he went through the Museum, relocking all the doors behind him."

"I understand that there is a tell-tale watch in each room?"

"Yes. That in the Greek Room registers four a.m., so that it was about then that he met his death. He had evidently opened the door communicating with the next room—that containing the broken glass-case; but he did not touch the detector and the door was found open this morning."

"Some one must have lain concealed there and sprung upon him as he entered."

"Impossible! There is no other means of entrance or exit. The three windows are iron-barred and they have not been tampered with. Moreover, the watch shows that he was there at three o'clock, and nothing larger than a mouse could find shelter in the place; there is nowhere a man could hide.''

"Then the murderer followed him into the Greek Room."

"Might I venture to point out that, had he done so, he would have been there this morning when Beale arrived? The door of the Greek Room was locked and the keys were found inside upon the floor!"

"The thief might have had a duplicate set."

"Quite impossible; but, granting the impossible, how did he get in, since the hall door was bolted and barred?"

"We must assume that he succeeded in concealing himself before the Museum was closed."

"The assumption is not permissible, in view of the fact that Beale and I both examined the rooms last night prior to handing the keys to Conway. However, again granting the impossible, how did he get out?"

The Scotland Yard man removed his hat and mopped his forehead with his handkerchief. "I must say, sir, it is a very strange thing," he said; "but how about the iron door here?"

"It leads to my own apartments. I, alone, hold a key. It was locked."

A brief examination served to show that exit from any of the barred windows was impossible.

"Well, sir," said the detective, "if the man had keys he could have come down into the hall and the lower room."

"Step down and look," was Coram's invitation.

The windows of the room on the ground floor were also heavily protected, and it was easy to see that none of them had been opened.

"Upon my word," exclaimed the inspector, "it's uncanny! He couldn't have gone out by the hall door, because you say it was bolted and barred on the inside."

"It was," replied Coram.

"One moment, sir," interrupted the plain-clothes man. "If that was so, how did you get in this morning?"

"It was Beale's custom," said Coram, "to come around by the private entrance to my apartments. We then entered the Museum together by the iron door into the Greek Room and relieved Conway of the keys. There are several little matters to be attended to in the morning before admitting the public, and the other door is never unlocked before ten o'clock."

"Did you lock the door behind you when you came through this morning?"

"Immediately on finding poor Conway."

"Could any one have come through this door in the night, provided he had a duplicate key?"

"No. There is a bolt on the private side."

"And you were in your rooms all last night?"

"From twelve o'clock, yes."

The police looked at one another silently; then the inspector gave an embarrassed laugh. "Frankly, sir," he said, "I'm completely puzzled!"

We passed upstairs again and Coram turned to the doctor. "Anything else to report about poor Conway?" he asked.

"His face is all cut by the broken glass and he seems to have had a desperate struggle, although, curiously enough, his body bears no other marks of violence. The direct cause of death was, of course, a broken neck."

"And how should you think he came by it?"

"I should say that he was hurled upon the floor by an opponent possessing more than ordinary strength!"

Thus the physician, and was about to depart when there came a knocking upon the iron door.

"It is Hilda," said Coram, slipping the key in the lock—"my daughter," he added, turning to the detective.

II

The heavy door swinging open, there entered Hilda Coram, a slim, classical figure, with the regular features of her father and the pale gold hair of her dead mother. She looked unwell, and stared about her apprehensively.

"Good-morning, Mr. Searles," she greeted me. "Is it not dreadful about poor Conway!"—and then glanced at Coram. I saw that she held a card in her hand. "Father, there is such a singular old man asking to see you."

She handed the card to Coram, who in turn passed it to me. It was that of Douglas Glade of the *Daily Cable*, and had written upon it in Glade's hand the words—

"To introduce Mr. Moris Klaw."

"I suppose it is all right if Mr. Glade vouches for him," said Coram. "But does anybody here know Moris Klaw?"

"I do," replied the Scotland Yard man, smiling shortly. "He's an antique dealer or something of the kind; got a ramshackle old place by Wapping Old Stairs—sort of a cross between Jamrach's and a rag shop. He's lately been hanging about the Central Criminal Court a lot. Seems to fancy his luck as an amateur investigator. He's certainly smart," he added grudgingly; "but cranky."

"Ask Mr. Klaw to come through, Hilda," said Coram.

Shortly afterwards entered a strange figure. It was that of a tall man, who stooped; so that his apparent height was diminished. A very old man who carried his many years lightly, or a younger man prematurely aged. None could say which. His skin had the hue of dirty vellum, and his hair, his shaggy brows, his scanty beard were so toneless as to defy classification in terms of colour. He wore an archaic brown bowler, smart, gold-rimmed pince-nez and a black silk muffler. A long, caped black cloak completely enveloped the stooping figure; from beneath its mud-spattered edge peeped long-toed continental boots.

He removed his hat.

"Good-morning, Mr. Coram," he said. His voice reminded me of the distant rumbling of empty casks; his accent was wholly indescribable. "Good-morning" (to the detective), "Mr. Grimsby. Good-morning, Mr. Searles. Your friend, Mr. Glade, tells me I shall find you here. Good-morning, Inspector. To Miss Coram I already have said good-morning."

From the lining of the flat-topped hat he took out one of those small cylindrical scent-sprays and played its contents upon his high, bald brow. An odour of verbena filled the air. He replaced the spray in the hat, the hat upon his scantily thatched crown.

"There is here a smell of dead men!" he explained.

"I turned aside to hide my smiles, so grotesque was my first impression of the amazing individual known as Moris Klaw.

"Mr. Coram," he continued, "I am an old fool who sometimes has wise dreams. Crime has been the hobby of a busy life. I have seen crime upon the Gold Coast, where the black fever it danced in the air above the murdered one like a lingering soul, and I have seen blood flow in Arctic Lapland, where it was frozen up into red ice almost before it left the veins. Have I your permit to see if I can help?"

All of us, the police included, were strangely impressed now.

"Certainly," said Coram; "will you step this way?"

Moris Klaw bent over the dead man.

"You have moved him!" he said sharply.

It was explained that this had been for the purpose of a medical examination. He nodded absently. With the aid of a large magnifying-glass he was scrutinising poor Conway. He examined his hair, his eyes, his hands, his finger-nails. He rubbed long, flexible fingers upon the floor beside the body—and sniffed at the dust.

"Some one so kindly will tell me all about it," he said, turning out the dead man's pockets.

Coram briefly recounted much of the foregoing, and replied to the oddly chosen questions which from time to time Moris Klaw put to him. Throughout the duologue, the singular old man conducted a detailed search of every square inch, I think, of the Greek Room. Before the case containing the harp he stood, peering.

"It is here that the trouble centres," he muttered. "What do I know of such a Grecian instrument? Let me think."

He threw back his head, closing his eyes.

"Such valuable curios," he rumbled, "have histories—and the crimes they occasion operate in cycles." He waved his hand in a slow circle. "If I but knew the history of this harp! Mr. Coram!"

He glanced towards my friend.

"Thoughts are things, Mr. Coram. If I might spend a night here —upon the very spot of floor where the poor Conway fell—I could from the surrounding atmosphere (it is a sensitive plate) recover a picture of the thing in his mind"—indicating Conway—"at the last!"

The Scotland Yard man blew down his nose.

"You snort, my friend," said Moris Klaw, turning upon him. "You would snort less if you had waked screaming, out in the desert; screaming out with fear of the dripping beaks of the vultures—the last, dreadful fear which the mind had known of him who had died of thirst upon that haunted spot!"

The words and the manner of their delivery thrilled us all.

"What is it," continued the weird old man, "but the odic force, the ether—say it how you please—which carries the wireless message, the lightning? It is a huge, subtle, sensitive plate. Inspiration, what you call bad luck and good luck—all are but reflections from it. The supreme thought preceding death is imprinted on the surrounding atmosphere like a photograph. I have trained this"— he tapped his brow—"to reproduce those photographs! May I sleep here to-night, Mr. Coram?"

Somewhere beneath the ramshackle exterior we had caught a glimpse of a man of power. From behind the thick pebbles momentarily had shone out the light of a tremendous and original mind.

"I should be most glad of your assistance," answered my friend.

"No police must be here to-night," rumbled Moris Klaw. "No

heavy-footed constables, filling the room with thoughts of large cooks and small Basses, must fog my negative!"

"Can that be arranged?" asked Coram of the inspector.

"The men on duty can remain in the hall, if you wish it, sir."

"Good!" rumbled Moris Klaw.

He moistened his brow with verbena, bowed uncouthly, and shuffled from the Greek Room.

III

Moris Klaw reappeared in the evening, accompanied by a strikingly beautiful brunette.

The change of face upon the part of Mr. Grimsby of New Scotland Yard was singular.

"My daughter—Isis," explained Moris Klaw. "She assists to develop my negatives."

Grimsby became all attention. Leaving two men on duty in the hall, Moris Klaw, his daughter, Grimsby, Coram and I went up to the Greek Room. Its darkness was relieved by a single lamp.

"I've had the stones in the Athenean Harp examined by a lapidary," said Coram. "It occurred to me that they might have been removed and paste substituted. It was not so, however."

"No," rumbled Klaw. "I thought of that, too. No visitors have been admitted here during the day?"

"The Greek Room has been closed."

"It is well, Mr. Coram. Let no one disturb me until my daughter comes in the morning."

Isis Klaw placed a red silk cushion upon the spot where the dead man had lain.

"Some pillows and a blanket, Mr. Klaw?" suggested the suddenly attentive Mr. Grimsby.

"I thank you, no," was the reply. "They would be saturated with alien impressions. My cushion it is odically sterilised! The 'etheric storm' created by Conway's last mental emotion reaches my brain unpolluted. Good-night, gentlemen. Good-night, Isis!"

We withdrew, leaving Moris Klaw to his ghostly vigil.

"I suppose Mr. Klaw is quite trustworthy?" whispered Coram to the detective.

"Oh, undoubtedly!" was the reply. "In any case, he can do no harm. My men will be on duty downstairs here all night."

"Do you speak of my father, Mr. Grimsby?" came a soft, thrilling voice.

Grimsby turned—and met the flashing black eyes of Isis Klaw.

"I was assuring Mr. Coram," he answered readily, "that Mr. Klaw's methods have several times proved successful!"

"Several times!" she cried scornfully. "What! has he ever failed?"

Her accent was certainly French, I determined; her voice, her entire person, as certainly charming—to which the detective's manner bore witness.

"I'm afraid I'm not familiar with all his cases, miss," he said. "Can I call you a cab?"

"I thank you, no." She rewarded him with a dazzling smile. "Good-night."

Coram opened the doors of the Museum, and she passed out. Leaving the men on duty in the hall, Coram and I shortly afterwards also quitted the Museum by the main entrance, in order to avoid disturbing Moris Klaw by using the curator's private door.

To my friend's study, Hilda Coram brought us coffee. She was unnaturally pale, and her eyes were feverishly bright. I concluded that the tragedy was responsible.

"Perhaps, to an extent," said Coram; "but she is studying music, and I fear overworking in order to pass a stiff exam."

Coram and I surveyed the Greek Room problem from every conceivable standpoint; but were unable to surmise how the thief had entered, how left, and why he had fled without his booty.

"I don't mind confessing," said Coram, "that I am very ill at ease. We haven't the remotest idea how the murderer got into the Greek Room nor how he got out again. Bolts and bars, it is evident, do not prevail against him, so that we may expect a repetition of the dreadful business at any time!"

"What precautions do you propose to take?"

"Well, there will be a couple of police on duty in the Museum for the next week or so, but, after that, we shall have to rely upon a night watchman. The funds only allow of the appointment of four attendants: three for day and one for night duty."

"Do you think you'll find any difficulty in getting a man?"

"No," replied Coram. "I know of a steady man who will come as soon as we are ready for him."

I slept but little that night, and was early afoot and around to the Museum. Isis Klaw was there before me, carrying the red cushion, and her father was deep in conversation with Coram.

Detective-Inspector Grimsby approached me.

"I see you're looking at the cushion, sir!" he said, smilingly. "But it's not a 'plant.' He's not an up-to-date cracksman. Nothing's missing!"

"You need not assure me of that," I replied. "I do not doubt Mr. Klaw's honesty of purpose."

"Wait till you hear his mad theory, though!" he said, with a glance aside at the girl.

"Mr. Coram," Moris Klaw was saying, in his odd, rumbling tones, "my psychic photograph is of a woman! A woman dressed all in white!"

Grimsby coughed—then flushed as he caught the eye of Isis.

"Poor Conway's mind," continued Klaw, "is filled with such a picture when he breathes his last—great wonder he has for the white woman and great fear for the Athenean Harp, which she carries!"

"Which she carries!" cried Coram.

"Some woman took the harp from its case a few minutes before Conway died!" affirmed Moris Klaw. "I have much research to make now, and with aid from Isis shall develop my negative! Yesterday I learnt from the constable who was on night duty at the corner of the Square that a heavy pantechnicon van went driving round at four o'clock. It was shortly after four o'clock that the tragedy occurred. The driver was unaware that there was no way out, you understand. Is it important? I cannot say. It often is such points that matter. We must, however, waste no time. Until you hear from me again you will lay dry plaster-of-Paris all around the stand of the Athenean Harp each night. Good-morning, gentlemen!"

His arm linked in his daughter's, he left the Museum.

IV

For some weeks after this mysterious affair, all went well at the Menzies Museum. The new night watchman, a big Scot, by name John Macalister, seemed to have fallen thoroughly into his duties, and everything was proceeding smoothly. No clue concerning the previous outrage had come to light, the police being clearly at a loss. From Moris Klaw we heard not a word. But Macalister did not appear to suffer from nervousness, saying that he was quite big enough to look after himself.

Poor Macalister! His bulk did not save him from a dreadful fate. He was found, one fine morning, lying flat on his back in the Greek Room—*dead!*

As in the case of Conway, the place showed unmistakable signs of a furious struggle. The attendant's chair had been dashed upon the floor with such violence as to break three of the legs; a bust of Pallas, that had occupied a corner position upon a marble pedestal, was found to be hurled down; and the top of the case which usually contained the Athenean Harp had been unlocked, and the priceless antique lay close by, upon the floor!

The cause of death, in Macalister's case, was heart-failure, an unsuspected weakness of that organ being brought to light at the inquest; but, according to the medical testimony, deceased must have undergone unnaturally violent exertions to bring death about. In other respects, the circumstances of the two cases were almost identical. The door of the Greek Room was locked upon the inside and the keys were found on the floor. From the detector watches in the other rooms it was evident that his death must have taken place about three o'clock. Nothing was missing, and the jewels in the harp had not been tampered with.

But, most amazing circumstance of all, imprinted upon the dry plaster-of-Paris which, in accordance with the instructions of the mysteriously absent Moris Klaw, had nightly been placed around the case containing the harp, *were the marks of little bare feet!*

A message sent, through the willing agency of Inspector Grimsby, to the Wapping abode of the old curio dealer, resulted in the discovery that Moris Klaw was abroad. His daughter, however, reported having received a letter from her father which contained the words—

"Let Mr. Coram keep the key of the case containing the Athenean Harp under his pillow at night."

"What does she mean?" asked Coram. "That I am to detach that particular key from the bunch or place them all beneath my pillow?"

Grimsby shrugged his shoulders.

"I'm simply telling you what she told me, sir."

"I should suspect the man to be an imposter," said Coram, "if it were not for the extraordinary confirmation of his theory furnished by the footprints. They certainly looked like those of a woman!"

Remembering how Moris Klaw had acted, I sought out the constable who had been on duty at the corner of South Grafton Square on the night of the second tragedy. From him I elicited a fact which, though insignificant in itself, was, when associated with another circumstance, certainly singular.

A Pickford traction-engine, drawing two heavy wagons, had been driven round the Square at three a.m., the driver thinking that he could get out on the other side.

That was practically all I learned from the constable, but it served to set me thinking. Was it merely a coincidence that, at almost the exact hour of the previous tragedy, a heavy pantechnicon had passed the Museum?

"It's not once in six months," the man assured me, "that any vehicle but a tradesman's cart goes round the Square. You see, it doesn't lead anywhere, but this Pickford chap he was rattling by before I could stop him, and though I shouted he couldn't hear me, the engine making such a noise, so I just let him drive round and find out for himself."

I now come to the event which concluded this extraordinary case, and, that it may be clearly understood, I must explain the positions which we took up during the nights of the following week; for Coram had asked me to take a night watch, with himself, Grimsby and Beale, in the Museum.

Beale, the commissionaire, remained in the hall and lower room—it was catalogued as the "Bronze Room"—Coram patrolled the room at the top of the stairs, Grimsby the next, or Greek, Room, and I the Egyptian Room. None of the doors were locked, and Grimsby, by his own special request, held the keys of the cases in the Greek Room.

We commenced our vigil on the Saturday, and I, for one, found it a lugubrious business. One electric lamp was usually left burning in each apartment throughout the night, and I sat as near to that in the Egyptian Room as possible and endeavoured to distract my thoughts with a bundle of papers with which I had provided myself.

In the next room I could hear Grimsby walking about incessantly, and, at regular intervals, the scratching of a match as he lighted a cigar. He was an inveterate cheroot smoker.

Our first night's watching, then, was productive of no result, and the five that followed were equally monotonous.

Upon Grimsby's suggestion we observed great secrecy in the matter of these dispositions. Even Coram's small household was kept in ignorance of this midnight watching. Grimsby, following out some theory of his own, now determined to dispense altogether with light in the Greek Room. Friday was intensely hot, and occasional fitful breezes brought with them banks of black thundercloud, which, however, did not break; and, up to the time that we assumed our posts at the Museum, no rain had fallen. At about twelve o'clock I looked out into South Grafton Square and saw that the sky was entirely obscured by a heavy mass of inky cloud, ominous of a gathering storm.

Returning to my chair beneath the electric lamp, I took up a work of Mark Twain's, which I had brought as a likely antidote to melancholy or nervousness. As I commenced to read, for the twentieth time, *The Jumping Frog*, I heard the scratch of Grimsby's match in the next room and knew that he had lighted his fifth cigar.

It must have been about one o'clock when the rain came. I heard the big drops on the glass roof, followed by the steady pouring of the deluge. For perhaps five minutes it rained steadily, and then ceased as abruptly as it had begun. Above the noise of the water rushing down the metal gutters, I distinctly detected the sound of Grimsby striking another match. Then, with a mighty crash, came the thunder.

Directly above the Museum it seemed as though the very heavens had burst, and the glass roof rattled as if a shower of stones had fallen, the thunderous report echoing and reverberating hollowly through the building.

As the lightning flashed with dazzling brilliance, I started from my chair and stood, breathless, with every sense on the alert; for, strangely intermingling with the patter of the rain that now commenced to fall again, came a low wailing, like nothing so much as the voice of a patient succumbing to an anesthetic. There was something indefinably sweet, but indescribably weird, in the low and mysterious music.

Not knowing from whence it proceeded, I stood undetermined what to do; but, just as the thunder boomed again, I heard a wild cry—undoubtedly proceeding from the Greek Room! Springing to the door, I threw it open.

All was in darkness, but, as I entered, a vivid flash of lightning illuminated the place.

I saw a sight which I can never forget. Grimsby lay flat upon the floor by the further door. But, dreadful as that spectacle was, it scarce engaged my attention; nor did I waste a second glance upon the Athenean Harp, which lay close beside its empty case.

For the figure of a woman, draped in flimsy white, was passing across the Greek Room!

Grim fear took me by the throat—since I could not doubt that what I saw was a supernatural manifestation. Darkness followed. I heard a loud wailing cry and a sound as of a fall.

Then Coram came running through the Greek Room.

Trembling violently, I joined him; and together we stood looking down at Grimsby.

"Good God!" whispered Coram; "this is awful. It cannot be the work of mortal hands! Poor Grimsby is dead!"

"Did you—see—the woman?" I muttered. I will confess it: my courage had completely deserted me.

He shook his head; but, as Beale came running to join us, glanced fearfully into the shadows of the Greek Room. The storm seemed to have passed, and, as we three frightened men stood around Grimsby's recumbent body, we could almost hear the beating of each other's hearts.

Suddenly, giving a great start, Coram clutched my arm. "Listen!" he said. "What's that?"

I held my breath and listened. "It's the thunder in the distance," said Beale.

"You are wrong," I answered. "It is some one knocking at the hall entrance! There goes the bell, now!"

Coram gave a sigh of relief. "Heavens!" he said; "I've no nerves left! Come on and see who it is."

The three of us, keeping very close together, passed quickly through the Greek Room and down into the hall. As the ringing continued, Coram unbolted the door...and there, on the steps, stood Moris Klaw!

Some vague idea of his mission flashed through my mind. "You are too late!" I cried. "Grimsby has gone!"

I saw a look of something like anger pass over his large pale features, and then he had darted past us and vanished up the stairs.

V

Having rebolted the door, we rejoined Moris Klaw in the Greek Room. He was kneeling beside Grimsby in the dim light—and Grimsby, his face ghastly pale, was sitting up and drinking from a flask!

"I am in time!" said Moris Klaw. "He has only fainted!"

"It was the ghost!" whispered the Scotland Yard man. "My God! I'm prepared for anything human—but when the lightning came and I saw that white thing...playing the harp..."

Coram turned aside and was about to pick up the harp, which lay upon the floor near, when—

"Ah!" cried Moris Klaw, "do not touch it! It is death!"

Coram started back as though he had been stung as Grimsby very unsteadily got upon his feet.

"Turn up lights," directed Moris Klaw, "and I will show you!"

The curator went out to the switchboard and the Greek Room became brightly illuminated. The ramshackle figure of Moris Klaw seemed to be invested with triumphant majesty. Behind the pebbles his eyes gleamed.

"Observe," he said, "I raise the harp from the floor." He did so. "And I live. For why? Because I do not take hold upon it in a natural manner—*by the top!* I take it by the side! Conway and Macalister took hold upon it at the top; and where are they—Conway and Macalister?"

"Mr. Klaw," said Coram. "I cannot doubt that this black business is all clear to your very unusual intelligence; but to me it is a profound mystery. I have, myself, in the past, taken up the harp in the way you describe as fatal, and without injury——"

"But not immediately after it had been played upon!" interrupted Moris Klaw.

"Played upon! I have never attempted to play upon it!"

"Even had you done so you might yet have escaped, provided you *set it down* before touching the top part! Note, please!"

He ran his long white fingers over the golden strings. Instantly there stole upon my ears that weird, wailing music which had heralded the strange happenings of the night!

"And now," continued our mentor, "whilst I who am cunning hold it where the ladies' gold feet join, observe the top—where the hand would in ordinary rest in holding it."

We gathered around him.

"A *needle-point*," he rumbled impressively, "protruding! The player touches it not! But who takes it from the hand of the player *dies!* By placing the harp again upon its base the point again retires! Shall I say what is upon that point, to drive a man mad like a dog with rabies, to stay potent for generations? I cannot. It is a secret buried with the ugly body of Caesar Borgia!"

"Caesar Borgia!" we cried in chorus.

"Ah!" rumbled Moris Klaw, "your Athenean Harp was indeed made by Paduano Zelloni, the Florentine! It is a clever forge! I have been in Rome until yesterday. You are surprised? I am sorry; for the poor Macalister died. Having perfected, with the aid of Isis, my mind photograph of the lady who plays the harp, I go to Rome to perfect the story of the harp. For why? At my house I have records, but incomplete, useless. In Rome I have a friend, of so old a family, and once so wicked, I shall not name it!

"He has recourse to the great Vatican Library—to the annals of his race. There he finds me an account of such a harp. In those priceless parchments it is called 'a Greek lyre of gold.' It is described. I am convinced. I am sure!

"Once the beautiful Lucrece Borgia play upon this harp. To one who is distasteful to her she says: 'Replace for me my harp.' He does so. He is a dead man! God! what cleverness!

"Where has it lain for generations before your Sir Menzies find it? No man knows. But it has still its virtues! How did the poor Menzies die? Throw himself from his room window, I recently learn. This harp certainly was in his room. Conway, after dashing, mad, about the place, springs head downward from the attendant's chair. Macalister dies in exhaustion and convulsions!"

A silence: when—

"What caused the harp to play?" asked Coram.

Moris Klaw looked hard at him. Then a thrill of new horror ran through my veins. A low moan came from somewhere hard by! Coram turned in a flash!

"Why, my private door is open!" he whispered.

"Where do you keep your private keys?" rumbled Klaw.

"In my study." Coram was staring at the open door, but seemed afraid to approach it. "We have been using the attendant's keys at night. My own are on my study mantelpiece now."

"I think not," continued the thick voice. "Your daughter has them!"

"My daughter!" cried Coram, and sprang to the open door. "Heavens! Hilda! Hilda!"

"She is somnambulistic!" whispered Moris Klaw in my ear. "When certain unusual sounds—such as heavy vehicles at night— reach her in her sleep (ah! how little we know of the phenomenon of sleep!), she arises, and, in common with many sleep-walkers, always acts the same. Something, in the case of Miss Hilda, attracts her to the golden harp——"

"She is studying music!"

"She must rest from it. Her brain is overwrought! She unlocks the case and strikes the cords of the harp, relocking the door, replacing the keys—I before have known such cases—then retires as she came. Who takes the harp from her hands, or raises it, if she has laid it down upon its side, dies! These dead attendants were brave fellows both, for, hearing the music, they came running, saw how the matter was, and did not waken the sleeping player. Conway was poisoned as he returned the harp to its case; Macalister, as he took it up from where it lay. Something to-night awoke her ere she could relock the door. The fright of so awaking made her to swoon.''

Coram's kindly voice and the sound of a girl sobbing affrightedly reached us.

''It was my yell of fear, Mr. Klaw!'' said Grimsby shamefacedly. ''She looked like a ghost!''

''I understand,'' rumbled Moris Klaw soothingly. ''As I see her in my sleep she is very awesome! I will show you the picture Isis has made from my etheric photograph. I saw it, finished, earlier to-night. It confirmed me that the Miss Hilda with the harp in her hand was poor Conway's last thought in life!''

''Mr. Klaw,'' said Grimsby earnestly, ''you are a very remarkable man!''

''Yes?'' he rumbled, and gingerly placed in its case the ''Greek lyre of gold'' which Paduano Zelloni had wrought for Caesar Borgia.

From the brown hat he took out his scent-spray, and squirted verbena upon his heated forehead.

''That harp,'' he explained, ''it smells of dead men!''

CASE OF THE POTSHERD OF ANUBIS,

In examining the mass of material which I have collated respecting Moris Klaw, several outstanding facts strike me, as being worthy of some special notice.

For instance, an unusual number of the cases in which he was concerned centred about curios and relics of various kinds. His personal tastes (he was, I think, primarily, an antiquarian) may have led him to examine such cases in preference to others. Then again, no two of his acquaintances agree upon the point of Moris Klaw's actual identity and personality. He was a master of disguise; and the grand secret of his life was one which he jealously guarded from all.

But was the Moris Klaw who kept the curio-shop in Wapping the real Moris Klaw? And to what extent did he believe in those psychical phenomena upon which professedly his methods were based? As particularly bearing upon this phase of the matter, I have selected, for narration here, the story of the potsherd.

Since the Boswell, in records of this kind, has often appeared, to my mind, to overshadow the Johnson, I have decided to present this episode in the words of Mr. J.E. Wilson Clifford, electrical engineer, of Copthall House, Copthall Avenue, E.C., to whom I am indebted for a full and careful account. I do not think I could improve upon his paper, and my own views might unduly intrude upon the story; therefore, with your permission, I will vacate the rostrum in favour of Mr. Clifford, for whom I solicit your attention.

I

MR. CLIFFORD'S STORY OF THE EGYPTIAN POTSHERD

During the autumn of 19__, I was sharing a pleasant set of rooms with Mark Lesty, who was shortly taking up an appointment at a London hospital, and it was, I think, about the middle of that month, that the extraordinary affair of Halesowen and his Egyptian potsherd came under our notice.

Our rooms (they were in a south-west suburb) overlooked a fine expanse of Common. Halesowen rented a flat commanding a similar prospect; and, at the time of which I write, he had but recently returned from a protracted visit to Egypt.

Halesowen was a tall, fair man, clean-shaven, very fresh coloured and wearing his hair cropped close to his head. He was well travelled, and no mean antiquary. He lived entirely by himself; and Lesty and I frequently spent the evening at his place, which was a veritable museum of curiosities. I distinctly recall the first time that he showed us his latest acquisitions.

Both the windows were wide open and the awning fluttered in the slight breeze. Dusk was just descending, and we sat looking out over the Common and puffing silently at our briars. We had been examining the relics that Halesowen had brought back from the land of the Pharaohs, the one, I remember, which had most impressed me, tyro that I was, being the mummy of a sacred cat from Bubastis.

"It wouldn't have been worth bringing back only for the wrapping," Halesowen assured me. "This, now, is really unique."

The object referred to was a broken pot or vase, upon which he pointed out a number of hieroglyphics and a figure with the head of a jackal. "A potsherd inscribed with the figure of Anubis," he explained. "Very valuable."

"Why?" Lesty inquired, in his lazy way.

"Well," Halesowen replied, "the characters of the inscription are of a kind entirely unfamiliar to me. I believe them to be a sort of secret writing, possibly peculiar to some brotherhood. I am risking expert opinion, although in every sense, I stole the thing!"

"How's that?" I asked.

"Well, Professor Sheraton—you'll see his name on a row of cases in the B.M.—excavated it. But it's a moral certainty he didn't intend to advise the authorities of his find. He was going to smuggle it out of Egypt into his private collection. I had marked the spot where he found it for inquiries of my own. This dishonest old fossil—"

Lesty laughed.

"Oh! my own motives weren't above suspicion! But any way the Professor anticipated me. Accordingly, I employed one Ali, a distinguished member of a family of thieves, to visit the learned gentleman's tent! Cutting the story—there's the pot!"

"Here! I say!" drawled Lesty. "You'll come to a bad end, young fellow!"

"The position is a peculiar one," replied Halesowen, smiling. "Neither of us had any legal claim to the sherd—whilst we were upon Egyptian territory. Therefore, even if the Professor learnt that I had the thing—and he may suspect—he couldn't prosecute me!"

"Devilish high-handed!" commented Lesty.

"Yes. But remember we were well off the map—miles away from Cook's route. The possession of this potsherd ought to make a man's reputation—any man who knows a bit about the subject. Curiously enough, a third party had had his eye upon the place where this much-sought sherd was found. And in some mysterious fashion he tumbled to the fact that it had fallen into *my* hands. He made a sort of veiled offer of a hundred pounds for it. I refused, but ran across him again, a week or so later, in Cairo, and he raised his price to two hundred."

"That's strange," I said. "Who was he?"

"Called himself Zeda—Dr. Louis Zeda. He quite lost his temper when I declined to sell, and I've not set eyes on him since."

He relocked the fragment in his cabinet, and we lapsed into silence, to sit gazing meditatively across the Common, picturesque in the dim autumn twilight.

"By the way, Halesowen," I said, "I see that the flat next door, same floor as this, is to let."

"That's so," he replied. "Why don't you men take it?"

"We'll think about it," yawned Lesty, stretching his long limbs. "Might look over it in the morning."

The following day we viewed the vacant flat, but found, upon inquiry of the agent, that it had already been let. However, as our own rooms suited us very well, we were not greatly concerned. Just as we finished dinner the same evening, Halesowen came in, and, without preamble, plunged into a surprising tale of uncanny happenings at his place.

"Take it slow," said Lesty. "You say it was after we came away?"

"About an hour after," replied Halesowen. "I had brought out the potsherd, and had it in the wooden stand on the table before me. I was copying the hieroglyphics, which are unusual, and had my reading-lamp burning only, the rest of the room being consequently in shadow. I was sitting with my back to the windows, facing the door, so no one could possibly have entered the room unseen by me. It was as I bent down to scrutinise a badly defaced character that I felt a queer sensation stealing over me, as though some one were standing close behind my chair, watching me!"

"Very common," explained Lesty; "merely nerves."

"Yes, I know; but not what followed. The sensation became so pronounced, that I stood up. No one was in the room. I determined to take a stroll, concluding that the fresh air would clear these uncanny cobwebs out of my brain. Accordingly, I extinguished the lamp and went out. I was just putting my cap on, when something prompted me to return and lock up the potsherd."

He fixed his eyes upon us with an expression of doubt.

"There was some one, or something, in the room!"

"What do you mean!" asked Lesty incredulously.

"I quite distinctly saw a hand and bare white arm pass away from the table—and vanish! It was dark in the room, remember; but I could see the arm well enough. I switched on the reading-lamp. Not a thing was to be seen. There was no one in the room and no one but myself in the flat, for I searched it thoroughly!"

Some moments of silence followed this remarkable story, and I sat watching Lesty, who, in turn was regarding Halesowen with the stolid, vacant stare which sometimes served to conceal the working of his keen brain.

"Pity you didn't let us know sooner," he said, rising slowly to his feet. "This is interesting."

II

Halesowen's nerves evidently had been shaken by the inexplicable incident. As the three of us strode across the corner of the Common, he informed us that the new tenant of the adjoining flat had moved in. "I have been away all day," he said; "but the stuff was bundled in some time during the afternoon."

We proceeded upstairs and into the cosy room which had been the scene of the remarkable occurrence related. As it was growing dark, Halesowen turned on the electric light, and, indicating a chair by the writing table, explained that it was there he had been seated at that time.

"Did you have the windows open?" asked Lesty.

"Yes," was the reply. "I left the chairs and the awning out, too, as it was a fine night; in fact, you can see that they still remain practically as you left them."

"When you returned, and saw, or thought you saw, the hand and arm—you would have to pass around to this side of the table in order to reach the lamp?"

"Yes."

Apparently Lesty was about to make some observation, when an interruption occurred, in the form of a ringing on the door bell, followed by a discreet fandango on the knocker.

"Who the deuce have we here!" muttered Halesowen. "I saw no one go in below."

As our host passed through the lighted room and into the hall, my friend and I both leant forward in our chairs, the better to hear what should pass; nor were we kept long in suspense, for, as we heard the outer door opened, an odd, rumbling voice came, with a queer accent:

"Ah, my dear Mr. Halesowen, it is indeed an intrusion of me! But when I find how we are neighbours I cannot resist to make the call and renew a so pleasant acquaintance!"

"Dr. Zeda!" we heard Halesowen exclaim, with little cordiality.

"Ever your devoted servant!" replied the courteous foreigner.

I glanced at Lesty, and we rose together and stepped through the open window in time to see a truly remarkable personage enter.

This was a large-framed man, with snow-white hair cut close to his skull, French fashion. He had a high and very wrinkled brow and wore gold-rimmed pince-nez. Jet black and heavy eyebrows were his, and his waxed moustache, his neat imperial, were likewise of the hue of coal. His complexion was pallid; and in his well-cut frock-coat, with a loose black tie overhanging his vest, he made a striking picture, standing bowing profoundly in the doorway.

Halesowen rapidly muttered the usual formalities; in fact, I remember mentally contrasting our friend's unceremonious manners with the courtly deportment of Dr. Zeda.

The latter explained that he had taken the adjacent flat, only learning, that evening, whom he had for a neighbour, and, despite the lateness of the hour, he said, he could not resist the desire to see Halesowen, of whose company in Egypt he retained such pleasant memories. Allowing for his effusiveness, there was nothing one could take exception to in his behaviour, and I rather wondered at the brusque responses of our usually polite host.

When, after a brief chat, the foreign gentleman rose to take his leave, he extended an invitation to all of us to lunch with him on the following day. "My place is in somewhat disorder," he said, smiling, "but you are Bohemian, like myself, and will not care!"

Though I half expected that Halesowen would decline, he did not do so; I, therefore, also accepted, as did Lesty. Whereupon, Zeda departed.

Halesowen, returning to the chair which he had vacated to usher out his visitor, lighted a cigarette, regarded it for a moment, meditatively, and then frankly expressed his doubts.

"He's been watching me!" he said; "and when he saw the next flat vacant he jumped at the chance."

"My dear chap," I retorted, "he must be very keen on securing your potsherd if he is prepared to take and furnish a flat next door to you simply with a view to keeping an eye on it!"

"You have no idea how anxious he is," he assured me. "If you had seen his face, in Cairo, when I flatly declined to sell, you would be better able to understand."

"Why not sell, then?"

"I'm dashed if I do!" said Halesowen stubbornly.

On the following day we lunched with Dr. Zeda, and were surprised at the orderly state of his establishment. Everything, from floor to ceiling, was in its proper place.

"It hasn't taken you long to get things straight," commented Lesty.

"Ah, no," replied the other. "These big firms they do it all in a day if you insist—and I insist, see?"

I thoroughly enjoyed my visit, for he proved an excellent host, and I think even Lesty grew less suspicious of him. During the weeks that followed, the doctor came several times to our rooms, and we frequently met at Halesowen's. The latter, who boldly had submitted photographs and drawings of the sherd to the British Museum, experienced no repetition of the mysterious phenomenon already described. Then, about seven o'clock one morning, when the mists hung low over the Common in promise of a hot day, a boy came for Lesty and myself with news of a fresh development. He was a lad who did odd jobs for Halesowen, and he brought word of an attempted burglary, together with a request that we should go over without delay.

Our curiosity keenly aroused, we were soon with our friend, and found him seated in the familiar room, before a large cabinet, with double glass doors, which, as was clearly evident, had been hastily ransacked. Other cases in which he kept various curios were also opened, and the place was in general disorder.

"What's gone?" asked Lesty, quickly.

"Nothing!" was the answer. "The potsherd is in the safe, and the safe is in my bedroom—or perhaps something might have gone!"

"You lock it up at night, then? I thought you kept it in the cabinet."

"Only during the day. It goes in the safe, with one or two other trifles, at night; but *everybody* doesn't know that!"

We looked at one another, silently; but the name that was on all our lips remained unspoken—for we were startled by a loud knocking and ringing at the door. Carter opening it, into the room ran Dr. Zeda!

"Oh, my dear friends!" he cried, in his hoarse, rumbling voice, "there has been to my flat a midnight robber! He has turned completely upside-down all my collections!"

Lesty coughed loudly; but, as I turned my head to look at him, his face was quite expressionless. Halesowen seemed stricken dumb by surprise; whilst, for my own part, as I watched the foreigner staring about the disordered room, and noted the growing look of bewilderment creeping over his pallid countenance, I was compelled to admit to myself that here was either a consummate actor or a man of whom we hastily had formed a most unwarrantable opinion.

"But, my friend—my good Halesowen," he exclaimed, with widely opened eyes and extended palms—"what is it that I see? You are as disordered as myself!"

Halesowen nodded. "The burglar gave me a call, too!" he said, grimly.

"My dear sir!" gasped Zeda, seizing the speaker's arm—"tell me quickly—you have lost nothing?"

Halesowen glanced at him rather hard. "No," he answered.

"Ah, what a relief! I feared," rumbled the doctor. "But perhaps you wonder for what it is they came?"

"I can guess!"

"You need no longer to guess; I will tell you. It is for your fragment of the sacred vase, and to me they come for mine!"

We were even more astonished by this assertion than we had been by the doctor's first. "*Your* fragment!" said Halesowen, slowly, with his eyes fixed on Zeda—"to what fragment do you refer?"

"To that which, together with your potsherd, makes up the complete vase! But you doubt?" he suggested, shrugging his shoulders. "Wait but for a moment and I will prove!"

He moved from the room; his gait had a mincing awkwardness,

quite indescribable; and we heard his retreating, heavy footsteps as he passed downstairs. Then we stood and gaped at one another. "His confounded ingenuity," rapped Halesowen, "has completely tied my hands."

Being interrupted, at this moment, by the re-entrance of the gentleman in question, further discussion of the subject was precluded. Zeda carried a small iron box, which he placed carefully upon the table and unlocked. A second box of polished ebony was revealed within, and this being unlocked in turn, was proved to contain, reposing in a nest of blue velvet, a fragment of antique pottery. Taking the fragment in his hand, the doctor begged that the potsherd be produced.

Halesowen, after a momentary hesitation, retired from the room, to return almost immediately with the broken vase in its wooden frame. Dr. Zeda, placing the portion which he held in his hand against that in the frame, but not so closely as to bring the parts in contact, turned to us with a triumphant smile. "They correspond, gentlemen, to a smallest fraction!" he declared; which, indeed, was perfectly true.

"And now," continued Zeda, evidently gratified by the surprise which we could not conceal, "I will relate to you a story. I do not ask that you shall credit it; I only say that I have given up my life to such studies, and that I am willing, as matters have so arrived, that you shall join me to prove false or true what I think of the potsherd of Anubis."

"Good!" said Lesty, and settled himself to listen, an example that was followed by Halesowen and myself. Zeda paused for a moment, evidently to collect his ideas, a pause upon which my stolid friend placed a dubious interpretation, for he cleared his throat, significantly.

III

"The date is no matter," said Dr. Zeda, "but there was at Gizeh, to the north of the Sphinx, a temple dedicated to Isis; but wherein the worship was different. We only know of this shrine by the monuments, but they prove it to have been—eh, Mr. Halesowen?"

Halesowen nodded.

"Here, then, the gods of the dead were adored—but the worship of Anubis took precedence, and was conducted at a shrine apart. Here, locked within three-and-thirty doors, having each its separate janitor who held the key, reposed a sacred symbol—a symbol, my friends, upon which was based the occult knowledge of the initiated; a symbol more precious than the lives of a hundred-hundred warriors—for so it is written!''

"I have never met with the inscription!'' said Halesowen drily.

Dr. Zeda smiled.

"You never are likely to meet it!'' he responded. "Your Belzoni and Lepsius, your Birch, Renouf, Brugsch and Petrie, is a mere unseeing vandal, blinded to the great truth—to the ultimate secret that Egypt holds for him who has eyes to see and a brain to realise!''

The mysterious foreign gentleman looked about him with a sort of challenge in his glance; then he quietly resumed his story.

"At the change of the moon in the sacred month, Methori, a maiden selected from a noble house for her beauty and purity, and for a whole year dedicated to the service of the gods, held in her hands the sacred thing—held it aloft that the initiated might worship, until the first white beam lit up the receptacle, when all bowed down their heads and chanted the 'Hymn of the souls who are passing.' Then was it locked again within the three-and-thirty doors, there to remain for another year. None saw the symbol itself but the high priest, who looked upon it when he was so ordained—for any other that gazed upon it died! It was contained in a holy vase!''

He paused impressively. We had all fallen under the peculiar fascination of the speaker's personality; we felt as though he spoke of matters wherein he had had personal concern. I could almost believe him to have witnessed the strange rites that he told of with such conviction.

"In a year so long ago,'' he softly resumed, his voice now a kind of jagged whisper, "that to speak of its date were to convey nothing to you, the highborn virgin on whom the exalted office was conferred, closed upon her unhappy soul the gates of paradise for ages unnumbered; called down upon her head the curse of the high priest and the anger of the most high gods; was rejected of Set himself!

"She let fall from her hands the sacred vase, and the holy symbol was lost to the children of earth for evermore! Lost was the key to the book of wisdom; closed was that book to man for all time!''

"Go on!'' said Halesowen, harshly, for Zeda had paused again.

"You do not grasp?'' asked the doctor. "Well, then, know that the sentence was 'Until the parts of this vase be made whole again.' Five fragments there were: a large one, which is your potsherd, and four smaller. The four smaller, after twenty years of untiring search, I have recovered and joined together. What if we now make whole that which was broken? May I not, by the exercise of such poor shreds of the lost wisdom as I have gathered up, summon before me that wandering spirit ere it return again to plead for rest at the judgment seat of Amenti?"

When I say that the man's words proved electrical, I do not exaggerate the effect which this astounding proposition had upon us. Halesowen was fairly startled out of his chair, and stood with his eyes fixed on the other in a fascinated gaze.

Zeda, entirely returning to his customary urbanity, shrugged and smiled. "You believe my story?"

Lesty was the first to recover himself, and his reply was characteristic. "Can't say I do," he drawled frankly. "I don't say that *you* may not, though," he added.

"Then do you not owe it to assist in proving my words? A little séance? You are sceptical, quite? Very well; I try to show you. If I fail, then it is unfortunate, but—I bow to an inevitable!"

We looked at each other, interrogatively, and then Halesowen answered: "All right. It's a queer yarn, but we leave the matter entirely in your hands."

The doctor bowed. "Shall we say to-night to begin?" he said tentatively.

"By all means."

The doctor expressed himself delighted, and, carefully relocking the fragment of the vase in its double case, he was about to depart, when a point occurred to me.

"Might I ask whom you suspect of the attempted burglary?" I said.

He turned, in the door, and fixed a strange glance upon me. "There are others," he replied, "who seek as I seek, and who do not scruple to gain their ends how they may. Of them we shall beware, my friends, for we know they design upon us!"

With that and a low bow he retired.

Little of interest occurred during the day, until about four in the afternoon, when Halesowen aroused us out of a lazy dose to show a letter just received from the British Museum.

It was in reply to one asking why he had received no acknowledgment of the photographs and drawings submitted; and it informed him that no such photographs and drawings had come to hand!

We usually took tea in the afternoon, and Halesowen joined us on this occasion, whilst, at about five o'clock, Dr. Zeda also looked in. He remained until it began to grow dusk, when we all went over to Halesowen's to arrange the first "sitting"—for so the doctor referred to the projected séance. Retiring, for a few minutes, to his own establishment, Zeda returned with the iron box and explained what he proposed to do.

"Around this small table we sit, as at séance," he said; "but no medium—only the potsherd. With these flexible bands I will attach, temporarily, the parts, and stand the vase in Mr. Halesowen's frame, here by the window—so. Beside it we will place the lamp, shaded thus—so that a dim light is upon it. We can just see from where we sit in the dark. We will now wait until it is more dusk."

Accordingly, we went out on to the balcony and smoked for an hour, Zeda polluting the clean air with the fumes of the long, black cigars he affected. They had an appearance as of dried twigs and an odour so wholly original as to defy simile. Between eight and nine o'clock he expressed himself satisfied with the light—or, rather, lack of it—and we all gathered around the table in the gloom, spreading our hands as he directed. For close upon an hour we sat in tense silence, the room seeming to be very hot. A slight breeze off the Common had wafted the fumes of Zeda's cigar in through the open windows, which he had afterwards closed, and the reek filled the air as with something palpable—and nauseous. I was growing very weary of the business, and Lesty, despite the doctor's warning against disturbing the silence, had begun to cough and fidget irritably, when the rumbling foreign voice came, so unexpectedly as to startle us all: "It is useless to-night; something is not propitious. Turn up the lights."

From the celerity with which Halesown complied, I divined that he, too, had been growing impatient.

"There is some not suitable condition," said Zeda, relocking his portion of the vase in its case. "To-morrow we shall make some changes in the order."

He seemed not at all disappointed, being apparently as confident as ever in the ultimate success of the séances. One of the windows, he suggested, should be left open on the following evening during our sitting; and this we were only too glad to agree upon, since it would possibly serve to clear the atmosphere, somewhat, of the odour emanating from the doctor's cigars. Several other points he also mentioned as being conceivably responsible for our initial failure—such as our positions around the table, and the relative distance of the potsherd. "We shall see, to-morrow," were his last words as he left us.

"A perfect monument of mendacity!" muttered Lesty, as we heard the retiring footsteps of our foreign friend on the gravel below; "and I think his accent is assumed. I don't know why we even seem to credit such an incredible fable."

"I don't know, either," said Halesowen, reflectively. "But he certainly possesses the missing part of the vase, and if he does not believe the story, himself, what earthly object can he hope to serve by these séances?"

"Give it up!" replied Lesty, promptly; and that, I think, rather aptly expressed the mental attitude of all three.

We saw nothing of Zeda throughout the following day, but he duly put in an appearance in the evening, and placed us around the table again, but in different order. One of the French windows was left open, and the potsherd, with the lamp beside it, placed somewhat to the left.

After persevering for about forty minutes, we were rewarded by a rather conventional phenomenon. The table rocked and gave forth cracking sounds. There was no other manifestation, and at about half-past ten, the doctor again terminated the séance.

"Excellent!" said Zeda enthusiastically, "excellent! We were *en rapport*, and within the circle there was power. To-morrow we shall triumph, my friends but there is again an alteration that occurs to me. You, Mr. Clifford, shall sit next to Mr. Lesty on the left. Mr. Halesowen shall be upon his right, and I, facing Mr. Lesty, between. Also, there is too much light from the lamps in the road. It is good, I think, to have open the windows, but this Japanese screen will keep out that too much light and shelter the vase. To-morrow we will observe these things."

This, then, concluded our second sitting, and brings me to the final episode of that affair which, strange enough in its several developments, was stranger still in its *dénouement*.

IV

Zeda, on the following day, entertained us to luncheon in town, followed by an afternoon concert, for which he had procured seats, being interested, or professing to be, in a certain fiddler who figured largely in the programme. We had arranged that Halesowen and the doctor should dine with us in the evening, before we went to the former's flat for the séance, and we accordingly returned direct to our rooms and chatted over the doings of the day until dinner was served. Zeda surpassed himself in brilliant conversation. He must, I remember thinking, have led a strange and eventful life.

At about nine o'clock, we walked over, in the dark, to our friend's flat, where we had to grope for and light an oil-lamp which he had, Zeda declaring that something in the atmosphere was propitious and that the electric light would tend to disturb these favourable conditions. He seemed to be strung to high tension, perhaps with expectancy, but was not so preoccupied as to forget his black cigars, one of which he lighted as he was about to go out for the iron box. He borrowed my matches for the purpose and forgot to return them.

It was, perhaps a quarter to ten before Zeda had matters arranged to his satisfaction, and so dark, by reason of the tall Japanese screen which stood before the open windows, that I could see neither Zeda, on my left, nor Lesty, who sat on my right. Halesowen was a dim silhouette against the patch of light cast by the oil reading-lamp beside the vase, which stood the whole length of the room away. I was conscious of a suppressed excitement, which I am sure was shared by my companions.

I heard a distant clock striking the half-hour, and then the three quarters; but still nothing had occurred. A motor-car drove around from the road and stopped somewhere at the outer end of the drive. I wondered, idly, if it were that of the surgeon who lived at Number 10. After that, everything was very quiet, and I was expecting to hear the hour strike, and straining my ears to catch the sound of the first chime, when the rocking and cracking of the table began. This was much more violent than hitherto, and Zeda's gruff tones came softly: "Whatever shall happen, do not remove your hands from the table!"

He ceased speaking, and the rocking motions, together with the rapping and cracking that had sounded from all about us, also ceased, with disconcerting suddenness. A silence fell, so short in duration as to be scarcely appreciable; for it was almost instantly broken by an unexpected sound.

It was a woman's voice, very low and clear, and it seemed to mutter something in a weird, rising cadence, with a high note at the end of every third bar or so, and this over and over again—an eerie thing, vaguely like a Gregorian chant.

"Triumph!" whispered Zeda. "The Hymn of the souls who are passing."

His speech seemed to disturb the singer, but only for a moment. The Hymn was continued.

This singular performance was proving too much for my nerves; at each recurrence of the quiet, clear note on the fourth beat of the third bar, a cold shudder ran down my spine. Then, as the very monotony of the thing was beginning to grow appalling, I suddenly became aware of a slim, white figure standing beside the vase!

The chant stopped, and I could hear nothing but the nervous breathing of my companions. Seated as they were, I doubted whether Halesowen or Lesty could see this apparition, but I was facing directly toward her—for it was a woman. I could see every line of her figure—the curves of her throat and arms and shoulders, the dull, metallic gleaming of her clustering hair. As she extended her hand toward the light, I distinctly saw the large, green stone set in a ring on her index finger. She must be very beautiful, I thought, and I was peering through the gloom in a vain endeavour to see her more clearly, when there came a disconcerting crash—and utter darkness! The table whereat we were seated was overturned, and I found myself capsized from my chair!

"Hold him!" yelled the voice of Lesty. "Hold him, Halesowen —Clifford!"

A door banged loudly.

"Confound it! I'm on the floor!"—from Halesowen.

I shouted for some one to turn up the light, at the same time scrambling through the gloom with that intent. After severely damaging my shins against the intervening furniture, I found the switch. It would not work!

"It's cut off!" I cried. "Strike a match, somebody."

"Haven't got any!" said Lesty.

"Zeda has mine!" responded Halesowen. "Open the door."

"Locked!" was Lesty's next report.

"Break it down!" shouted Halesowen, hurling aside the Japanese screen. *"The potsherd is gone!"*

Lesty applied his shoulder to the oak—once—twice—thrice. Then all together we attacked it, and it flew open with a splintering crash.

"Round to his flat!" panted Halesowen, running downstairs.

Out on to the drive we sprinted, into the next entrance and up to the first landing. Knocking and ringing proved ineffectual, and the door was too strong to be burst open. We stood in dismayed silence, staring at one another.

"Off your balcony, on to his and through the French window!" said Lesty, suddenly; so back we all ran again.

I had never before realised how easy it was to get from one balcony to another, until I saw Lesty swing himself across. Halesowen and I followed in a trice and we all blundered into the dark room through the open window and made for the electric switch beside the mantelpiece. We turned on the light. The room was unfurnished!

"Good Lord!" breathed Halesowen, hurrying into the next.

That, too, was quite bare, as were all the rest! The outer door was locked.

"While we were fooling at that concert, he had every scrap of stuff removed!" I said. "He probably had the lot on hire from a big furnishing firm—curios and all. I remember noticing that his curiosities were of a very ordinary character, considering his extensive travels and the nature of his studies."

"No doubt whatever," agreed Lesty. "His burglary proved a failure (and, I think, must have been interrupted), though I am compelled to admire the neat manner in which he handled the very delicate situation that resulted. His more recent and elaborate device has turned out all that could be desired—from Zeda's point of view!"

"But how has he got away?" said Halesowen, in bewilderment.

"Motor waiting at the corner," replied Lesty, promptly. "Heard it come up. When the reading-lamp was capsized, and whoever had crept from his balcony to yours and in behind the screen had returned the same way—with the vase!—Zeda overturned the table and pushed you two men backwards in your chairs. Then, before I could reach him, he bolted out and locked the door after him. For, having lulled my suspicions by two practically uneventful séances, he cunningly placed himself nearest to the door and me farthest away. He probably removed the key when he went out for the box and placed it outside in the lock when he returned. His accomplice had run straight through Zeda's flat and out to the waiting car, and there he joined her. They may be thirty miles away by now!"

Being unable to open the door, we perforce returned to Halesowen's balcony by the same way that we had come, our friend bewailing his lost potsherd and exclaiming: "The cunning, cunning scamp!"

"I knew he had some deep game in hand," said Lesty; "but I hadn't bargained for this move. Of course, I had noticed the dodge of borrowing all our matches, but I didn't grasp its importance until too late. It never occurred to me that he'd disconnected the electric light (which he probably did some time in the night, by the way). I was a fool not to realise it, too, when he insisted on our only using the oil-lamp. Then, again, I was slow not to go straight through the window and into Zeda's flat that way. It is just possible I might have caught the lady songster if I had done that in the first place. The possibility, however, had not been overlooked, since she took the precaution to lock the door after her.''

''A clever rogue!'' I declared. ''But wasn't the first attempt—for I suppose we must classify the mysterious arm under that head— more than a trifle indiscreet?''

''No doubt,'' agreed Lesty. ''But we didn't know, then, that Zeda was in London, and the flat was still unfurnished. Also, they may have thought Halesowen was in bed; or the woman (whom he has so cleverly kept out of sight) may have exceeded her instructions in attempting to touch the potsherd while any one remained in the room.''

''But,'' said Halesowen, slowly, ''we don't know that there *was* any woman!''

''Eh?'' queried Lesty.

''Did you see her?''

''No.''

''I did. She was lovely, very lovely—for a woman!''

Lesty stared curiously. ''You surprise me,'' he commented, drily.

''Zeda was a strange man,'' pursued the other, ''and there were certainly things occurred as we sat round that table that need a lot of explaining.''

''Very ordinary three-and-six-a-head phenomena!'' was the reply. ''Merely a blind.''

''Then what was the reason of his burning desire to secure my potsherd, if not to complete the vase?''

''Do you mean to tell me,'' asked Lesty, ''that you are going to credit that story about the priestess—*now*, after he has shown his hand? Do you wish to suggest that he was aided by a spirit?''

''Then why was he so keen to get the thing?'' persisted Halesowen.

Lesty looked at him, looked at me, shrugged his shoulders and began to load his pipe. Having done so, he sat smoking and staring at the brilliant moon.

''Well?'' inquired our host.

''Give it up!'' admitted Lesty.

(CONCLUSION OF MR. CLIFFORD'S ACCOUNT)

V

One of my visits to the Wapping curio-shop of Moris Klaw was made in company with Mr. Halesowen, who, with the others mentioned in the foregoing narrative, I subsequently had met.

Somewhere amid the misty gloom of this place, where loot of a hundred ages, of every spot from pole to pole, veils its identity in the darkness, sits a large grey parrot. Faint perfumes and scuffling sounds tell of hidden animal life near to the visitor; but the parrot proclaims itself stridently—

"Moris Klaw! Moris Klaw! The devil's come for you!"

That signal brings Moris Klaw from his hiding-place. He shuffles into the shop, a figure appropriate to its surroundings. Imagine a tall, stooping man, enveloped in a very faded blue dressing-gown. His skin is but a half-shade lighter than that of a Chinaman; his hair, his shaggy brows, his scanty beard, defy one to name their colour. He wears pince-nez.

When upon this particular occasion I introduced my companion, and Moris Klaw acknowledged the introduction in his rumbling voice, I saw Halesowen stare.

Klaw produced a scent-spray from somewhere and sprayed verbena upon his high, yellow brow.

"It is very stuffy—in this shop!" he explained. "Isis! Isis! Bring for my visitors some iced drinks!"

He invoked a goddess, and a goddess appeared: a brilliantly beautiful brunette, with delightfully curved scarlet lips and flashing eyes, whose fire the gloom could not dim.

"Good God!" cried Halesowen—and fell back.

"My daughter, Isis," rumbled Moris Klaw. "This is Mr. Halesowen, from whom we rescue the Egyptian potsherd!"

"*What!*"

Halesowen leant forward across the counter.

"You recognize my daughter?" continued Moris Klaw; "but not Dr. Zeda, eh? Or only his poor old voice? You gave us great trouble, Mr. Halesowen. Once, you came in just as Isis, who has climbed on to your balcony, is about to take the potsherd——"

"There was no one in the room!"

"*I* was in the room!" interrupted the girl coolly. "I was draped in black from head to foot, and I slipped behind the window hangings, unseen, whilst you fumbled with your lamp!"

"It was indiscreet," continued Moris Klaw—"and made it harder for me; because, afterwards, you lock up the treasure and my search is unavailing. Also, I am interrupted. Pah! I am clumsy! I waste time! But, remember, I offered to buy it!"

"Suppose," said Halesowen, slowly, "I give you both in charge?"

"You cannot," was the placid reply; "for you cannot say how

you came into possession of the sherd! Professor Sheraton was in a similar forked stick—and that is where *I* come in!''

''What! you were acting for him?''

''Certainly! I happen to be in Egypt at the time, and he is a friend of mine. Your thief, Ali, left a small piece of the pot behind, and I am entrusted to make it complete!''

''You have succeeded!'' said Halesowen, grimly, all the time furtively watching the beautiful Isis.

''Yes,'' rumbled Moris Klaw. ''I am the instrument of poetic justice. Isis, those cool beverages. Let us drink to poetic justice!''

He sprayed his ample brow with verbena.

In conclusion: you may ask if the value of the potsherd justified the elaborate and costly mode of its recovery.

I reply: upon what does the present fame of Professor Sheraton rest? His *New Key to the Egyptian Book of the Dead.* Upon what is that work founded? Upon the hieroglyphics of the Potsherd of Anubis—which (no questions being asked of so distinguished a savant) was recently acquired from the Professor by the nation at a cost of £15,000!

Third Episode

CASE OF THE CRUSADER'S AXE

I

I have heard people speak of Moris Klaw's failures. So far as my information bears me, he never experienced any. "What," I have been asked, "of the Cresping murder case? He certainly failed there."

Respecting this question of his failure or success in the sensational case which first acquainted the entire country with the existence of Crespie Hall, and that brought the old world village of Cresping into such unwonted prominence, I shall now invite your opinion.

The investigation—the crime having baffled the local men—ultimately was placed in the hands of Detective-Inspector Grimsby; and through Grimsby I was brought into close touch with the matter. I had met Grimsby during the course of the mysterious happenings at the Menzies Museum, and at that time I also had made the acquaintance of Moris Klaw.

Thus, as I sat over my breakfast one morning reading an account of the Cresping murder case, I was no more than moderately surprised to see Inspector Grimsby walk into my rooms.

He declined my offer of a really good Egyptian cigarette.

"Thanks all the same," he said; "but there's only one smoke I can think on."

With that he lighted one of the cheroots of which he smoked an incredible quantity, and got up from his chair, restlessly.

"I've just run up from Cresping by the early train," he began abruptly. "You've heard all about the murder, of course?"

I pointed to my newspaper, conspicuous upon the front page of which was—

THE MURDER AT CRESPIE HALL

"Ah, yes," he said, absently. "Well, I've been sent down, and to tell you the white and unsullied truth I'm in a knot!"

37

I passed him a cup of coffee.

"What are the difficulties?" I asked.

"There's only one," he rapped back: "who did it!"

"It looks to me a very clear case against Ryder, the ex-butler."

"So it did to me," he agreed—"until I got down there! I'd got a warrant in my pocket all ready. Then I began to have doubts!"

"What do you propose to do?"

Grimsby hesitated.

"Well," he replied, "it wouldn't do any good to make a mistake in a murder case; so what I should *like* to do would be to get another opinion—not official, of course!"

I glanced across at him.

"Mr. Moris Klaw?"

He nodded.

"Exactly!"

"You've changed your opinion respecting him?"

"Mr. Searles, his investigation of the Menzies Museum outrages completely stood me on my head! I'm not joking. I'd always thought him a crank, and in some ways I think so still; but at seeing through a brick wall I'd put all I've got on Moris Klaw any day!"

"But surely you are wasting time by coming to me?"

"No, I'm not," said Grimsby, confidently. "Moris Klaw, for all his retiring habits, is not a man that wants his light hidden under a bushel! He knows that you are collecting material about his methods, and he's more likely to move for you than for me."

I saw through Grimsby's plan. He wanted me to invite Moris Klaw to look into the Crespie murder case, in order that he (Grimsby) might reap any official benefit accruing without loss of self-esteem! I laughed.

"All right, Grimsby!" I said. "Since he has made no move, voluntarily, it may be that the case does not interest him; but we can try."

Accordingly, having consulted an A.B.C. we presently entrained for Wapping, and as a laggard sun began to show up the dinginess and the dirtiness of that locality, sought out a certain shop, whose locale I shall no more closely describe than in saying that it is close to Wapping Old Stairs.

One turns down a narrow court, with a blank wall on the right and a nailed-up doorway and boarded-up window on the left. Through the cracks of the latter boarding, the inquiring visitor may catch a glimpse, beyond a cavernous place which once was some kind of warehouse, of Old Thames tiding muddily.

The court is a *cul de sac*. The shop of Moris Klaw occupies the blind end. Some broken marble pedestals stand upon the footway, among seatless chairs, dilapidated chests and a litter of books, stuffed birds, cameos, ink-stands, swords, lamps, and other unclassifiable rubbish. A black doorway yawns amid the litter.

Imagine Inspector Grimsby and I as entering into this singular Cumean cave.

Our eyes, at first, failed to penetrate the gloom. All about moved rustling suggestions of animal activity. The indescribable odour of old furniture assailed our nostrils together with an equally indescribable smell of avian, reptilian, and rodent life.

"Moris Klaw! Moris Klaw! the devil's come for you!"

Thus, the scraping voice of the parrot. A door opened, admitting a little more light and Moris Klaw. The latter was fully dressed; whereby I mean that he wore his dilapidated caped black cloak, his black silk muffler and that rarest relic of his unsavoury reliquary, the flat-topped brown bowler.

In that inadequate light his vellum face looked older, his shaggy brows, his meagre beard, more toneless, than ever. Through the gold-trimmed pince-nez he peered for a moment, downwards from his great height. He removed the bowler.

"Good-morning, Mr. Searles! Good-morning, Inspector Grimsby! I am just from Paris. It is so good of you to call so early to tell me all about the poor murdered man of Cresping! Good-morning! Good-morning!"

II

Moris Klaw's sanctum is certainly one of the most remarkable apartments in London. It is lined with shelves, which contain what I believe to be a unique library of works dealing with criminology—from Moris Klaw's point of view. Strange relics are there, too; and all of them have histories. A neat desk, with flowers in a silver vase, and a revolving chair standing upon a fine tiger-skin are the other notable items of furniture.

The contrast on entering was startling. Moris Klaw placed his hat upon the desk, and from it took out the scent-spray without which he never travels. He played the contents upon his high, yellow forehead—filling the air with the refreshing odour of verbena.

"That shop!" he said, "it smell very strong this morning. It is not so much the canaries as the rats!"

"I trust," began Grimsby, respectfully, "that Miss Klaw is quite well?"

"Isis will presently be here to say for herself," was the reply. "And now—this bad business of Cresping. It seems I am just back in time, but, ah! it is a fortnight old!"

Grimsby cleared his throat. "You will have read—"

"Ah, my friend!" Moris Klaw held up a long, tapering, white hand. "As though you do not know that I never confuse my poor brain with those foolish papers. No, I have not read, my friend!"

"Oh!" said Grimsby, something taken aback. "Then I shall have to tell you the family history—"

Isis Klaw entered.

From her small hat, with its flamingo-like plume, to her dainty shoes, she was redolent of the Rue de la Paix. She wore an amazingly daring toilette; I can only term it a study in flame-tones. A less beautiful woman could never have essayed such a scheme; but this superb brunette, with her great flashing eyes and taunting smile had the lithe carriage of a Cleopatra, the indescribable *diablerie* of a *ghaziyeh*.

Inspector Grimsby greeted her with embarrassed admiration. Greetings over—

"We must hurry, father!" said the girl.

Moris Klaw reclaimed his archaic bowler.

"Mr. Searles and Inspector Grimsby will perhaps be joining us?" he suggested.

"Where?" began Grimsby.

"Where but by the 9.5 train for Uxley!" said Klaw. "Where but from Uxley to Cresping! Do I waste time, then—I?"

"You have been retained?" suggested Grimsby.

"Ah, no!" was the reply. "But I shall receive my fee, nevertheless!"

At the end of the court a cab was waiting. Outside the cavernous door a ramshackle man with a rosy nose bowed respectfully to the proprietor.

"You hear me, William," said Moris Klaw, to this derelict. "You are to sell nothing—unless it is the washstand! Forget not to change the canaries' water. The Indian corn is for the white rats. If there is no mouse in the trap by eight o'clock, give the owl a herring. And keep from the drink; it will be your ruin, William!"

We entered the cab. My last impression of the place was derived from the invisible parrot, who gave us God-speed with—

"Moris Klaw! Moris Klaw! the devil's come for you!"

As we drove stationward, Grimsby, his eyes rarely leaving the piquant face of Isis Klaw, outlined the history of the Crespie family to the silent Moris. In brief it was this—

The late Sir Richard Crespie, having become involved in serious monetary difficulties, employed such methods of drowning his sorrows as were far from conducive to domestic felicity; and after a certain unusually violent outburst the home was broken up. His son, Roland, was the first to go; and he took little with him but his mother's blessing and his father's curses. Then Lady Crespie went away to her sister in London, only surviving her departure from the Hall by two years. Alone, and deserted, first by son and then by wife, the debauched old baronet continued on his course of heavy drinking for some years longer. The servants left him, one by one, so that in the end, save for faithful old Ryder, the butler, whose family had served the Crespies for time immemorial, he had the huge mansion to himself. Apoplexy closed his unfortunate career; and, since nothing had been heard of him for years, it was generally supposed that the son had met his death in Africa, whence he had gone on leaving home.

With the passing of Sir Richard came Mr. Isaac Heidelberger, and he wasted no time in impressing his noxious personality upon the folks of Cresping. He was a German Jew, large and oily, with huge coarse features and a little black moustache that had been assiduously trained in a futile attempt to hide a mouth that had well befitted Nero. A week after Sir Richard's burial, Mr. Heidelberger took possession of the Hall.

The new occupant brought with him one Heimer, a kind of confidential clerk, and, old Ryder the butler having been sent about his business, the two Jewish gentlemen proceeded to make themselves comfortable. The nature of their business was soon public property: the grand old Hall was to be turned into a "country mansion for paying guests."

Very strained relations existed between the big Jew and the ex-butler, who, having a little money saved, had settled down in Cresping. One night, at the "Goblets"—the historic village inn— Heidelberger having swaggered into the place, there arose an open quarrel. Said Ryder—

"Sir Richard, with all his faults, was once a good English gentleman, and, but for such as you, a good English gentleman he might have died!"

"It was exactly a week later that the tragedy occurred.

"We come to it now, eh?" interrupted Moris Klaw at this point. "So—we also come to the station! I will ask you to reserve us a first-class carriage!"

Grimsby made arrangements to that end. And, as the train moved out of the station, resumed his story.

"What I gather is this," he said.

[I condense his statement and append it in my own words.]

The "Goblets" was just closing its doors, and the villagers who nightly met there were standing in a group under the swinging sign, when a man came running down the street from the direction of the Hall, and, observing the gathering, ran up. It was Heimer, Isaac Heidelberger's secretary. He was hatless and his flabby face, in the dim light, was ghastly.

"Quick!" he rasped, hoarsely. "Where does the doctor live?"

"Last house but one," somebody said. "What's the matter?"

"Murder!" cried Heimer, as he rushed off down the village street.

Such was the dramatic manner in which the news of the subsequently notorious case was first carried to the outside world. The facts, as soon made known throughout the length and breadth of the land, were, briefly, as follows.

Heidelberger and his secretary, who were engaged in making an inventory of the contents of the Hall and in arranging for such alterations of the rooms and laying out of the neglected grounds as they considered necessary, had practically reached the end of their task. In fact, had nothing intervened, Cresping would, on the following day, have seen the old mansion in the hands of an army of London workmen.

At about half-past seven in the evening, Heidelberger had entered the room occupied by Heimer and had mentioned that he expected a visitor. The secretary, who had more work than he could well accomplish, did not pause to inquire concerning him, believing the other to allude either to the architect or to Heidelberger's man, who was coming down from London. Heidelberger had then gone up to the library, saying that he should not require Heimer again that night.

Between eight and half-past—Heimer was not sure of the time—there was a ring at the bell (that of the tradesmen's entrance). Knowing that Heidelberger could admit the visitor directly to the library, Heimer, hearing nothing more, concluded that the two were closeted there.

The first intimation that he received of anything amiss was a loud and angry cry, apparently proceeding from the old banqueting-hall directly overhead, and unmistakably in the voice of Heidelberger. Springing from his chair, he took a step towards the door, and then paused in doubt. There was an angry murmur from above, the tones of the Jew being clearly distinguishable; then a sudden scuffle and an oscillation of the floor as though two heavy men were at handigrips; next, a crash that shook the room, and a high-pitched cry of which he only partially comprehended the last word. This he asserted to be "holy."

That Heimer stood transfixed at the open door throughout all this, suffices to brand him a coward. It was, in fact, only his stories of shadowy figures in the picture gallery and his general disinclination to leave his room after dusk that had prompted Heidelberger—a man of different mettle—to wire to London for the servant.

At this juncture, however, moved as much by a fear of the sudden silence as by any higher motive, he took a revolver from the table drawer, and, holding it cocked in one hand and seizing the lamp in the other, he crept, trembling, up a narrow little stair that led to a door beneath the minstrels' gallery. To open it he had to place the lamp on the floor, and, at the moment of doing so, he heard a sound inside the hall like the grating of a badly oiled lock.

Then, with the lamp held high above his head, he peered inside; and, considering the character of the man, it is worthy of note that he did not faint on the spot, for the feeble light, but serving, as it did, to intensify the gloom of the long and shadowy place, revealed a scene well calculated to shake the nerves of a stouter man than Heimer.

Less than six feet from where he stood, and lying flat on his back, with his head towards the light, was Heidelberger in a perfect pool of blood, his skull cleft almost to the chine! Beside him on the floor lay the fearful weapon that had wrought his end—an enormous battle-axe, a relic of the Crusades such as none but a man of herculean strength could possibly wield.

Sick with terror, and scarcely capable of keeping his feet, Heimer gave one glance around the gloomy place, which showed him that, save for the murdered man, it was empty; then he staggered down the narrow stairs and let himself out into the grounds. Slightly revived by the fresh night air, but fearful of pursuit by the unknown assassin, he ran, as fast as his condition would allow, into the village.

"Here it is—Uxley!" jerked Moris Klaw.

III

"Ah!" cried Moris Klaw, in a species of fanatic rapture—"look at the blood!"

We stood in the ancient banqueting-hall of Crespie. By a distant door I could see a policeman on duty. A ghostly silence was the marked feature of the place. Klaw's harsh, rumbling voice echoed eerily about that chamber sacred to the shades of departed Crespies.

Isis Klaw stood beside her father. They were a wildly incongruous couple. The girl looked down at the bloodstained flooring with the calm scrutiny of an experienced criminologist.

"This spot must be alive with odic impressions," she said softly.

A local officer, who formed one of the group, stared uncomprehendingly. Moris Klaw instinctively turned to him.

"You stare widely, my friend!" he said. "It is clear you know nothing of the psychology of crime! Let me, then, enlighten you. First: all crime" (he waved one long hand characteristically) "operates in cycles. Its history repeats itself, you understand. Second: thoughts are *things*. One who dies the violent death has, at the end, a strong mental emotion—an etheric storm. The air—the atmosphere—retains imprints of that storm."

"Indeed!" said the officer.

"Yes, indeed! I shall not sleep in this place—as is my usual custom in such inquiries. Why? Because I am afraid of the *shock* of experiencing such an emotion as was this late Heidelberger's! Ah! you are dense as a bull! Once, my bovine friend, I slept upon a spot in desolate Palestine where a poor woman had been stoned to death. In my dreams those merciless stones struck me! Upon the head and the face they crashed! And I was helpless—bound—as was the unhappy one who for her poor little sins had had her life crushed from her tender body!"

He ceased. No one spoke. In such moments, Moris Klaw became a magician; a weaver of spells. The most unimpressionable shuddered as though the strange things which this strangest of men told of, lived, moved, before their eyes. Then—

"Yonder is the axe, sir," said the local man, with a sudden, awed respect.

Klaw walked over to where the huge battle-axe stood against a post of the gallery.

"Try to lift it, Mr. Klaw," said Grimsby. "It will give you some idea of what sort of man the murderer must have been! I can't raise it upright by the haft with one hand."

Moris Klaw seized the axe. Whilst Grimsby, the local man and myself stared amazedly, he swung it about his head as one swings an Indian club! He struck with it—to right—to left; he laid it down.

"My father has a wrist of steel!" came the soft voice of Isis. "Did you not know that he was once a famous swordsman?"

Klaw removed his hat, took out the scent-spray and bathed his forehead with verbena.

"That is a *man's* axe!" he said. "Isis, what do we know of such an axe? We, who have so complete a catalogue of such relics?"

Isis Klaw produced from her bag a bulky notebook.

"It is the third one," she replied calmly, passing the open book to her father; "the one we thought!"

"Ah," rumbled Klaw, adjusting his pince-nez, "Black Geoffrey's axe!" He turned again to Palmer, the local officer. "All such antiques," he said, "have histories. I collect those histories, you understand. This axe was carried by 'Black Geoffrey,' a very early Crespie, in the first Crusade. It slew many Saracens, I doubt not. But this does not interest me. In the reign of Henry VIII. we find it dwelt, this great axe, at Dyke Manor, which is in Norfolk. It was not until Charles II. that it came to Crespie Hall. And what happened at Dyke Manor? One, Sir Gilbert Myerly was slain by it! Who wielded it? Patience, my friends! All is clear to me! What a wonderful science is the Science of Cycles!"

Behind the pebbles his eyes gleamed with excitement. It seemed as though his notes (how obtained I was unable to conjecture) had furnished him with a clue; although to me they seemed to have not the slightest bearing upon the case.

"Now, Mr. Grimsby," continued Moris Klaw: "In a few words, what is the evidence against Ryder, the butler?"

"Well," was the reply, "you will note where the axe used to hang, up there before the rail of the minstrels' gallery. The theory is that the murderer rushed up, wrenched the axe from its fastening—"

"Theories, my friend, "interrupted Moris Klaw, "are not evidence!"

Isis gazed at Mr. Grimsby with a smile. He looked embarrassed.

"Sorry!" he said, humbly. "Here are the facts, then. In the right hand of the dead man was an open pocket knife. It is assumed... sorry! Several spots of blood were found on the knife. Do you want to see it?"

Moris Klaw shook his head.

"It has been ascertained," continued Grimsby, "that Ryder

went out at eight o'clock on the night of the murder and didn't
return until after ten. He was interrogated. Listen to this, Mr.
Klaw, and tell me why I haven't arrested him! He admitted that
he was the man who rang the bell; he admitted being closeted with
Heidelberger in the library; and he admitted that he was in the hall
when the Jew met his death!''

"Good!" said Moris Klaw. "And he is still at large?"

"He is! He's made no attempt to run away. I had his room
searched, and found a light coat with both sleeves bloodstained!
He had a cut on his left hand such as might be caused by the slash
of a pocket knife! He said he had caught his hand on a doorlatch,
but blankly declined to say what he was doing here on the night of
the murder! Yet, I didn't arrest him! Why?"

"Why?" said Moris Klaw. "Tell me."

"Because I didn't think it feasible that a man of his age could
wield that axe—and I hoped to use Ryder as a trap to catch his
accomplice!"

"Ah! clever!" rumbled Moris Klaw. "French, Mr. Grimsby!
Subtle! But you have just seen what a poor old fool can do with
that axe!"

I have never observed a man so suddenly lose faith in himself as
did Grimsby at those words. He flushed, he paled; he seemed to
become speechless.

"Tell me, Mr. Grimsby," said Klaw, "what does the suspected
man do that is suspicious? What letters does he write? What letters
does he receive?"

"None!" replied the now angry Grimsby. "But he visits Dr.
Madden, in Uxley, every day."

"What for, eh?"

"The doctor says the interviews are of a purely professional
nature; and I can't very well suspect a man in his position!"

"You have done two silly things," rumbled Moris Klaw. "You
have wasted much time in the matter of Ryder, and you have
accepted, unquestioned, the word of a doctor. Mr. Grimsby, I have
known doctors who were most inspired liars!"

"Then you are of opinion—"

Klaw raised his hand.

"It is Dr. Madden we shall visit," he said. "This Ryder cannot
escape us. Isis, my child, I need not have troubled you. This is so
simple a case that we need no 'mental negatives' to point out to us
the culprit!"

"Mr. Klaw——" began Grimsby, excitedly.

"My friend," he was answered, "I shall make a few examinations and then we shall be off to Uxley. The assassin returns to London with us by the 3.45 train!"

IV

As we drove through the village street, in the car which Grimsby had hired, upon the gate of one of the last cottages a tall, white-haired old man was leaning. His clear-cut, handsome features wore an expression of haggard sorrow.

"There he is!" rapped Grimsby. "Hadn't I better make the arrest at once?"

"Ah, no, my friend!" protested Klaw. "But stop—I have something to say to him."

The car stopping, Moris Klaw descended and approached the old man, who perceptibly paled at sight of us.

"Good-day, Mr. Ryder!" Klaw courteously saluted the ex-butler.

"Good-day to you, sir," replied the old man civilly.

Whereupon Moris Klaw said a simple thing, which had an astounding effect.

"How is he to-day?" he inquired.

Ryder's face became convulsed. His eyes started forth. He made a choking sound, staring, as one possessed, at his questioner.

"What... what... do you mean?" he gasped.

"Never mind, Mr. Ryder—never mind!" rumbled Klaw. "Isis, my child, remain with this gentleman and tell him all we know about the axe of 'Black Geoffrey.' He will be glad to hear it!"

The beautiful Isis obeyed without question. As the rest of us drove on our way, I could see the flame-coloured figure passing up the garden path beside the tall form of the old butler. Grimsby, a man badly out of his depth, watched until both became lost to view.

"I've got evidence," he suddenly burst out, "that Ryder declared Heidelberger to be the direct cause of Sir Richard's downfall! And I've got witnesses who heard him say, 'Please God! the Jew won't be here much longer!'"

"Good!" rumbled Moris Klaw. "Very good!"

During the remainder of the journey, Grimsby talked on incessantly, smoking cheroots the whole time. But Moris Klaw was silent.

Dr. Madden had but recently returned from his morning visits. He was a typical country practitioner, fresh-faced and clean-shaven, with iron-grey hair and a good head. He conveyed the impression, in some way, that he knew himself to be in a tight corner.

"What can I do for you, gentlemen?" he said, briskly.

"We have called, Dr. Madden," rumbled Moris Klaw, wagging his finger impressively, "to tell you that Ryder is in imminent danger—imminent danger—of arrest!"

The doctor started.

"And therefore we want a word with one of your patients!"

"I do not understand you. Which of my patients?"

Moris Klaw shook his head.

"Let us be intelligent," he said, "you and I, and not two old fools! You understand so perfectly which of your patients."

Dr. Madden drummed his fingers on the table.

"Are you a detective?" he snapped.

"I am not!" replied Moris Klaw. "I am a student of the Science of Cycles—not motor cycles; and a humble explorer of the etheric borderland! You lay yourself open to grave charges, doctor!"

The doctor began to fidget nervously.

"If indeed I am culpable," he said, "my culpability only dates from last night."

"So!" rumbled Klaw. "He has been insensible?"

Dr. Madden started up.

"Mr. Klaw," he replied. "I do not know whom you may be; but your penetration is uncanny. He had lost his memory!"

"What?—lost his memory! How is that?"

"He was thrown from his horse! Come; I see it is useless, now, to waste time. I will take you to him."

As we filed out to the waiting car, I glanced at Grimsby. His stupefaction was almost laughable.

"What in heaven's name is it all about, Mr. Searles?" he whispered to me. "I feel like a man in a strange country. People talk, and it doesn't seem to mean anything!"

En route:

"Tell me, doctor," said Moris Klaw, "about your patient."

The doctor, without hesitation, now explained that he had been called to attend a Mr. Rogers, an artist, who was staying at Hinxman's Farm, off the Uxley Road. On the evening of the tragedy

Mr. Rogers went out on Bess, a mare belonging to the farm, and, not having returned by ten, some anxiety was felt concerning him, the mare possessing a very bad reputation. At about a quarter-past ten the animal returned, riderless, and Rogers was brought home later, in an insensible condition, by two farm hands, having been found beside the road some distance from the farm.

For some time Mr. Rogers lay in a critical condition, suffering from concussion. Finally, a change for the better set in, but the patient was found to have lost his memory.

"Last Saturday," added the doctor, "a specialist whom I had invited to come down from London performed a successful operation."

"Ah," rumbled Moris Klaw; "so we can see him?"

"Certainly. He is quite convalescent. His memory returned to him completely last night."

In a state of uncertainty which can well be imagined, we arrived at, and entered, Hinxman's farm. Seated in the shade of the verandah, smoking his pipe, was a bronzed young man who wore a bandage about his head. He was chatting to the farmer when we arrived.

Moris Klaw walked up the steps, beside Dr. Madden.

"Good-day, Mr. Farmer," he said amiably. (A rosy-cheeked girl-face was thrust from an open window)—"Good-day, Miss Farmer!" He removed the brown bowler. He turned to the bronzed young man. "Good-day, *Sir Roland Crespie!*"

V

When Grimsby and I had somewhat recovered from the shock of this dramatic meeting, and Sir Roland, Madden and Moris Klaw had talked together for a few moments, said Moris Klaw—

"And now Sir Roland will tell us all about the death of Mr. Heidelberger!"

Inspector Grimsby was all eyes when the young baronet began—

"You must know, then, that I, together with three others, have been engaged, since my departure from England, in a mining venture in West Africa. Up to the time when I left, and, for the sake of my health, came to England, our efforts had been attended by only moderate success. Thus, on arriving in Cresping, and taking lodgings with Hinxman as 'Mr. Rogers'—for the circumstances under which I left home made me desirous of remaining unknown in the village—I, on learning that my father had just died and that the Hall had fallen into Heidelberger's hands, realised that my slender capital would not allow of my buying him out. The facts of the case came as a great shock to me: and, without revealing my identity—the beard which I had cultivated in Africa, but which the doctors have removed, acting as an effectual disguise—I made inquiries concerning Ryder. I had little difficulty in finding him, and he alone, in Cresping, knew whom I really was.

"I now come to the events that immediately preceded Heidelberger's death. There was one object in the old place for which I determined to negotiate, and which, owing to its associations, I particularly desired to retain. This was my mother's portrait. I may mention here that, for certain reasons which I would prefer not to specify, I had rather have burnt the picture than see it fall into the hands of the Jew.

"With this object in view, then, I enlisted the services of Ryder, though from none other than myself would he have accepted the task. This brings me to the day prior to Heidelberger's death, and, on that morning, I received news from Africa which led me to hope that I might, after all, be able to save my old home from an igno-minious fate. Herein my hopes have since been realised, for I learnt to-day that the mine has made rich men of us all; and I assume that some ill-advised remark upon the part of Ryder, regarding Heidelberger's possible expulsion, gave rise to the idea that the old man contemplated a violent deed.

"It therefore came about that he made an appointment with Heidelberger, an appointment which he duly kept; and it was solely due to my anxiety on Ryder's behalf, and lest he should meet with some ill-treatment from the Jew—whom I knew for a man of most brutal disposition—that I took certain steps which, indirectly, brought about the tragedy.

"In common with most old mansions of the period, the Hall has its hidden entrances and exits—though, in accordance with certain ancient traditions, the secret of their existence is strictly preserved among the family. With a view, therefore, to becoming an unseen witness of the transactions between Ryder and Heidelberger, I made use of a passage that opens into a shrubbery some fifty yards from the west wing. Entering, and mounting the steps at whose foot the tunnel terminates, I found myself at the back of an old painting in the banqueting-hall. The frame of this picture forms a door which opens upon pressing a spring, but the apparatus, owing to its great age, works very stiffly. From this position, then, I could hear all that took place in the hall, where, I had anticipated, the negotiations would be conducted, as my mother's picture hangs there.

"This proved to be the case; for I had but just gained the top of the steps when I heard the two enter the hall. Heidelberger spoke first.

" 'Think of *you* wanting to buy Lady Crespie's picture, you sentimental old fool!' he said. 'If it had been another I could name who wanted it, the case would have been different!'

"Then I heard Ryder's voice. 'What do you mean, Mr. Heidelberger?' he asked.

"I awaited the Jew's reply with some curiosity. As I had anticipated, it consisted of a foul and unfounded imputation against my poor mother. It was, in fact, more than I could bear in silence, and the tolerance of old Ryder, too, had reached its limit. For, at the moment that I wrenched open the panel and sprang into the room to confront this slanderer, I heard the sound of a blow, followed by an animal-like roar of anger from Heidelberger.

"The next moment, he seized the old man by the throat. Before he had time to proceed further I struck him heavily with my fist, so that he released his grip and turned to face his new assailant.

"One tribute I must pay to Heidelberger. He was, seemingly, incapable of fear; for this sudden attack by a person he had not known to be present seemed only to arouse a new resentment. His face, as he turned and looked me up and down, contained no trace of fear.

" 'So it's you that wants the picture, is it?' he sneered. 'I suppose you are——'

" 'Stop!' I said. 'I am Roland Crespie, and can listen to no more of your foul slanders!'

"For a second he hesitated, looking from me to Ryder and then toward the picture, dimly discernible in the light of the candle which he had brought with him. Then, before I could divine his intention, he drew a knife from his pocket, and, opening a blade, took a step in the direction of the portrait. 'You shall never have it!' he said.

"He had actually inserted the blade in the canvas—as an examination will show—when I came upon him, and we closed in a desperate struggle.

"In what followed, one can almost trace the finger of destiny. Heidelberger was a more powerful man than myself, but in his fury he endeavoured to stab me with the knife which he held in his hand!

"I seized his wrist, but he wrenched it from my grasp. I leapt back from him—as he struck down with the knife—and to the left of one of the posts supporting the minstrels' gallery.

"In the blindness of his anger, Heidelberger failed to perceive the proximity of this post. Moreover it was very dark under the gallery. He threw himself forward savagely—and struck his shoulder against the post. The impact was tremendous.

"Gentlemen! I tremble, now, to relate what happened! The axe of Black Geoffrey, which had hung for centuries before the rail above, was shaken from its place by the shock and its time-worn fastenings were torn bodily from their hold. At the instant that Heidelberger's huge body struck the post, the great axe, as though detached by invisible hands, fell, blade downward, cleaving the head of the unfortunate man and remaining, with quivering shaft, upright in the oaken floor!

"The suddenness of the tragedy almost dazed me, and I was awakened to its awful reality by old Ryder's cry—'Oh, Master Roly!' As Master Roly I had always been known to the old butler, and this name it was which some one stated to be 'holy.'

"Our subsequent action was, perhaps, ill-advised. Removing the axe and raising the head of the victim, examination showed him to be dead, and, hearing hesitating footsteps upon the narrow stair beneath the gallery, we seized the candle and retreated through the secret panel, Ryder severely cutting his hand in endeavouring to force the rusty bolt into place. It was not until we stood in a lane bordering the grounds, where I had tethered the mare upon which I had ridden from the farm, that the seemingly guilty nature of our action dawned upon me. Now, however, was too late to atone for what I attribute to a momentary panic; and requesting Ryder to keep silence until he received instructions from me, I mounted the mare, intending to return to my lodgings and think the matter quietly over.

"By an unlucky accident, the brute threw me, at some distance from the farm, thereby all but bringing about a second tragedy; and what followed is already known to you.

"Of Ryder I need only say that rather than incriminate me he was prepared to pay the penalty for a deed which was in truth a visitation of God. Dr. Madden recognised me, of course, and to him also I am eternally indebted. I had proposed to make this statement before a magistrate later to-day."

"You see," said Moris Klaw, "I have done nothing! It would all have happened the same if I had been in Peru!"

Grimsby cleared his throat.

"Without casting any doubt upon Sir Roland's word," he began, "there's no evidence to go to a jury that he didn't—"

"Pull down the axe himself?" suggested Klaw.

Grimsby looked uncomfortable.

"Well—*is* there?"

"There is!" rumbled Moris Klaw. "I am he! This case most triumphantly substantiates my theory of Cycles! Almost parallel it occurred hundreds of years ago, at Dyke Manor! The axe has repeated itself!"

"H'um!" said Grimsby. "Your theory of Cycles wouldn't hold water with twelve good men and true, I'm afraid, Mr. Klaw!"

"Yes?" replied Moris Klaw. "No? You think not, eh? Well then, there is another little point. I am an old crank-fool, eh? So? But you? You are sublimely mad, my Grimsby! You say he, or Mr. Ryder, may have snatched down the black axe? Yes? Have you tried to reach the spot where it hung before the rail?"

"No," confessed Grimsby, with the light as of the dawning of an unpleasant idea in his eyes.

"No," said Klaw, placidly; "but *I* have. Mr. Grimsby, it is impossible to reach within three feet of the spot, from the stair or from the gallery; and no live thing but a giraffe could reach it from the floor!"

We were seated in the train, homeward-bound.

"For this case," grumbled Klaw, "I get no credit. It will be said that it all came out without aid from you or from me. Never mind—I have my fee!"

He patted the haft of the great axe, which ghastly relic in some way he had arranged to appropriate. Grimsby was watching Isis Klaw out of the corner of his eye. From a dainty gold case she offered him a cigarette. Grimsby is no cigarette smoker, but he accepted, with alacrity.

The beautiful Isis took one also, and lay back puffing sinuous spirals from between her perfect red lips.

Fourth Episode

CASE OF THE IVORY STATUE

I

Where a case did not touch his peculiar interest, appeals to Moris Klaw fell upon deaf ears. However dastardly a crime, if its details were of the sordid sort, he shrank within his Wapping curio-shop as closely as any tortoise within its shell.

"Of what use," he said to me on one occasion, "are my acute psychic sensibilities to detect who it is with a chopper that has brained some unhappy washerwoman? Shall I bring to bear those delicate perceptions which it has taken me so many years to acquire in order that some ugly old fool shall learn what has become of his pretty young wife? I think not—no!"

Sometimes, however, when Inspector Grimsby of Scotland Yard was at a loss, he would induce me to intercede with the eccentric old dealer, and sometimes Moris Klaw would throw out a hint.

Beyond doubt the cases that really interested him were those that afforded scope for the exploiting of his pet theories; the Cycle of Crime, the criminal history of all valuable relics, the indestructibility of thought. Such a case came under my personal notice on one occasion, and my friend Coram was instrumental in enlisting the services of Moris Klaw. It was, I think, one of the most mysterious affairs with which I ever came in contact, and the better to understand it you must permit me to explain how Roger Paxton, the sculptor, came to have such a valuable thing in his studio as that which we all assumed had inspired the strange business.

It was Sir Melville Fennel, then, who commissioned Paxton to execute a chryselephantine statue. Sir Melville's museum of works of art, ancient and modern, is admittedly the second finest private collection of the kind in the world. The late Mr. Pierpont Morgan's alone took precedence.

The commission came as something of a surprise. The art of chryselephantine sculpture, save for one attempt at revival, in Belgium, has been dead for untold generations. By many modern critics, indeed, it is condemned, as being not art but a parody of art.

Given carte-blanche in the matter of cost, Paxton produced a piece of work which induced the critics to talk about a modern Phidias. Based upon designs furnished by the eccentric but wealthy baronet, the statue represented a slim and graceful girl reclining as in exhaustion upon an ebony throne. The ivory face, with its wearily closed eyes, was a veritable triumph, and was surmounted by a head-dress of gold intertwined among a mass of dishevelled hair. One ivory arm hung down so that the fingers almost touched the pedestal; the left hand was pressed to the breast as though against a throbbing heart. Gold bracelets and anklets, furnished by Sir Melville, were introduced into the composition; and, despite the artist's protest, a heavy girdle, encrusted with gems and found in the tomb of some favourite of a long-dead Pharaoh, encircled the waist. When complete, the thing was, from a merely intrinsic point of view, worth several thousand pounds.

As the baronet had agreed to the exhibition of the statue prior to its removal to Fennel Hall, Paxton's star was seemingly in the ascendant, when the singular event occurred that threatened to bring about his ruin.

The sculptor gave one of the pleasant little dinners for which he had gained a reputation. His task was practically completed, and his friends had all been enjoined to come early, so that the statue could be viewed before the light failed. We were quite a bachelor party, and I shall always remember the circle of admiring faces surrounding the figure of the reclining dancer—warmed in the soft light to an almost uncanny semblance of fair flesh and blood.

"You see," explained Paxton, "this composite work although it has latterly fallen into disrepute, affords magnificent scope for decorative purposes; such a richness of colour can be obtained. The ornaments are genuine antiques and of great value—a fad of my patron's."

For some minutes we stood silently admiring the beautiful work-manship; then Harman inquired: "Of what is the hair composed?"

Paxton smiled. "A little secret I borrowed from the Greeks!" he replied, with condonable vanity "Polyclitus and his contempo-raries excelled at the work."

"That jewelled girdle looks detachable," I said.

"It is firmly fastened to the waist of the figure," answered the sculptor. "I defy any one to detach it inside an hour."

"From a modern point of view the thing is an innovation," remarked one of the others, thoughtfully.

Coram, curator of the Menzies Museum, who up to the present had stood in silent contemplation of the figure, now spoke for the first time. "The cost of materials is too great for this style of work ever to become popular," he averred. "That girdle, by the way, represents a small fortune, and together with the anklets, armlets and head-dress, might well tempt any burglar. What precautions do you take, Paxton?"

"Sleep out here every night," was the reply; "and there is always some one here in the daytime. Incidentally, a curious thing occurred last week. I had just fixed the girdle, which, I may explain, was once the property of Nicris, a favourite of Ramses III., and my model was alone here for a few minutes. As I was returning from the house I heard her cry out, and when I came to look for her she was crouching in a corner trembling. What do you suppose had frightened her?"

"Give it up," said Harman.

"She swore that Nicris—for the statue is supposed to represent her—had moved!"

"Imagination," replied Coram; "but easily to be understood. I could believe it, myself, if I were here alone long enough."

"I fancy," continued Paxton, "that she must have heard some of the tales that have been circulated concerning the girdle. The thing has a rather peculiar history. It was discovered in the tomb of the dancer by whom it had once been worn; and it is said that an inscription was unearthed at the same time containing an account of Nicris's death under particularly horrible circumstances. Seton—you fellows know Seton—who was present at the opening of the sarcophagus, tells me that the Arabs, on catching sight of the girdle, all prostrated themselves and then took to their heels. Sir Melville Fennel's agent sent it on to England, however, and Sir Melville conceived the idea of this statue."

"Luckily for you," added Coram.

"Quite so," laughed the sculptor; and, carefully locking the studio door, he led the way up the short path to the house.

We were a very merry party, and the night was far advanced ere the gathering broke up. Coram and I were the last to depart; and having listened to the voices of Harman and the others dying away as they neared the end of the street, we also prepared to take our leave.

"Just come with me as far as the studio," said Paxton, "and having seen that all's well I'll let you out by the garden door."

Accordingly, we donned our coats and hats, and followed our

host to the end of the garden, where his studio was situated. The door unlocked, we all three stepped inside the place and gazed upon the figure of Nicris—the pallid face and arms seeming almost unearthly in the cold moonlight, wherein each jewel of the girdle and head-dress glittered strangely.

"Of course," muttered Coram, "the thing's altogether irregular—a fact which the critics will not fail to impress upon you; but it is unquestionably very fine, Paxton. How uncannily human it is! I don't entirely envy you your bedchamber, old man!"

"Oh, I sleep well enough," laughed Paxton. "No luxury, though; just this corner curtained off and a camp bedstead."

"A truly Spartan couch!" I said. "Well, goodnight, Paxton. We shall probably see you to-morrow—I mean later to-day!"

With that we parted, leaving the sculptor to his lonely vigil at the shrine of Nicris, and as my rooms were no great distance away, some half-hour later I was in bed and asleep.

I little suspected that I had actually witnessed the commencement of one of the most amazing mysteries which ever cried out for the presence of Moris Klaw.

II

Some few minutes subsequent to retiring—or so it seemed to me; a longer time actually had elapsed—I was aroused by the ringing of my telephone bell. I scrambled sleepily out of bed and ran to the instrument.

Coram was the caller. And, now fully awake, I listened with an ever-growing wonder to his account of that which had prompted him to ring me up. Briefly, it amounted to this: some mysterious incident, particulars of which he omitted, had aroused Paxton from his sleep. Seeking the cause of the disturbance, the artist had unlocked the studio door and gone out into the garden. He was absent but a moment and never out of earshot of the door; yet, upon his return, *the statue of Nicris had vanished!*

"I have not hesitated to 'phone through to Wapping," concluded Coram, "and get a special messenger sent to Moris Klaw. You see, the matter is urgent. If the statue cannot be recovered, its loss may spell ruin for Paxton. He had heard me speak of Moris Klaw, and of the wonders he worked in the Greek Room mysteries and accordingly called me up. I knew, if Klaw came, you would be anxious to be present."

"Certainly," I replied, "I wouldn't miss one of his inquiries for anything. Shall I meet you at Paxton's?"

"Yes."

I lost little time in dressing. From Coram's brief account, the mystery appeared to be truly a dark one. Would Moris Klaw respond to this midnight appeal? There was little chance of a big fee; for Paxton was not a rich man; but in justice to the remarkable person whom it is my privilege to present to you in these papers, I must add that monetary considerations seemingly found no place in Klaw's philosophy. He acted, I believe, from sheer love of the work; and this affair, with its bizarre details—the ancient girdle of the dancing girl—the fear of the model, who had declared that the statue moved—was such, I thought, as must appeal to him.

Ten minutes later I was at Paxton's house. He and Coram were in the hall, and Coram admitted me.

"Do you mean," he asked of Paxton, pursuing a conversation which my advent had interrupted, "that the statue melted into the empty air?"

"The double doors opening on to the street were securely locked and barred; that of the garden was also locked; I was in the garden, and not ten yards from the studio," was Paxton's reply. "Nevertheless, Nicris had vanished, leaving no trace behind!"

Incredible though the story appeared, its confirmation was to be found in the speaker's face. I was horrified to see how haggard he looked.

"It will ruin me!" he said, and reiterated the statement again and again.

"But, my dear fellow," I cried, "surely you have not given up hope of recovering the statue? After all, such a robbery as this can scarcely have been perpetrated without leaving some clue behind."

"Robbery!" repeated Paxton, looking at me strangely: "you would be less confident that it is a case of robbery, Searles, if you had heard what I heard!"

I glanced at Coram, but he merely shrugged his shoulders.

"What do you mean?" I said.

"Then Coram has not told you?"

"He has told me that something aroused you in the night and that you left the studio to investigate the matter."

"Correct, so far. Something did arouse me; and the thing was a voice!"

"A voice?"

"It would be, I suppose, about two hours after you had gone, and I was soundly asleep in the studio, when I suddenly awoke and sat up to listen—for it seemed to me that I heard a cry immediately outside the door.''

"What kind of cry?"

"Of that I was not, at first, by any means certain; but after a brief interval the cry was repeated. It sounded more like the voice of a boy than that of a man and it uttered but one word: 'Nicris!' ''

"And then?"

"I sprang on to the floor, and stood for a moment in doubt—the thing seemed so uncanny. The electric light is not, as you know, installed in the studio, or I should have certainly switched it on. For possibly a minute I hesitated, and then, as I pulled the curtains aside and stood by the door to listen, for the third occasion the cry was repeated, this time coming indisputably from immediately outside."

"You refer to the door that opens on to the garden?"

"Exactly—close to which stands my bed. This, then, decided me. Taking up the small revolver which I have always kept handy since Nicris was completed, I unlocked the door and stepped out into the garden—''

A vehicle, cab or car, was heard to draw up outside the house. Came the sound of a rumbling voice. Coram sprang to the door.

"Moris Klaw!" I cried.

"Good-morning, Mr. Coram!" said the strange voice, from the darkness outside. "Good-morning, Mr. Searles!"

Moris Klaw entered.

He wore his flat-topped, brown bowler of effete pattern; he wore his long, shabby, caped coat; and from beneath it gleamed the pointed, glossy toe-caps of his continental boots. Through his gold-rimmed glasses he peered into the shadows of the hall. His scanty, colourless beard appeared less adequate than ever to clothe the massive chin. The dim light rendered his face more cadaverous and more yellow even than usual.

"And this," he proceeded, as the anxious sculptor came forward, "is Mr. Paxton, who has lost his statue? Good-morning, Mr. Paxton!"

He bowed, removing the bowler and revealing his great, high brow. Coram was about to reclose the door.

"Ah, no!" Moris Klaw checked him. "My daughter is to come yet with my cushion!"

Paxton stared, not comprehending, but stared yet harder when Isis Klaw appeared, carrying a huge red cushion. She was wrapped in a cloak which effectually concealed her lithe figure, and from the raised hood her darkly beautiful face looked out with bewitching effect. She divided between Coram and myself one of her dazzling smiles.

"It is Mr. Paxton," said her father, indicating the sculptor. Then, indicating the girl: "It is my daughter, Isis. Isis will help us to look for Nicris. Why am I here, an old fool who ought to be asleep? Because of this girdle your statue wore. I so well remember when it was dug up. I cannot know its history; but be sure it is evil. From the beginning, please, Mr. Paxton!"

"I am awfully indebted to you! Won't you come in and sit down?" said Paxton, glancing at the girl in bewilderment.

"No, no!" replied Klaw, "let us stand. It is good to stand, and stand upright; for it is because he can do this that man is superior to the other animals!"

Coram and I knew Klaw's mannerisms, but I could see that Paxton thought him to be a unique kind of lunatic. Nevertheless he narrated something of the foregoing up to the point reached at Moris Klaw's arrival.

"Proceed slowly, now," said Klaw. "You left the door open behind you?"

"Yes; but I was never more than ten yards from it. It would have been physically impossible for any one to remove the statue unknown to me. You must remember that it was no light weight."

"One moment," I interrupted. "Are you sure that the statue was in its place before you came out?"

"Certain! There was a bright moon, and the figure was the first thing my eyes fell upon when I pulled the curtain aside."

"Did you *touch* it?" rumbled Moris Klaw.

"No. There was no occasion to do so."

"How much to be regretted, Mr. Paxton! The sense of touch is so exquisite a thing!"

We all wondered at his words.

"Stepping just outside the door," Paxton resumed, "I looked to right and left. There was no one in sight. Then I walked to the wall—a matter of some ten yards—and, pulling myself up by my hands, looked over into the street. It was deserted, save for a constable on the opposite corner. I know him, slightly, and his presence convinced me that no one could either have come into or gone out of the garden by way of the wall. I did not call him, but immediately returned to the studio door."

"In all, you were absent from the studio about how long?" asked Moris Klaw.

"Not a second over half a minute!"

"And on returning once more to the door?"

"A single glance showed me that the statue had gone!"

"Good Heavens!" I said; "it sounds impossible. Was the constable on point duty?"

"He was; there is always an officer there. He stood in sight of the double doors opening on to the street during the whole time, so that 'Nicris' unquestionably came out by way of the garden or melted into thin air. Since the only exit from the garden also opens on to the street, how, but by magic, can the statue have been removed from the premises?"

"Ah, my friend," said Moris Klaw, "you talk of magic as one talks of onions! How little you know"—he swept wide his arms, looking upward—"of the phenomena of the two atmospheres! Proceed!"

"The throne," continued Paxton, who was becoming impressed as was evident by the uncanny sense of power which emanated in some way from Moris Klaw—"remains."

"And the statue—it was attached to it?"

"As to the figure being attached, I may say that it was only partially so. Materials for completing the work were to have arrived to-day."

"How long would it have taken to detach it?" growled Klaw.

"Granting some knowledge of the nature of the work, not long—for, as I have said, in this respect it was incomplete. Half an hour or so, I should have believed!"

"Then," I said, "the matter, in brief, stands thus: In the course of thirty seconds, during which time a constable was in view of one entrance and you were ten yards from the other, some one detached the statue from the throne—an operation involving half an hour's skilled labour—and unseen by yourself or the officer, removed it from the premises."

"Oh, the thing is impossible!" groaned Paxton. "There is something unearthly in the affair. I wish I had never set eyes upon that accursed girdle!"

"Curse not the girdle," rumbled Moris Klaw. "Curse instead its wearer, and inform us on finding Nicris to be missing, what did you do?"

"I hastily searched the studio. A brief investigation convinced me that neither statue nor thief was concealed there. I then came out, locked the door, and having examined the garden, hailed the constable. He had been on duty for four hours at that point and had observed absolutely nothing of an unusual nature. He saw you fellows come out by the garden entrance, and from that time until I hailed him, nothing, he declared, had come in or gone out!"

"He heard no cry?"

"No; it was not loud enough to be audible from the corner."

"Lastly," said Klaw, "have you informed Scotland Yard?"

"No," answered the sculptor; "nor will the constable lodge information; moreover, I withheld from him the object of my inquiries. If this business gets into the papers I shall be a ruined man!"

"I have hopes," Klaw assured him, "that it will get in no papers. Let us proceed now to the scene of these wonderful happenings. It is my custom, Mr. Paxton, to lay my old head down upon the scene of a mystery, and from the air I can sometimes recover the key to the labyrinth!"

"So I have heard," said Paxton.

"You have heard so, yes? You shall see! Lead on, Mr. Paxton! No time must be wasted. I am another like Napoleon, and can sleep on an instant. I do not know insomnia! Lead on. Isis, my child, be careful that it brushes against no object in passing—my odically sterilised cushion!"

We proceeded to the studio.

"I feel that I am responsible for dragging you here at this unearthly hour," said Paxton to Isis Klaw.

She turned her fine eyes upon him.

"My father is indebted for the opportunity," she replied; "and since he has need of me, I am here. I, too, am indebted."

Her supreme self-possession and tone of finality silenced the artist. So far as I could see, everything in the studio was exactly as before, save that Nicris's throne was vacant. The top of the studio was partially glazed, and Moris Klaw peered up at it earnestly.

"From above," he rumbled, "I should wish to look down into below. How do I reach it?"

"The only step-ladder is that in the studio," answered Paxton. "I will bring it out."

He did so. The grey light of dawn was creeping into the sky and against that sombre background we watched Moris Klaw crawling about the roof like some giant spider.

"Did you find anything?" asked Paxton, anxiously, as the investigator descended.

"I find what I look for," was the reply; "and no man is entitled to find more. Isis, my child, place that cushion in the ebony chair."

The girl stepped on to the dais, and disposed the red cushion as directed.

"You see," explained Moris Klaw, "whoever has robbed you, Mr. Paxton, runs some one great danger, however clever his plans.

There is, in every criminal scheme, one little point that only Fate can decide—either to hitch or to smooth out—to bring success and riches or whistling policemen and Brixton Gaol! Upon that so critical point his or her mind will concentrate at the critical moment. The critical moment, here, was that of getting Nicris out of your studio.

"I sleep upon that throne where she reclined—the ivory dancer. This sensitive plate—" he tapped his brow—"will reproduce a negative of that critical moment as it seemed in the mind of the one we look for. Isis, return in the cab that waits and be here again at six o'clock."

He placed his quaint bowler upon a table and laid beside it his black cloak. Then, a ramshackle figure in shabby tweed, reclined upon the big ebony chair, his head against the cushion.

"Place my cloak about me, Isis."

The girl did so.

"Good-morning, my child! Good-morning, Mr. Searles! Good-morning, Mr. Coram and Mr. Paxton!"

He closed his eyes.

"Excuse me," began Paxton.

Isis placed her finger to her lips, and signed to us to withdraw silently.

"Ssh!" she whispered. "He is asleep!"

III

At five minutes to six sounded Isis Klaw's ring upon the door bell. Paxton, Coram, and I had spent the interval in discussing the apparently supernatural happening which threatened to wreak the artist's ruin. Again and again he had asked us: "Should I call in the Scotland Yard people? If Moris Klaw fails, consider the price-less time lost!"

"If Moris Klaw fails," Coram assured him, "no one else will succeed!"

We admitted Isis, who wore now a smart tweed costume and a fashionable hat. Beyond doubt, Isis Klaw was strikingly beautiful.

At the door of the studio stood her father, staring straight up to the morning sky, as though by astrological arts he hoped to solve the mystery.

"What times does your model come?" he asked, ere Paxton could question him.

"Half-past ten. But, Mr. Klaw—" began our anxious friend.

"Where does it lead to," Klaw rumbled on, "that lane behind the studio?"

"Tradesmen's entrance to the next house."

"Whose house?"

"Dr. Gleeson."

"M.D.?"

"Yes. But tell me, Mr. Klaw—tell me, have you any clue?"

"My mind, Mr. Paxton, records for me that Nicris was not stolen away, but *walked!* Plainly, I feel her go tip-toe, tip-toe, so silent and cautious! She is concerned, this barbaric dancing-girl who escapes from your studio, with two things. One is some very big man. She thinks, as she tip-toes, of one very tall; six feet and three inches at least! So it is not of you she thinks, Mr. Paxton. We shall see of whom it is. Tell me the name of your acquaintance, the point-policeman."

We were all staring at Moris Klaw, spellbound with astonishment. But Paxton managed to mumble—

"James—Constable James."

"We shall seek him, this James, at the section-house of the police depot," rumbled Klaw. "Be silent, Mr. Paxton; let no one know of your loss. And hope."

"I can see no ground for hope!"

"No? But I? I recognise the clue, Mr. Paxton! What a great science is that of mental photography!"

What did he mean? None of us could surmise, and I could see that poor Paxton reposed no faith whatever in the eccentric methods of the investigator. He would have voiced his doubts, I think, but he met a glance from the dark eyes of Isis Klaw which silenced him.

"My child," said Klaw to his daughter, "take the cushion and return. My negative is a clear one. You understand?"

"Perfectly," replied Isis with composure.

"Breakfast—" began Paxton, tentatively.

But Moris Klaw waved his hands, and enveloped himself in the big cloak.

"There is no time for such gross matters!" he said. "We are busy."

From the brown bowler he took out a scent-spray, and bedewed his high, bald forehead with verbena.

"It is exhausting, that odic photography!" he explained.

Shortly afterwards he and I walked around to the local police depot. Something occurred to me, *en route.*

"By the way," I said, "what was the other thing of which you spoke? The thing that you declared Nicris to be thinking of, though I don't understand in the least how one can refer to the 'thoughts' of an ivory statue!"

"Ah," rumbled my companion, "it is something I shall explain later—that other fear of the missing one."

Arriving at the police depot, "Shall I ask for Constable James?" I said.

"Ah, no," replied Klaw. "It is for the constable that he relieved at twelve o'clock I am looking."

Inquiry showed that the latter officer—his name was Freeman—had just entered the section-house. Moris Klaw's questions elicited the following story—although its bearing upon the matter in hand was not evident to me.

Towards twelve o'clock, that is, shortly before Freeman was relieved, a man, supporting a woman, came down the street and entered the gate of Dr. Gleeson's house. The woman was enveloped in a huge fur cloak which entirely concealed her face and figure, but from her feeble step the constable judged her to be very ill. Considering the lateness of the hour, also, he concluded that the case must be a serious one; he further supposed the sick woman to be resident in the neighbourhood, since she came on foot.

He had begun to wonder at the length of the consultation, when, nearly an hour later, the man appeared again from the shadows of the drive, still supporting the woman. Pausing at the gate he waves his hand to the policeman.

Constable Freeman ran across the road immediately.

"Fetch me a taxicab, officer!" said the stranger, supporting his companion and exhibiting much solicitude.

Freeman promptly ran to the corner of Beira Road, and returned with a cab from the all-night rank.

"Open the door!" directed the man, who was a person of imposing height—some six-feet-three, Freeman averred.

"Ha, ha!" growled Moris Klaw, "six-feet-three! What a wondrous science!"

He seemed triumphant; but I was merely growing more nonplussed.

With that, carefully wrapping the cloak about the woman's figure, the big man took her up in his arms and placed her inside the cab—the only glimpse of her which the constable obtained being that of a small foot clad in a silk stocking. She had apparently dropped her shoe.

Tenderly assisting her to a corner of the vehicle, the man, having

bent and whispered some word of encouragement in her ear, directed the cabman to drive to the Savoy.

"Did you give him your assistance?" asked Moris Klaw.

"No. He did not seem to require it."

"And the number of the cabman?"

Freeman fetched his notebook and supplied the required information.

"Thank you, Constable Freeman," said Klaw. "You are a very
alert constable. Good-morning, Constable Freeman!"

Again satisfaction beamed from behind my companion's glasses.
But to my eyes the darkness grew momentarily less penetrable.
For these inquiries bore upon matters which had occurred prior to
twelve o'clock; and, Coram, myself, and Paxton had seen the
statue in its usual place considerably after midnight! My brain was
in a turmoil.

Said Moris Klaw: "That cab was from the big garage at Brixton.
We shall ring up the Brixton garage and learn where the man may
be found. Perhaps, if Providence is with us—and Providence is
with the right—he has not yet again left home."

From a public call-office we rang up the garage, and learned
that the man we wanted was not due to report for duty until ten
o'clock. We experienced some difficulty in obtaining his private
address, but finally it was given to us. Thither we hastened, and
aroused the man from his bed.

"A big gentleman and a sick lady," said Moris Klaw, "they
hired your cab from Dr. Gleeson's, near Beira Road, at about
twelve o'clock last night, and you drove them to the Savoy Hotel."

"No, sir. He changed the address afterwards. I've been wondering why. I drove him to Number 6A, Rectory Grove, Old Town,
Clapham."

"Was the lady by then recovered—no? Yes?"

"Partly, sir. I heard him talking to her. But he carried her into
the house."

"Ah," said Moris Klaw, "there is much genius wasted; but what
a great science is the science of the mind!"

IV

Many times Moris Klaw knocked upon the door of the house in
Clapham Old Town, a small one standing well back from the road-
way. Within we could hear some one coughing.

Then the door was suddenly thrown open, and a man appeared

who must have stood some six feet three inches. He had finely chiselled features, was clean-shaven and wore pince-nez.

Klaw said a thing that had a surprising effect.

"What!" he rumbled, "has Nina caught cold?"

The other glared, with a sudden savagery coming into his eyes, fell back a step, and clenched his great fists.

"Enough, Jean Colette!" said Moris Klaw, "you do not know me, but I know you. Attempt no tricks, or it is the police and not a meddlesome, harmless old fool who will come. Enter, Jean! We follow."

For a moment longer the big man hesitated, and I saw the shadows of alternate resolves passing across his fine features. Then clearly he saw that surrender was inevitable, shrugged his shoulders, and stared hard at my companion.

"Enter, messieurs," he said, with a marked French accent.

He said no more, but led the way into a long, bare room at the rear of the house. To term the apartment a laboratory would be correct but not inclusive; for it was, in addition, a studio and a workshop. Glancing rapidly around him, Moris Klaw asked: "Where is it?"

The man's face was a study as he stood before us, looking from one to the other. Then a peculiar smile, indescribably winning, played around his lips. "You are very clever, and I know when I am beaten," he remarked; "but had you come four hours later it would have been one hour too late."

He strode up the room to where a tall screen stood, and, seizing it by the top, hurled it to the ground.

Behind, on a model's dais, reclined the statue of Nicris, in a low chair!

"You have already removed the girdle and one of the anklets," rumbled Klaw.

This was true. Indeed, it now became evident that the man had been interrupted in his task by our arrival. Opening a leather case that stood upon the floor by the dais, he produced the missing ornaments.

"What action is to be taken, messieurs?" he asked, quietly.

"No action, Jean," replied Moris Klaw. "It is impossible, you see. But why did you delay so long?"

The other's reply was unexpected.

"It is a task demanding much time and care, if the statue is not to be ruined; otherwise I should have performed it in Mr. Paxton's studio instead of going to the trouble of removing the figure—

and—Nina's condition has caused me grave anxiety throughout the night.'' He stared hard at Moris Klaw. We could hear the sound of coughing from some room hard by. "Who are you, m'sieur?'' he asked pointedly.

"An old fool who knew Nina when she posed at Julien's, Jean,'' was the reply, "and who knew you, also, in Paris.''

V

Paxton, Coram, myself, and Moris Klaw sat in the studio, and all of us gazed reflectively at the recovered statue.

"It was so evident,'' explained Klaw, "that since you were absent from here but thirty seconds, for any one to have removed the statue during that time was out of the question.''

"But some one did—''

"Not during that time,'' rumbled Moris Klaw. "Nicris was removed whilst you all made merry within the house!''

"But, my dear Mr. Klaw, Searles, Coram and I saw the statue long after that—some time about one o'clock!''

"Wrong, my friend! You saw the *model!*''

"What! Nina?''

"Madame Colette, whom you knew in Paris as Nina—yes! Listen—when I drop off to sleep here and dream that I am afraid for what may happen to some very large man, I dream, also, that I fear to be *touched!* I look down at myself, and I am beautiful! I am ivory of limb and decked with gold! I creep, so cautiously, out of the studio (in my dream; *you* would call it a dream) and I know, when I wake, that I must have been Nicris! Ah, you wonder! Listen.

"At about midnight, whilst your party is amiable together, comes one, Jean Colette, a clever scamp from that metropolis of such perverted genius—Paris. Into Dr. Gleeson's he goes, supporting Madame—your model. This is seen by Constable Freeman. When the trees hide them they climb over the fence into the lane and over the wall into your garden. Nina has a cast of the studio key. How easy for her to get it!

"Jean, a clever rogue with his hands, and a man who promised to be, once, a great artist, detaches the figure from the throne and arrays it as Madame—in Madam's outer garb! Beneath her cloak, Madame is Nicris—with copies of the jewels and all complete. He is clever, this Jean! He is, too, a man of vast strength—a modern Crotonian Milo. Not only does he carry that great piece of ivory from the studio, he lifts it over the wall—did Madame assist?—and into Dr. Gleeson's drive. He bears it to the gate, wrapped in Nina's furs. He calls a policeman! Ah, genius is here! He gives the wrong address. He is as cool as an orange!

"Do they escape now? Not so! He sees that you, finding Nicris missing, will apply to the point-policeman and get hold upon a thread. He says, 'I will make it to appear that the robbery took place at a later time. I will thus gain hours! Another policeman will be on duty when the discovery is made; he will know nothing. He leaves Nina to pretend to be Nicris!

"Ah! she has courage, but her fears are many. Most of all she dreads that you will *touch* her! You do not. And Jean, the ivory statue safe at Clapham, returns for Nina. He comes into the doctor's drive by the further gate—where the point-policeman cannot see him. He wears rubber shoes. He mounts to the studio roof. He lies flat upon the ledge above the door. His voice is falsetto. He calls 'Nicris!'

"Presently, you come out. You peep over the wall. Ah! out, also, is Madame! She stretches up her white arms—so like the real ivory!—he stretches down his steel hands. He raises her beside him! Name of a dog, he is strong!

"Why to the roof and not over the wall? The path is of gravel and her feet are bare. On the roof, to prove me correct, upon the grime are marks of small, bare feet; are marks of men's rubber shoes; are, half-way along, marks of smaller rubber shoes—which he had brought for Nina. He has forethought. They retire by the further gate of your neighbour's drive.

"No doubt he bring her furs as well—no doubt. But she contracts a chill, no wonder! Ah! he is cool, he is daring, he is a great man—"

A maid entered the studio.

"A gentleman to see you, sir."

"Ask him to come along here."

A short interval—and Jean Colette entered, hat in hand!

"These two wedges, m'sieur—" he bowed to Paxton—"which help to attach the girdle. I forgot to return them. Adieu!"

He placed the wedges on a table, and amid a dramatic silence withdrew.

Moris Klaw took out the cylindrical scent-spray from the lining of the brown bowler.

"A true touch of Paris!" he rumbled. "Did I not say he was a great man?"

CASE OF THE BLUE RAJAH

I

Inspector Grimsby called upon me one evening, wearing a great glumness of countenance.

"Look here," said he. "I'm in a bit of a corner. You'll have heard that a committee of commercial magnates has been formed to buy, and on behalf of the City of London to present to the Crown, the big Indian diamond?"

I nodded and pushed the box of cigarettes towards him.

"Well," he continued, thoughtfully selecting one, "they are meeting in Moorgate Street to-morrow morning to complete the deal and formally take over the stone. Sir Michael Cayley, the Lord Mayor, will be present, and he's received a letter, which has been passed on to me."

He fumbled for his pocket-case. Grimsby is a man who will go far. He is the youngest detective-inspector in the service, and he has that priceless gift—the art of using other people for the furtherance of his own ends. I do not intend this criticism unkindly. Grimsby does nothing dishonourable and seeks to rob no man of the credit that may be due. There is nothing underhand about Grimsby, but he is exceedingly diplomatic. He imparts official secrets to me with an ingenuousness entirely disarming—but always for reasons of his own.

"Here you are," he said, and passed a letter to me.

It read as follows—

> *"To the Right Hon. the Lord Mayor of London.*
>
> "My Lord,
>
> "Beware that the Blue Rajah is not stolen on Wednesday the 13th inst. Do not lose sight of it for one moment.
>
> "Your Lordship's obedient servant,
>
> "Moris Klaw."

"You see," continued Grimsby, "Wednesday the thirteenth is to-morrow, when the thing is being brought to Moorgate Street. Naturally, Sir Michael communicated with the Yard, and as I'm in the know about Moris Klaw, I got the job of looking into the matter. I was at the Mansion House this morning."

"I suppose Sir Michael regards this note with suspicion?"

"Well, he's not silly enough to suppose that anybody who thought of stealing the diamond would drop him a line advising him of the matter! But he'd never heard of Moris Klaw until I explained about him. When I told him that Klaw had a theory about the Cycle of Crime, and his letter probably meant that, according to said theory, on Wednesday the thirteenth the Blue Rajah was due to be lifted, so to speak, he laughed. You'll have noticed that people mostly laugh at first about Moris Klaw?"

"Certainly. You did, yourself!"

"I know it—and I'm suffering for it! Klaw won't lift his little finger when I ask him; and as for his daughter, she giggles as though she was looking at a comedian when she looks at *me!* She thinks I'm properly funny!"

"You've been to Wapping, then?"

"Yes, this afternoon. The Lord Mayor wanted a lot of convincing that Moris Klaw was on the straight after I'd told him that the old gentleman was a dealer in curios in the East End. Finally, he suggested that I should find out what the warning meant exactly. But I couldn't get to see Klaw; his daughter said he was out."

"I suppose every precaution will be taken?"

"To-morrow morning we have arranged that I and two other C.I.D. men are to accompany the party to the Safe Deposit vaults to fetch the diamond and we shall guard it on the way back afterwards."

"Who's going to fetch it?"

"Sir John Carron, representing the India Office, Mr. Mark Anderson—the expert—representing the City, and Mr. Gautami Chinje, representing the Gaekwar of Nizam. I was wondering"—he surveyed the burning end of his cigarette—"if you had time to run down to Wapping yourself, and find out from what direction we ought to look for trouble?"

"Sorry, Grimsby," I replied; "I would do it with pleasure, but my evening is fully taken up. Personally, it appears to me that Moris Klaw's warning was a timely one. You seem to be watching the stone pretty closely."

"Like a cat watches a mouse!" he rapped. "If any one steals the Blue Rajah to-morrow, he'll be a clever fellow."

II

Basinghall House, Moorgate Street, is built around a courtyard. You enter under an archway, and find offices before you, offices to right and offices to left. As a matter of fact, Basinghall House was designed for an hotel, but subsequently let off in suites of chambers. The offices of Messrs. Anderson and Brothers are on the left, as you enter, and from the window of the principal's sanctum you may look down into the courtyard.

The room chosen for the meeting on Wednesday morning, however, was one opening off this. In common with the adjoining office—as I have said, that of the principal—it had a second door, opening on a corridor. This latter door, however, was never used and was always kept double-locked. Thus, the doorway from the other office was really its only means of entrance or egress. A large window offered a prospect of the courtyard.

At a quarter to eleven on Wednesday morning, Mr. Anderson (one of the City Aldermen) entered his own private office from the corridor. He was accompanied by Sir John Carron, Mr. Gautami Chinje, and Inspector Grimsby. These three had come with him from the Safe Deposit vaults. Mr. Anderson had possession of the case containing the diamond.

In the office, already awaiting the party, were Sir Michael Cayley (the Lord Mayor), Mr. Morrison Dell, of the Goldsmiths and Silversmiths Company, Sir Vernon Rankin (ex-Lord Mayor), Mr. Werner, of the great engineering firm, and Mr. Anderson, junior. These constituted the Presentation Committee duly appointed by the City of London (excluding, of course, Sir John Carron, of the India Office, Mr. Chinje, representing the vendor of the jewel, and Mr. Grimsby, representing New Scotland Yard).

"We are all present, gentlemen," said Mr. Anderson. "But before we proceed to the business which brings us here, we will enter the inner room, where we shall be quite private."

Accordingly the party of eight passed through the doorway; and Mr. Anderson, senior, entering last, relocked the door behind him. Inspector Grimsby remained alone in the private office.

Eight oaken chairs and a small oaken table bearing a pewter inkpot, two pens and a blotting-pad, represents, with a square of red carpet and a framed photograph bearing the legend: "Jagersfontein Diamond Workings, Orange Free State, 1909," an inventory of the furniture.

The company being seated, Mr. Anderson, by the table, rose and said—

"Gentlemen, our business this morning can be briefly dealt with. I have here"—he produced a leather case, opened it and placed it on the table before him—"the diamond known as the Blue Rajah. Its history may be summarised thus: It appeared in the year 1680, and is supposed to have been found in the Kollur Mine, on the Kostna. It had a weight of 254½ carats in the rough, but was reduced to 132 carats in the cutting. It has been successively owned by Nadir Shah, Princess de Lamballe, the Sultan Abdúl Hámid, Mr. Simon Rabstein of New York, and, finally, the Gâekwâr of Nizam. It has no flaws; in fact, two of the original facets were retained when the stone passed through the cutter's hands. It is rose cut and its colour is of the finest water, having the rare blue tint."

He paused, raising the diamond from its receptacle, and holding it in his hand. The sunlight, pouring in through the window, struck flame-spears from the wonderful thing.

"In fact, gentlemen," he concluded, "the Blue Rajah is a fitting offering for the City of London to make to the Crown."

"Hear, hear!" chorused the others; and the diamond was passed from hand to hand. The formal business of making over the stone to the Committee was then transacted. A huge cheque was placed in the pocket-case of Mr. Gautami Chinje, autographs were affixed to two formidable documents; and the Blue Rajah became the property of the loyal City of London.

"You see," said Sir John Carron, holding the stone daintily between thumb and forefinger, and pointing, lecturer-fashion, "the diamond is perfectly proportioned, being a full three-fifths as deep as it is broad."

"Quite so," agreed Mr. Morris Dell, looking over his shoulder.

"It is the most perfectly proportioned stone I have ever handled, Sir John," said the younger Mr. Anderson—and he stood back surveying the gem with the caressing glance of a connoisseur.

Sir John turned and tenderly laid the diamond in its case. At which moment, exactly, arose a blood-curdling scream in the courtyard below.

"Good Lord!" cried Mr. Werner, "What is that?"

There was a crowded rush to the window—those in the second rank peering over the heads and shoulders of those in the first. The horrid cries continued, in a choking yet shrill crescendo.

"Ah! God in Heaven! You are killing me! No! No! Mercy!... Mercy!... Mercy!..."

"It is some one in the archway," said Sir Vernon Rankin, excitedly. "Can any of you see him?"

No one could, though all craned necks vigorously.

"Unfortunately the window cannot be opened," cried Mr. Anderson. "The catch has jammed in some way. I am having it removed immediately."

The cries ceased. People were running about below, and the blue uniform of a City constable showed among the group in the archway.

"I'll run down and see what has happened," said Mr. Chinje, stepping to the door which opened on the corridor. "Hullo! it is locked!"

Young Mr. Anderson turned to him with a smile.

"Both doors are locked, Mr. Chinje," he said. "For the time being we are virtually prisoners."

"Give me the case," said his father, selecting the key of the door communicating with his private office. "There is no occasion for further delay."

The Lord Mayor turned from the window, through which he had still been vainly peering, and stepped to the table.

"Mr. Anderson!"

"Yes?" said the latter, glancing back, keys in hand.

"Have you the diamond?"

"Certainly not!"

"Then who has it?"

No one had it. But the case was empty!

III

Mr. Anderson replaced the keys in his pocket. His ruddy face suddenly had grown pale. Sir Michael Cayley, the empty case in his hand, stood staring across the room like a man dazed. Then he forced speech to his lips.

"Gentlemen," he said, "since it is physically impossible for the diamond to have left this room, in this room it must be searched for—and found. First, is it by any chance upon the floor?"

A brief examination showed that it was not.

"Then," continued Sir Michael, "the painful conclusion is unavoidable that it is upon some one's person!"

An angry murmur arose. Mr. Anderson raised his hand.

"Gentlemen," he said, "Sir Michael states no more than the fact."

And, his face remaining very pale, he removed his coat and waistcoat and threw them upon the table, emptied his trouser-pockets and turned out the linings.

"Be good enough to examine them, gentlemen," he said.

There was a momentary hesitation; but the Lord Mayor stepped forward and in a businesslike way examined the contents of the several pockets. He turned to Mr. Anderson.

"Thank you," he said. "If the others are satisfied, I am."

There was a murmur of assent; and as the owner of the office picked up his property, Sir Michael, in turn, submitted himself to examination. All the others followed suit, without further hesitation. And the result of the inquiry was *nil*.

Eight anxious faces surrounded the little table.

"I suggest," said Mr. Anderson, quietly, "that we admit the detective who is in my office. His experience may enable him to succeed where we have failed."

All agreeing, the communicating door was opened. Mr. Anderson, without quitting the room, called to Inspector Grimsby. The inspector entered. The door was relocked.

"Inspector," said Mr. Anderson, "the diamond is missing!"

Whereupon Grimsby's eyes opened widely in amazement.

"Are you sure, sir?"

"Unfortunately I cannot doubt it."

"When did you last see it?"

"At the moment when that uproar broke out, below," said Mr. Dell.

"Ah," murmured Grimsby, thoughtfully. "You all rushed to the window, I expect?"

"Exactly."

"Leaving the diamond on the table?"

"Yes."

"That's when it was stolen!"

"Very possibly, Inspector," said the Lord Mayor, a stoutly built man with an imperious manner. "But who took it and where did he conceal it?"

"You must all submit to be searched, gentlemen!"

"We have already done so."

"I am more used to that sort of thing. Do you all agree to being searched by me?"

All did. The previous performance was repeated. Grimsby not only searched the garments but passed his hands all over the persons of the eight, even making them open their mouths and tapping at their teeth with a lead pencil!

"I did some I.D.B. work in South Africa," he explained. "It's wonderful where a clever man can hide a diamond."

But no diamond was found!

The better to bring home to those who read these records the truly amazing nature of this circumstance, I will explain again, here, the construction and furniture of the apartment.

It was a small room, some fourteen feet by eighteen. It contained eight oak chairs and an oak table; a red carpet; its walls were distempered and bare, save for the framed photograph previously mentioned. The one window was closed and fastened. The door opening on the corridor was double-locked. Save when it had been opened to admit Grimsby, the door communicating with the next office had also been locked throughout the course of the meeting. There was no fireplace. Ventilation was provided for by a small, square ventilator above the corridor door.

Having convinced himself that the diamond was not upon the person of any one present, Inspector Grimsby took but two or three minutes to satisfy himself that it was not concealed elsewhere.

"Gentlemen," he said, slowly, "the Blue Rajah is not in this room!"

The Lord Mayor glared. He was a director of the company with which the diamond was insured.

"My good man," he said, "it isn't humanly possible for anything—anything—to have gone out of this room since we entered it!"

"I'm disposed to agree with you, sir," replied Grimsby. "But at the same time I'll stake my reputation that the diamond isn't inside these four walls! Although my search of you gentlemen was a mere formality, I assure you it was thorough. I've searched a few score Kaffirs and I know my business. As to the room itself, it's as bare as a drawing-board. A child could find the smallest bead in it inside twenty seconds. You can take it from me as a stone certainty that the diamond has gone!"

"Then we are wasting precious time!" cried Sir Michael. "Commence the pursuit at once, Inspector!"

Grimsby's jaw shot out doggedly.

"If you could give me a hint where to begin, sir," he said. "I shouldn't waste another second!"

"Hang it all, that's your business, my man!"

"I know it is, sir. But I'm only a poor human policeman, after all. We shan't gain anything by getting angry, shall we? This room, to all intents and purposes, is a locked box from which something has been extracted without lifting the lid. That's a conjuring trick, and as puzzling to me as it is to you."

Sir Michael softened. Inspector Grimsby is not a man who can be browbeaten.

"Quite right, Inspector," he said; "I recognise the difficulties. But this loss is horrible. It reflects upon all of us—all of us. If the news of this theft leaks out—if the stone cannot be recovered—a certain stigma—I cannot blind myself to the fact—a certain stigma will attach to our commercial integrity. Clean as our records may be, we cannot hope to escape it. For God's sake, Inspector, set your wits to work."

Indeed, those were anxious faces that surrounded the detective. Suddenly—

"Ah!" cried the Lord Mayor, "the man Klaw! On his own showing he knows something of this matter! Mr. Grimsby——"

Grimsby held up his hand and nodded.

"With your permission, gentlemen," he said, "I will try to get into communication with Moris Klaw at once."

"Good," said Mr. Anderson; "and meanwhile, whilst we await the result of your efforts, Inspector, I suggest, in the interests of all, that we lunch in my office. It may be inconvenient for many of you, but for my own part I am anxious to remain on these premises until we have news of the whereabouts of the diamond."

The proposal was carried unanimously. No one of those substantial men of affairs was anxious to lay himself open to the suspicion of having removed the great Blue Rajah from the office! For, as Sir Michael quite justly had pointed out, where a diamond worth an emperor's ransom is concerned, reputations melt like ice beneath a tropical sun.

In this way, then, I found myself concerned in the case; for Grimsby hastened to call me up, begging me to urge the retiring Moris Klaw to quit his Wapping haunt, to which he clung like Diogenes to his wooden cavern, and to journey to Moorgate Street. Fortunately I was in my rooms, and, willing enough to enjoy an opportunity of studying Klaw at work, I despatched a district messenger to him, trusting that he would be at his shop.

Since evidently he had apprehended that an attempt would be made this morning, I did not doubt that he would be at home. Indeed, he rang me up less than half-an-hour later and arranged to meet me at Mr. Anderson's office.

"I warned him—that Lord Mayor," came his rumbling continental tones along the wire, "how he must not let it out of his sight. He ignored me. So! Ring him up immediately, and tell him to have ready for me hot black coffee. It stimulates the inner perception, when green tea is not obtainable."

Without delay I followed Moris Klaw's instructions, and then

hurried out and into a cab. My duties, as Klaw's biographer—
self-appointed—forbade my delaying.

We arrived at Basinghall House simultaneously. Our cabs drew
up one behind the other. Except for the presence of Inspector
Grimsby at the entrance, there was nothing to show that a stupen-
dous robbery had been committed there less than an hour before.
As I descended, Grimsby ran and opened the door of the other
cab. He offered his hand to the beautiful girl who was within,
according her all the nervous deference due to a queen.

And indeed no queen of ancient times could have looked more
queenly than Isis Klaw—no Hatshepsu could have carried herself
more regally. She wore a dark, close-fitting costume and ermine
furs. In contrast to the snowy peltry, her large, black eyes and perfect red lips rendered her a study for the brush of a painter, but,
like her Oriental grace, defied the pen of the scribe.

Moris Klaw's daughter, her dazzling beauty enhanced by all the
feminine arts of Paris, was a rare exotic one would not have sought
in the neighbourhood of Wapping Old Stairs. But her father
afforded a contrast at least as singular as her residence.

Behind this seductive vision he appeared, enveloped in his caped
coat, his yellow bearded face crowned by the brown bowler of
Early Victorian pattern—indeed apparently of Early Victorian
manufacture. He peered at the taximeter through his gold-rimmed
pince-nez.

"Two and tenpence," he rumbled, hoarsely. "That meter re-
quires inspection, my friend. I have watched it popping up those
two pennies, and I have perceived that it does so every time the cab
bumps upon a drainhole. I am to pay, then, for all the drains between Wapping and Moorgate Street. Here it is—three shillings.
One and fourpence for the company and one and eightpence for
yourself."

He turned aside, raising his hat.

"Good-morning, Mr. Searles! Good-morning, Mr. Grimsby! I
shall charge the City of London one and sixpence for drains. Let us
walk on as far as the courtyard I see yonder, and you shall tell me
all the facts before I interview those others, who will be, of course,
so prejudiced by their misfortune."

We passed on, and many a clerkly glance followed the furry
figure of Isis beneath the archway. Hemmed in by offices, a certain
quietude prevailed in the court yard.

"It is a chilly morning," said Moris Klaw; "but here we will stop
and talk."

Accordingly Grimsby related the known facts of the case, more often addressing his story to the girl than to her father.

"Yes, yes," growled the latter, when the tale was told; "and this crying out—this screaming of murder—what occasioned it?"

"That's the mystery!" explained the detective. "I wish I had run out at once. I might have learned something. As it is, all I can find out amounts to nothing. The clerks and porters and other people who came flocking to the scene found no one here who knew anything about it!"

"The screamer was missing, eh?"

"Vanished! I can't help thinking it was a ruse; though what anybody profited by it isn't clear."

"It is not clear, you say?" rumbled Moris Klaw. "Ah! you have a fog of the mentality, my friend!"

Grimsby flushed.

"Of course," he added, hurriedly, "I can see that it served to divert the attention of the people who ought to have been guarding the diamond. But as both the doors and the window were locked, how did it help to get the stone out of the office?"

Moris Klaw pulled reflectively at his scanty beard.

"We shall see," he rumbled. "Let us ascend."

We entered the lift and went up to the office of Messrs. Anderson and Brothers. The Presentation Committee were awaiting the mysterious Moris Klaw, but had not anticipated a visit from a pretty woman. They were prepared to adopt towards the man who would seem to have had some foreknowledge of the robbery a certain attitude of suspicion. It was amusing to note the change of front when Isis entered. Moris Klaw singled out the Lord Mayor, and the owner of the office, with unerring instinct. He removed his hat.

"Good-morning, Mr. Anderson!" he said. "Good-morning, Sir Michael! Good-morning, gentlemen!"

"This is Mr. Moris Klaw," explained Grimsby, "and Miss Klaw. Mr. Searles."

Mr. Anderson hastened to place chairs. We became seated. Following a short interval, Sir Michael Cayley cleared his throat.

"We are—er—indebted to you, Mr. Klaw," he began, "for taking this trouble. But, in view of your note to me——"

Moris Klaw raised his hand.

"So simple," he said, whilst the Committee watched him, puzzled and surprised—that is, those who were not watching Isis, did so. "I have a library, you understand, of records dealing with such

historic gems. To show you that I have made some study of these
matters I will tell you that the diamond called the Blue Rajah was
discovered on the morning of April the thirteenth, 1680, in the
Kollur Mine, and stolen the same evening!''

"What is your authority for the exact date, Mr. Klaw?" asked
Anderson, with interest; "and for the statement that the diamond
was stolen on the day of its discovery?"

"Fact, Mr. Anderson, is my authority," was the rumbling reply,
"and I can tell you more. The diamond is the birth-stone of the
month of April, and this diamond was itself born on the thirteenth
of that month. To illustrate how its history is associated with April,
I shall only tell you of the beautiful and unhappy Marie de Lamballe. This great diamond was presented to her on the ninth of
April, 1790, and taken from her on the twelfth of April, 1792,
after her return from England, and only six months before her fair
head was stuck upon a pike and held up to the Queen's window!''

He paused impressively, waving his long hands in the air.

"I could recount to you," he resumed, "many such incidents
in the history of the Blue Rajah—and all took place within a week
of its birthday! What day is to-day?"

"Why, it's the thirteenth of April!" said Sir Michael Cayley,
with a start.

"The thirteenth of April," rumbled Moris Klaw. "For many
years the diamond has been too closely guarded for any new incident to occur, but when I learn how to-day it is to be brought here,
how many hands will touch it, how many eyes will look upon it, I
know that there is danger! Its history repeats. These incidents—"
again he waved his hands—"proceed in cycles. I warned you. But it
was perhaps inevitable. The Cycle of Crime is as inevitable and
immutable as the cycle of the ages. Man's will has no power to
check it."

Every one in the room was deeply impressed. Indeed, no one
could have failed to recognise in the speaker a man of powerful
mind, one of penetrating and unusual intellect.

"Had I had the good fortune to have met you, Mr. Klaw," said
the Lord Mayor, "I should have attached a greater, and—er—a
different, significance to your note. Your theories are strange ones,
but to-day they have received strange and ample substantiation. I
can only hope—and I do so with every confidence in your great
ability" (Moris Klaw rose and bowed), "that you will be able to
recover the diamond whose loss you so truly predicted."

"I will ask you," replied Moris Klaw, "to have sent into me the

black coffee. Myself, my daughter, Mr. Searles, and Mr. Grimsby
will view the room from which the robbery took place."

"You would wish us to remain here?" asked Mr. Anderson,
glancing at the others.

"I would so wish it, yes."

"I hope, Mr. Klaw," said Sir Michael Cayley, "that you will
not hesitate to send me an account of your fee and expenditures."

"I shall not so hesitate," replied Moris Klaw.

IV

We entered the small room from which the Blue Rajah had been
spirited away. Grimsby, who was badly puzzled, was evidently glad
of Klaw's cooperation. Moris Klaw's letter of warning, leading to
the request for Moris Klaw's attendance, had enabled the Scotland
Yard man to summon that keen intellect to his aid without com-
promising his professional reputation. He would lose no credit that
might accrue if the gem were recovered, and in short was congratu-
lating himself upon a diplomatic move.

"It's beyond me," he said, "how the thing was got out of the
room. With this door shut, the window fastened, and the other
door double-locked, as it always is, practically the place is a box."

Moris Klaw, from its hiding-place in the lining of his hat, took
out the scent-spray and squirted verbena upon his face.

"A box—yes," he rumbled; "and so stuffy. No air."

"There's no ventilation," explained Grimsby. "That square hole
over the door is intended for ventilation, but as there's no corresponding aperture over the window or elsewhere it's useless. Anyway, it only opens on the passage."

"Ah. You searched them all quite thoroughly?"

"Certainly; like Kaffirs. But I didn't expect to find it."

"Blessed is he who expecteth little. Isis, my child, there is some
one knocking."

Isis opened the door communicating with Mr. Anderson's office
and a boy entered carrying a tray, with a coffee pot and cup upon it.

"Good," said Moris Klaw. "I shall not sleep in this room, Mr.
Searles. It is difficult to sleep in the morning and I cannot wait for
night. I shall sit here at this table for one hour with my mind a
perfect blank. I shall think of nothing. That is a great art, Mr.
Searles—to think of nothing. Few people but ascetics can do it. Try
it for yourself, and you will find that thinking of trying not to think

is the nearest you will get to it! I shall expose my mind, a sensitive blank, to the etheric waves created here by mental emotion.

"I shall secure many alien impressions of horror at finding the Blue Rajah to be missing. That is unavoidable. But I hope, amongst all these, to find that other thought-thing—the fear of the robber at the critical moment of his crime! That should be a cogent and forceful thought—keener and therefore stronger to survive, because a thought of danger, but of gain, than the thoughts of loss with which this atmosphere is laden."

He stood up, removing his caped coat and revealing the shabby tweed suit which he wore. A big French knot, of black silk, looked grotesquely out of place beneath his yellow face with its edging of toneless beard.

"Isis," he said, "lay my cloak carefully upon that chair by the window. I will sit there."

Grimsby stepped forward to assist.

"No, no!" said Isis, but smiled enchantingly. "No hand but mine must touch it until my father has secured his impression!"

She laid the coat upon the chair, completely covering it; and Moris Klaw sat down.

"Another cup of coffeè," he said; and his daughter poured one out and handed it to him. "This is Java coffee and truly not coffee at all. There is no coffee but *Mocha*—a thing you English will never learn. Return in an hour, gentlemen. Isis, ask that no disturbing sound is allowed within or without. That Committee, it can go home. None of it has the diamond."

"And the other gentlemen?" asked Grimsby. "They'll be anxious to get about their business, too. There's Sir John Carron from the India Office and Mr. Gautami Chinje—the Gaekwar's representative."

"Of course—certainly," mused Moris Klaw. "But, of course, too, they will all be anxious to know immediately the result of my inquiries. Listen—Mr. Anderson will remain; he can represent the City. Mr. Chinje, you will perhaps ask him to remain, to represent the Gaekwar—the vendor; and Sir John Carron, he might be so good. Make those arrangements, Mr. Grimsby, and let nothing again disturb me."

We left him, returning to the outer office.

Sir John Carron expressed himself willing to remain.

"If I may use your telephone for a moment, Mr. Anderson," he said, "I can put off an engagement."

Mr. Chinje had no other engagement, and Mr. Anderson's duties had detained him in any event. There was some general, but subdued, conversation before the rest of the party left; but finally Sir John, Chinje, Grimsby, Isis Klaw and myself found ourselves in a waiting-room on the opposite side of the corridor, provided with refreshments and the gentlemen of the party with cigars, whilst the hospitable and deeply anxious Messrs. Anderson piled the table with periodical literature for our entertainment.

It was a curious interlude, which I shall always remember.

Sir John Carron, a tall, bronzed military man, middle-aged and perfectly groomed, surveyed Isis Klaw through his monocle with undisguised admiration. She bore this scrutiny with the perfect composure which was hers, and presently engaged the admiring baronet in some conversation about India, wherein Mr. Chinje presently joined. Chinje had all the quiet self-possession of a high-caste Hindu; and his darkly handsome face exhibited no signs of annoyance when Sir John adopted that tone of breezy patronage characteristic of some Anglo-Indian officers who find themselves in the company of a well-bred native. Grimsby, with recognition of his social inferiority written largely upon him, smoked, for the most part, in silence—Isis having given him permission to light up. Seeing his covert glances at this intimate trio, I ultimately succeeded in making the conversation a general one, thereby earning the Scotland Yard man's evident gratitude.

"You know, Inspector Grimsby," said Sir John, "I never was searched before to-day! But, by Jove, you did it very efficiently! I was dreadfully tempted to strike you when you calmly turned out my purse! Your method was far more workmanlike than Sir Michael Cayley's a few minutes earlier. He forgot to look in my watch-case, but you didn't!"

Grimsby smiled.

"There's more in a simple thing like searching a man than most people take into consideration," he replied. "I've known a Kaffir in the mines who—excuse me, Miss Klaw—wore no more than Adam, to walk off with stones worth my year's wages."

"I'm prepared to accept your assurance, Inspector," said Sir John, "that none of us had the diamond about our persons."

"My father has accepted it," added Isis Klaw; "and that is conclusive."

Which brought us face to face again with the amazing problem that we were there to solve. How, by any known natural law, had the Blue Rajah been taken out of the room? None of us could conjecture. That the detective was hopelessly mystified, his inaction, awaiting the result of Moris Klaw's séance, was sufficient proof. I wondered if the Commissioner would have approved of his passive attitude and entire dependence upon the efforts of an amateur, yet failed to perceive what other he could adopt. One thing was certain; if the diamond was recovered, its recovery would be recorded among Detective-Inspector Grimsby's successful cases! And there he sat placidly smoking one of Mr. Anderson's cabañas.

At the expiration of the hour specified, Isis Klaw rose and walked across to Mr. Anderson's office. Mr. Anderson, his ruddy face—typically that of a lowland Scot—a shade paler than was its wont, I fancy, was glancing from his watch to the clock.

Isis knocked on the inner door, opened it and entered. Sir John Carron was watching with intense interest. Mr. Chinje met my glance and smiled a little sceptically.

Moris Klaw came out with his caped coat on and carrying his bowler in his hand.

"Gentlemen," he said, "I have secured a mental negative, somewhat foggy, owing to those other thought-forms with which the atmosphere is laden. But I have identified him—the thief!"

A sound like a gasp repressed came from somewhere immediately behind me. I turned. Mr. Anderson and Mr. Anderson, junior, stood at my elbow, close by were Mr. Chinje, Grimsby and Sir John Carron.

"Who snorts?" rumbled Moris Klaw, peering through his pince-nez.

"Not I," said Sir John, staring about him.

We all, in turn, denied having uttered the sound.

"Then there is in this office a ghost," declared Klaw, "or a liar!"

"Excuse me, Mr. Klaw," began Mr. Anderson, with some heat.

Moris Klaw raised his hand. His daughter's magnificent eyes blazed defiance at us all.

"No anger," implored the rumbling voice. "No anger. Anger is a misuse of the emotions. There are present eight persons here. Some one snorted. Eight persons deny the snort. It is a ghost or a liar. Am I evident to you?"

"Your logic is irrefutable," admitted the younger Mr. Anderson, glancing from face to face. "It pains me to have to admit that you are right!"

In turn, I examined the faces of those present. Grimsby was a man witless with wonder. Both the Andersons were embarrassed and angry. Isis Klaw was scornfully triumphant, her father was, as ever nonchalant. Sir John Carron looked ill at ease. Mr. Chinje appeared to have changed his opinion of the eccentric investigator and now studied him with the calm interest of the cultured Oriental.

"I shall now make you laugh," said Moris Klaw. "I shall tell you what he was thinking of at the psychological instant—that mysterious thief. He was thinking of two things. One was a very pretty, fair young lady and the other was a funny thing. He was thinking of throwing twelve peanuts into a parrot's cage!"

V

There are speeches so entirely unexpected that their effect is unappreciable until some little time after the utterance. This speech of Moris Klaw's was of that description. For some moments no one seemed to grasp exactly what he had said, simple though his words had been. Then, it was borne home to us—that grotesque declaration; and I think I have never seen men more amazed.

Could he be jesting?

"Mr. Klaw——" began Sir John Carron. "But—"

"One moment, Sir John," interrupted Klaw. "Let all remain here for one moment. I shall return."

Whilst we stared, like so many fools, he shuffled from the office with his awkward gait. During his brief absence no one spoke. We were restrained, undoubtedly, by the presence of Isis Klaw, who, one hand upon her hip and with the other swinging her big ermine muff, smiled at us with a sort of pitying scorn for our stupidity.

Moris Klaw returned.

"Let me see," he rumbled, reflectively, "have you, Sir John Carron or Mr. Chinje, a specimen of the handwriting of the Gaekwar of Nizam?"

Chinje and Sir John stared.

"At the office—possibly," replied Sir John.

"I have my instructions, signed by him," said Mr. Chinje. "But not here."

"At your hotel, yes?"

"Yes," replied Chinje, shortly.

He gave me the impression that he resented Moris Klaw's catechising as that of a fool and an incompetent meddler with affairs of great importance.

"Then, gentlemen," said Klaw, "we must adjourn to examine that signature."

"Really," the younger Mr. Anderson burst out, "I must protest against this! You will pardon me, Mr. Klaw; I believe you to be sincere in your efforts on our behalf, but such an expedition can be no more than a wild-goose chase! What can the Gaekwar's signature have to do with the theft of the diamond?''

"I will tell you something, my feverish friend," said Moris Klaw, slowly. "The Blue Rajah is not on these premises. It is gone! It went before I came. If it is ever to come back you will put on your hat and accompany me to examine the signature to Mr. Chinje's instructions."

"I must add my protest to Mr. Anderson's," remarked Chinje. "This is mere waste of time."

"Mr. Grimsby," resumed Klaw, placidly, "it is a case to be hushed up, this. There must be no arrests!"

"Eh?" cried Grimsby.

"Sir John Carron will ring up the Commissioner and he will say that Detective-Inspector Grimsby has traced the Blue Rajah, which was stolen, but that for reasons of state, Detective-Inspector Grimsby will make a confidential report and no arrest!"

"Really——" began Sir John.

"Mr. Klaw," cried Anderson, interrupting excitedly. "You are jesting with men who are faced by a desperate position! I ask you, as man to man, if you know who stole the Blue Rajah and where it is?"

"I reply," rumbled Moris Klaw, "that I suspect who stole it, that I am doubtful how it was stolen, and that when I have examined the Gaekwar's signature I may know where it is!"

His reply had a tone of finality quite unanswerable. His attitude was that of a stone wall; and he had, too, something of the rugged strength of such a wall—of a Roman wall, commanding respect.

Sir John got into communication with the Commissioner, as desired by Klaw, and we all left the office and went down in the lift to the hall.

"Two cabs will be needful," said Moris Klaw; and two cabs were summoned.

Sir John Carron, the Andersons and Moris Klaw entered one; Isis Klaw, Grimsby, Chinje and I the other.

"The Hôtel Astoria," directed Chinje.

Throughout the drive to the Strand, Isis chatted to Grimsby, to his great delight. Mr. Chinje contented himself with monosyllabic replies to my occasional observations. He seemed to be disgusted with the manner in which the inquiry was being conducted. When the two cabs drove into the courtyard of the hotel, the one in which I was seated followed the other. Mr. Chinje, on my left, descended first, and Moris Klaw also descended first from the cab in front.

As he did so he stumbled on the step and clutched at Chinje for support. Isis leapt forward to his assistance.

"Ah," growled Klaw, hobbling painfully, and resting one hand upon Chinje's shoulder and the other upon his daughter's. "That foolish ankle of mine! How unfortunate! An accident, Mr. Chinje, which I met with in Egypt. I fell quite twenty feet in the shaft of a tomb and broke my ankle. At the least strain, I suffer yet."

"Allow me, Mr. Chinje," said Grimsby, stepping forward.

"No, no!" rumbled Klaw. "If you will hand me my hat which I have dropped, and see that my verbena has not fallen out—thank you—Mr. Chinje and Isis will be so good as to walk with me to the lift. A few moments' rest in Mr. Chinje's apartments will restore me."

This arrangement accordingly was adopted, and we presently came to the rooms occupied by the Gaekwar's representative, upon the fourth floor of the hotel. At the door, Mr. Chinje asked me to take his place whilst he found his key.

I did so and Chinje opened the door. To my great surprise he entered first. To my greater surprise, Moris Klaw, scorning my assistance and apparently forgetting his injury, rapidly followed him in. The rest of us flocked behind, possessed with a sense of something impending. We little knew *what* impended.

One thing, as I entered the little sitting-room, struck my vision with a sensation almost of physical shock. It was a large, empty parrot cage standing on the table!

I had an impression that Chinje dashed forward in a vain attempt to conceal the cage ere Moris Klaw entered. I saw, as one sees figures in a dream, a pretty, fair-haired girl in the room. Then the Hindu had leapt to an inner door—and was gone!

"Quick!" cried Klaw, in a loud voice. "The door! the door!"

He brushed the girl aside with a sweep of his arm and hurled himself against the locked door.

"Mr. Grimsby! Mr. Searles! Some one! Help with this door. Isis! hold her back, this foolish girl!"

The inner meaning of the scene was a mystery to us all, but the urgency of Moris Klaw's instructions brooked no denial. With a shrill scream the girl threw herself upon him, but Isis, exhibiting unsuspected strength, drew her away.

Then Sir John Carron joined Klaw at the door and they applied their combined weights to the task of forcing it open.

Once, they put their shoulders to it; twice—and there was a sound of tearing woodwork; a third time—and it flew open, almost precipitating them both into the room beyond. Hard on the din of the opening rang the crack of a pistol shot. A wisp of smoke came floating out.

"Ah, just God!" said Moris Klaw, hoarsely, "we are too late!"

And, at his words, with a leap like that of a wild thing, the fair girl broke from Isis, and passing us all, entered the room beyond. Awed, and fearful, we followed and looked upon a pitiful scene.

Gautami Chinje lay dead upon the floor, a revolver yet between his nerveless fingers and a red spot in his temple. Beside him knelt the girl, plucking with both hands at her lower lip, her face as white as paper and her eyes glaring insanely at the distorted features.

"Dearest," she kept whispering, in a listless way, "my dearest— what is the matter? I have the diamond—I have it in my bag. What is it, my dearest?"

We got her away at last.

"He had only been in London six months," Moris Klaw rumbled in my ear, "and you see, she adored him—helped him to steal. It is wonderful, snake-like, the power of fascination some Hindus have over women—and always over blondes, Mr. Searles, always blondes. It is a psychological problem."

So ended the case of the Blue Rajah robbery, one of the most brief in the annals of Moris Klaw. The great diamond we found in the girl's handbag, wrapped in a curious little rubber covering, apparently made to fit it.

"You see," explained Moris Klaw, later, to his wondering audience, "this girl—I have yet to find out whom she is—was perhaps married to Mr. Chinje. He would, of course, have deserted her directly he returned to India. But here at the Astoria she was known as Mrs. Chinje. Who would have been the losers by the robbery? The insurance company, if I do not mistake the case. For the Gaekwar, through his representative, Chinje, had the diamond insured for all the time it was his property and in England, and the Committee had it insured from the time it became their property. It had become their property. The Gaekwar would have got his cheque. He gets it now; it is in Chinje's pocket-case. The City would have lost their Blue Rajah, and the insurance company would have paid the City for the loss!

"The next office along the corridor from Mr. Anderson's is the Central London Electric Lighting Company. Many consumers call. Mrs. Chinje was not suspected of any felonious purpose when she was seen in that corridor—and she was seen by a clerk and by an engineer. After my mental negative had told me of a pretty young lady of whom the thief thinks at the moment of his theft, I went to inquire—you recall?—if such a one had been seen near the office.

"From the first my suspicions are with Chinje. The emotions have each a note, distinct, like the notes of a piano, though only audible to the trained mind. Both Isis and myself detect from Chinje the note of *fear*. I arrange, then, that he remains. My talk of examining the Gaekwar's writing is a ruse. It is Chinje's apartment and the fair lady I expect to find there that I am anxious to see.

"Then, in spite that he is the most cool of us all, I see that he suspects me and I have to hold him fast; for, if he could have got first to his room, and hidden the parrot cage, where had been our evidence? Indeed, only that I have the power to secure the astral negative, there had been no evidence at all. There is a third accomplice—him who howled in the courtyard; but I fear, as he so cleverly vanished, we shall never know his name.

"And how was it done, and why did this some one howl?"

Moris Klaw paused and looked around. We awaited his next words in tense silence.

"He howled because Chinje had looked out from the window (which, though hidden, the howler was watching) and made him some signal. The signal meant: 'The Blue Rajah has been placed upon the table—*howl!*'

"The one below obeyed, and the Committee, like foolish sheep —yes, gentlemen, like no-headed cattle-things!—flocked to the window. But Chinje did not flock with them! Like a deft-handed conjurer he was at the table, the diamond was in the little rubber purse held ready, and Mrs. Chinje, with her large handbag open, was waiting outside the door, in the corridor, like some new kind of wicket-keeper. Chinje tossed the diamond through the little square ventilator!

"He had been practising for weeks—ever since he knew that the Committee would meet in that room—tossing peanuts into the square opening of a parrot-cage, placed at the same height from the floor as the ventilator over Mr. Anderson's doorway! He had practised until he could do it twelve times without missing. He had nerves like piano-wires, yet he was a deadly anxious man; and he knew that a woman cannot catch!

"But she caught—or, if she dropped it, no one saw her pick it up.

"Gentlemen, these Hindus are very clever, but talking of their cleverness makes one very thirsty. I think I heard Mr. Anderson make some cooling speech about a bottle of wine!"

Sixth Episode

CASE OF THE
WHISPERING POPLARS

I

One afternoon Moris Klaw walked into my office and announced that "owing to alterations" he had temporarily suspended business at the Wapping emporium, and thus had found time to give me a call. I always welcomed a chat with that extraordinary man, and although I could conceive of no really useful "alteration" to his unsavoury establishment other than that of setting fire to it, I made no inquiries, but placed an easy chair for him and offered a cigar.

Moris Klaw removed his caped overcoat and dropped it upon the floor. Upon this sartorial wreckage he disposed his flat-topped brown bowler, and from it extracted the inevitable scent-spray. He sprayed his dome-like brow and bedewed his toneless beard with verbena.

"So refreshing," he explained, "a custom of the Romans, Mr. Searles. It is a very warm day."

I admitted that this was so.

"My daughter Isis," continued Klaw, "has taken advantage of the alterations and decorations to run over so far as Paris."

I made some commonplace remark, and we drifted into a conversation upon a daring robbery which at that time was flooding the press with copy. We were so engaged when, to my great surprise (for I had thought him at least a thousand miles away), Shan Haufmann was announced. As my old American friend entered, Moris Klaw modestly arose to depart. But I detained him and made the two acquainted.

Haufmann hailed Klaw cordially, exhibiting none of the ill-bred surprise which so often greeted my eccentric acquaintance of singular aspect. Haufmann had all that *bonhomie* which overlooks the clothes and welcomes the man. He glanced apologetically at his right hand which hung in a sling.

"Can't shake, Mr. Klaw," said the big American, a good-humoured smile on his tanned, clean-shaven face. "I stopped some lead awhile back and my right is still off duty."

Naturally I was anxious at once to know how he had come by the hurt; and he briefly explained that in the discharge of certain official duties he had run foul of a bad gang, two of whom he had been instrumental in convicting of murder, whilst the third had shot him in the arm and escaped.

"Three dagoes," he explained in his crisply picturesque fashion, "been wanted for years. Helped themselves to a bunch of my colts this Fall; killed one of the boys and left another for dead. So I went after them hot and strong. We rounded them up on the Mexican border, and got two, Schwart Sam and one of the Costas; but the younger Costa—we call him Corpus Chris—broke away and found me in the elbow with a lump of lead!"

"So you've come for a holiday?"

"Mostly," replied Haufmann. "Greta hustled me here. She got real ill when I said I wouldn't come. So we came! I'm centring in London for six months. Brought the girls over for a look round. I'm not stopping at a hotel. We've rented a house a bit outside; it's Lal's idea. Settled yesterday. All fixed. Expect you to dinner to-night! You, too, Mr. Klaw! Is it a bet?"

Moris Klaw was commencing some sort of a reply, but what it was never transpired, for Haufmann, waving his sound hand cheerily, quitted the office as rapidly as he had entered, calling back:

"Dine seven-thirty. Girls expecting you!"

That was his way; but so infectious was his real geniality that few could fail to respond to it.

"He is a good fellow, that Mr. Haufmann," rumbled Moris Klaw. "Yes, I love such natures. But he has forgotten to tell us where he lives!"

It was so! Haufmann, in his hurry and impetuosity, had overlooked that important matter; but I thought it probable that he would recall the oversight and communicate, so prevailed upon Klaw to remain. At last, however, I glanced at my watch, and found it to be nearly six o'clock, whereupon I looked blankly at Moris Klaw. That eccentric shrugged his shoulders and took up the caped coat. Then the 'phone-bell rang. It was Haufmann.

I was glad to hear his familiar accent as he laughingly apologised for his oversight. Rapidly he acquainted me with the whereabouts of The Grove—for so the house was called.

"Come now," he said. "Don't stop to dress; you've only just got time," and rang off.

I thought Moris Klaw stared oddly through his pince-nez when I

told him the address, but concluded, as he made no comment, that
I had been mistaken. There was just time to catch our train, and
from the station where we alighted it was only a short drive to the
house. Haufmann's car was waiting for us, and in less than three-
quarters of an hour from our quitting the Strand, we were driving
up to The Grove, through the most magnificent avenue of poplars
I had ever seen.

"By Jove!" I cried, "what fine trees!"

Moris Klaw nodded and looked around at the towering trunks
with a peculiar expression, which I was wholly at a loss to account
for. However, ere I had leisure to think much about the matter, we
found ourselves in the hall, where Haufmann and his two fascinating daughters were waiting to greet us. I do not know which of
the girls looked the more charming; Lilian with her bright mass of
curls and blue eyes dancing with vivacity, or Greta in her dark and
rather mystic beauty. At any rate, they were dangerous acquaintances for a susceptible man. Even old Moris Klaw showed unmistakably that his mind was not so wholly filled with obscure sciences
as to be incapable of appreciating the society of a pretty woman.

Greta I noticed looking thoughtfully at him, and during dinner
she suddenly asked him if he had read a book called *Psychic
Angles.*

Rather unwillingly, as it seemed to me, Klaw admitted that he
had, and the girl displayed an immediate and marked interest in
psychical matters. Klaw, however, though usually but too willing to
discuss this, his pet subject, foiled her attempt to draw him into a
technical discussion, and rather obviously steered the conversation
into a more general channel.

"Don't let her get away on the bogey tack, Mr. Klaw," said
Haufmann, approvingly. "She's a perfect demon for haunted
chambers and so on."

Laughingly the girl pleaded guilty to an interest in ghostly sub-
jects. "But I'm not frightened about them!" she added in pre-
tended indignation. "I should just love to see a ghost."

"O Greta!" cried her sister. "What a horrid idea."

"You have perhaps investigated cases yourself, Mr. Klaw?"
asked Greta.

"Yes," rumbled Klaw, "perhaps so. Who knows?"

Since he thus clearly showed his wish to drop the subject, the
girl made a little humourously wry face, whereat her father laughed
boisterously; and no more was said during the evening about
ghosts. I could not well avoid noticing two things, however, in

regard to Moris Klaw: one, his evident interest in Greta; and the
other a certain preoccupation which claimed him every now and
again.

We left at about ten o'clock, declining the offer of the car, as we
had ample time to walk to the station. Haufmann wanted to come
along, but we dissuaded him, with the assurance that we could find
the way without any difficulty. Klaw, especially, was very insistent
on the point, and when at last we swung sharply down the avenue
and, rounding the bend, lost sight of the house, he pulled up and
said:

"For this opportunity, Mr. Searles, I have been waiting. It may
not, of course, matter, but this house where the good Haufmann
resides was formerly known as The Park."

"What of that?" I asked, turning on him sharply.

"It is," he replied, "celebrated as what foolish people call a
haunted house. No doubt that is the reason why the name has been
changed. As The Park it has been dealt with many times in the
psychical journals."

"The Park"—I mused. "Is it not included in that extraordinary
work on the occult—*Psychic Angles*— of which Miss Haufmann
spoke to-night—the place where the monk was supposed to have
been murdered, where an old antiquary died, and some young girl,
too, if I remember rightly?"

"Yes," replied Moris Klaw, "yes. I will tell you a secret. *Psychic
Angles* is a little book of my own, and so, of course, I know about
this place."

His words surprised me greatly, for the book was being generally
talked about. He peered around him into the shadows and seemed
to sniff the air suspiciously.

"Setting aside the question of any supernatural menace," I said,
"directly the servants find out, as they are sure to do from others
in the neighbourhood, they will leave *en bloc*. It is a pleasant way
servants have in such cases."

"We must certainly tell him, the good Haufmann," agreed
Klaw, "and he will perhaps arrange to quit the place without letting
the ladies to know of its reputation. That Miss Greta she has the
sympathetic mind"—he tapped his forehead—"the plate so sensitive, the photo film so delicate! For her it is dangerous to remain.
There is such a thing, Mr. Searles, as sympathetic suicide! That
girl she is mediumistic. From The Park she must be removed."

"There is no time to lose," I said. "We must decide what to do
to-night. Suppose you come along to my place?"

Moris Klaw agreed, and we resumed our walk through the poplar grove.

Although the night was very still, an eerie whispering went on without pause or cessation along the whole length of the avenue. Against the star-spangled sky the tall trees reared their shapes in a manner curiously suggestive of dead things. Or this fancy may have had birth in the associations of the place. It was a fatally easy matter mentally to fashion one of the poplars into the gaunt form of a monk; and no one, however unimaginative, being acquainted with the history of The Grove, could fail to find, in the soft and ceaseless voices of the trees, something akin to a woman's broken sighs. In short, I was not sorry when the gate was passed, and we came out upon the high road.

Later, seated in my study, we discussed the business thoroughly. From my book-case I took down *Psychic Angles* and passed it to Moris Klaw.

"There we are," he rumbled, turning over the leaves. I read: "On August 8th, 1858, a Fra Giulimo, of a peculiar religious brotherhood who occupied this house from 1851 to 1858, was found strangled at the foot of a poplar close by the entrance gate." "I could never find out much about them, this brotherhood," he added, looking up; "but they were, I believe, decent people. They left the place almost immediately after the crime. No arrest was ever made. Then" (referring to the book), " 'about the end of February or early in the March of 1863, a Mr. B——J——took the house. He was an antiquarian of European repute and a man of retired habits. With only two servants—an old soldier and his wife—he occupied The Park'—(that is The Grove)—'from the spring of '63 to the autumn of '65.' Then follow verbatim reports by the well-known Pepley of interviews with people who had heard Mr. J——declare that a hushed voice sometimes called upon him by name in the night, from the poplar grove. Also, an interview with his man-servant and with wife of latter, corroborating other statements. Mr. B——J——was found one September morning dead in the grove. Cause of death never properly established. The house next enters upon a period of neglect. It is empty; it is shunned. From '65 right up to '88 it stood so empty. It was then taken by a Mr. K——; but he only occupied it for two months, this K——. Three other tenants subsequently rented the place. Only one of them actually occupied it—for a week; the other, hearing, we presume, of its evil repute, never entered into residence. Seventeen years ago the last tragedy connected with the unpleasant Grove took place. An eccentric old bachelor took the house, and, in the summer of '03, had a niece there to stay with him. The evidence clearly indicates to me that this unhappy one was highly neurotic— oh, clearly; so that the tragedy explains itself. She fell, or sprang, from her bedroom window to the drive one night in June, and was picked up quite dead at the foot of the first poplar in the Grove *Sacré!* it is a morgue, that house!''

He returned the book and sat watching me in silence for some moments.

"Did you spend any time in the house, yourself?" I asked.

"On four different occasions, Mr. Searles! It is only from certain of the rooms that the whispering is audible, and then only if the windows are open. You will notice, though, that all the tragedies occurred in the warm months when the windows would be so open.''

"Did you note anything supernormal in this whispering?"

"Nothing. You have read my explanation."

II

Haufmann looked rather blank when we told him.

"Just my luck!" he commented. "Greta's read your book, Mr. Klaw, and if she hasn't fixed it yet she's sure to come to it that The Park and The Grove are one and the same. It was largely because of her I arranged this trip," he added. "The trouble I've told you about got on her nerves and she had the idea some guy was tracking her around. The medicos said it was a common enough symptom and ordered a change. Anyhow, I quitted, to give her a chance to tone up. Confound this business!"

He ultimately left quite determined to change his place of residence. But so averse was his practical mind from the idea of inconveniencing onself on such ghostly grounds, that two weeks slipped by, and still the Haufmanns occupied The Grove. The decoration of Moris Klaw's establishment being presumably still in progress, Klaw accompanied me on more than one other occasion to visit Shan Haufmann and the girls. At last, one afternoon, Greta asked him point-blank if he thought the house to be that dealt with in *Psychic Angles.*

Of course, he had to admit that it was so; but far from exhibiting any signs of alarm, the girl appeared to be delighted.

"How dense I have been!" she cried. "I should have known it

from the description! As a matter of fact I might never have found out, but this morning the servants resigned unanimously!''

Klaw looked at me significantly. All was befalling as we had foreseen.

"They told you, then!" he said. "Yes? No?"

"They said the house was haunted," she replied, "but they didn't seem to know much more about it. That simple fact was enough for them!"

Haufmann came in and in answer to our queries declared himself helpless.

"Lal and Greta won't wait," he declared; "so what's to do? I've cabled for servants from home. Meanwhile we're at the mercy of day-girls and char-women!"

The concern evinced by Moris Klaw was very great. He seized an early opportunity of taking Haufmann aside and questioning him relative to the situation of the rooms occupied by the family.

"My room overlooks the avenue," replied Haufmann, "and so does Greta's. Lal's is on the opposite side. Come up and see them!"

Klaw and I accompanied him. It was a beautiful, clear day, and from his window we gazed along the majestic ranks of poplars, motionless as a giant guard in the still summer air. It was difficult to conjure up a glamour of the uncanny, with the bright sunlight pouring gladness upon trees, flowers, shrubs and lawn.

"This is the room from which the whisper is the most clearly audible!" said Moris Klaw. "I could tell you—ah! I spent several nights here!"

"The devil you did," rapped Haufmann. "I must sleep pretty soundly. I've never heard a thing. Greta's room is next on the right. She has said nothing."

Klaw looked troubled.

"There is no sound unusual to hear," he answered. "I quite convinced myself of that. But it is the tradition that speaks, Mr. Haufmann! In those silent watches, even so insensible an old fool as I can imagine almost anything, aided by such gruesome memories. Excepting the monk, who probably fell foul of a prowler-thief, the tragedies are easily to be explained. The old antiquity died of syncope, and the poor girl, in all probability, fell from the balcony in her sleep. She had a tremendously neurotic temperament.''

"It's bad, now Greta knows," mused Haufmann. "Her nerves are all unstrung. It's just the thing I wanted to avoid!"

"Can't you induce her at any rate to change her room?" I suggested.

"No! She's as obstinate as a pony! Her poor mother was the same. It's the Irish blood!"

Such was the situation when we left. No development took place for a couple of days or so, then that befell which we had feared and half expected.

Haufmann walked into my office with—

"It's started! Greta says she hears it every night!"

Prepared though I had been for the news, his harshly spoken words sent a cold shudder through me.

"Haufmann!" I said sternly. "There must be no more of this. Get the girls away at once. On top of her previous nerve trouble this morbid imagining may affect her mind."

"You haven't heard me out," he went on, more slowly than was his wont. "You talk of morbid imagining. What about this: *I've* heard it!"

I stared at him blankly.

"That's one on you!" he said, with a certain grim triumph. "After Greta said there was something came in the night that wasn't trees rustling, I sat up and smoked. First night I read and nothing happened. Next night I sat in the dark. There was no breeze and I heard nothing for my pains. Third night I stayed in the dark again, and about twelve o'clock a breeze came along. All mixed up with the rustling and sighing of the leaves I heard a voice calling as plain as I ever heard anything in my life! And it called *me!*"

"Haufmann!"

"It blame-well called *me!* I'd take my oath before a jury on it!"

"This is almost incredible!" I said. "I wish Moris Klaw were here."

"Where is he?"

"He is in Paris. He will be away over the weekend."

"I met a man curiously enough," continued Haufmann, "just outside the Charing Cross Tube, on my way here, who's coming down to have a look into the business; a hot man on mysteries." He mentioned the name of a celebrated American detective agency. "I'm afraid it's right outside his radius, but he volunteered and I was glad to have him. I'd like Klaw down though."

"What about the girls?"

"I was going to tell you. They're at Brighton for awhile. Greta didn't want to quit, but poor Lal was dead scared! Anyway I got them off."

The uncanny business claimed entire possession of my mind, and
further work was out of the question. I accordingly accompanied
Haufmann to the hotel where the detective was lodged and made
the acquaintance of Mr. J. Shorter Ottley. He was a typical New
Yorker, clean-shaven and sallow complexioned with good, grey
eyes and an inflexible mouth.

"We don't deal in ghosts!" he said, smilingly; "I never met a
ghost that couldn't stop a bullet if it came his way!"

"I'll make a confession to you," remarked Haufmann. "When
I heard that soft voice calling, I hadn't the sand to go and look out!
How's that for funk?"

"Not funk at all," replied Ottley, quietly. "Maybe it was
wisdom!"

"How do you mean?"

"I've got an idea about it, that's all. Did Miss Haufmann hear
it the same night?"

"Not the same night I did—no. She seems to have dozed off."

"When she *did* hear it, was it calling you?"

"She couldn't make out what it called!"

"Did she go to the window?"

"Yes, but she only looked out from behind the blind."

"See anything?"

"No."

"I should have very much liked an interview with her," said
Ottley, thoughtfully.

"She could tell you no more than I have."

"About that no! There's something else I would like to ask her."

That evening we all three dined at The Grove, dinner being prepared by a woman who departed directly we were finished. A
desultory game of billiards served to pass the time between twilight
and darkness, and the detective and I departed, leaving Haufmann
alone in the house. This was prearranged by Ottley, who had some
scheme in hand. Side by side we tramped down the poplar avenue,
went out by the big gate, and closed it behind us. We then skirted
the grounds to a point on the side opposite the gate, and, scaling
the wall, found ourselves in a wilderness of neglected kitchen garden. Through this the American cautiously led the way towards the
house, visible through the tangle of bushes and trees in sharp silhouette against the sky. On all fours we crossed a little yard and
entered a side-door which had been left ajar for the purpose, closing it softly behind us. So, passing through the kitchen, we made
our way upstairs and rejoined Haufmann.

A post had been allotted to me in the room next to his and I was enjoined to sit in the dark and watch for anything moving among the trees. Haufmann departed to a room on the west front with similar injunctions, and the detective remained in Haufmann's room.

As I crept cautiously to the window, avoiding the broad moonbeam streaming in, I saw a light on my left. Ottley was acting as Haufmann would have done if he had been retiring for the night. Three minutes later the light vanished, and the nervous vigil was begun.

There was very little breeze, but sufficient to send up and down the poplar ranks waves of that mysterious whispering which Klaw and I had previously noted. The moon, though invisible from that point, swam in an absolutely cloudless sky, and the shadow of the house lay black beneath me, its edge tropically sharp. A broad belt of moonbright grass and grave succeeded, and this merged into the light-patched gloom of the avenue. On the right of the poplars lay a shrubbery, and beyond that a garden stretching to the east wall. Just to the left, an outbuilding gleamed whitely. Some former occupant had built it for a coach-house and it now housed Haufmann's car. The apartments above were at present untenanted.

I cannot say with certainty when I first detected, mingled with the whistling of the branches, something that was not caused by the wind. But ultimately I found myself listening for this other sound. With my eyes fixed straight ahead and peering into the shadows of the poplars I crouched, every nerve at high tension. A slight sound on my left told of a window softly opened. It was Ottley creeping out on to the balcony. He, too, had heard it!

Then, with awful suddenness, the inexplicable happened.

A short, shrill cry broke the complete silence, succeeding one of those spells of whispering. a shot followed hot upon it—then a second. Somebody fell with a muffled thud upon the drive—and I leapt to the window, threw it widely open and stepped out on the balcony.

"Ottley!" I cried. "Haufmann!"

A door banged somewhere and I heard Haufmann's muffled voice:

"Downstairs! Come down!"

I ran across the room, out on to the landing, and down into the hall. Haufmann was unfastening the bolts. His injured arm was still stiff, and I hastened to assist him.

"My God!" he cried, turning a pale face toward me. "It's Ottley gone! Did you see anything?"

"No! Did you?"

"Curse it! No! I had just slipped away from the window to get my repeater! You heard the voice?"

"Clearly!"

The door was thrown open and we ran out into the drive.

There was no sign of Ottley, and we stood for a moment, undecided how we should act. Then, just inside the shadow belt we found the detective lying.

Thinking him dead, we raised and dragged him back to the house. Having re-fastened the door, we laid him on a sofa in the morning-room. His face was deathly and blood flowed from a terrible wound on his skull. Strangest of all, though, he had a gaping hole just above the right wrist. The skin about it was discoloured as if with burning. Neither of us could detect any sign of life, and we stood, two frankly frightened men, looking at one another over the body.

"It's got to be done!" said Haufmann slowly. "One of us has to stay here and do what he can for him, and one has to go for a doctor! There's no telephone!"

"Where's the nearest doctor?" I asked.

"There's one at the corner of the first road on the right."

"I'll go!" I said.

Without shame I confess that from the moment the door closed behind me, I ran my hardest down the poplar avenue until I had passed the gate! And it was not anxiety that spurred me, for I did not doubt that Ottley was dead, but stark fear!

III

Moris Klaw deposited a large grip and a travelling-rug upon the verandah.

"Good-day, Mr. Haufmann! Good-day, Mr. Searles!" At an open window the white-aproned figure of a nurse appeared. "Good-day, Nurse! I am direct from Paris. This is a case which cannot be dealt with under the head of the Cycle of Crime, and I do not think it has any relation with the history of The Park. But thoughts are things, Mr. Haufmann. How helpful that is!"

Forty-eight hours had elapsed since Haufmann and I had picked up Ottley for dead in the poplar avenue. Now he lay in a bed made up in the billiard-room, hovering between this world and another. I had a shrewd suspicion that the doctor who attended him was mystified by some of the patient's symptoms.

Haufmann stared oddly at Moris Klaw, not altogether comprehending the drift of his words.

"If only Ottley could tell us!" he muttered.

"He will tell us nothing for many a day," I said; "if, indeed, he ever speaks again."

"Ah," interrupted Moris Klaw, "to *me* he will speak! How? With the mind! Something—we have yet to learn what—struck him down that night. The blow, if it was a blow, made so acute an impression upon his brain that no other has secured admittance yet! Good! That blow, it still resides within his mind. To-night, I shall sleep beside his bed. I shall be unable odically to sterilise myself, but we must hope. From amid the phantasms which that sick brain will throw out upon the astral film—upon the surrounding ether—I must trust that I find the thought, the last thought before delirium came!"

Haufmann looked amazed. I had prepared him, to some extent, for Klaw's theories, but nevertheless he was tremendously surprised. Klaw, however, paid no attention to this. He looked around at the trees.

"I am glad," he rumbled impressively, "that you managed to hush up. Distinctly, we have now a chance."

"A chance of what?" I cried. "The thing seems susceptible of no ordinary explanation! How can you account for what happened to Ottley and for his condition? What incredible thing came out from the poplars?"

"No thing!" answered Moris Klaw. "No thing, my good friend!"

"Then what did he fire at?"

"At the coach-house!"

I met the gaze of his peculiar eyes, fixed upon me through the pince-nez.

"If you will look at the coach-house chimney," he continued, "you will see it—the hole made by his bullet!"

I turned quickly, and even from that considerable distance the hole was visible; a triangular break on the red-tiled rim.

"What on earth does it mean?" I asked, more hopelessly mystified than ever.

"It means that Ottley is a clever man, who knows his business; and it means, Mr. Searles, that we must take up this so extraordinary affair where the poor Ottley dropped it!"

"What do you propose?"

"I propose that you invite yourself to a few days' holiday, as I have done. You stay here. Do not allow even the doctor to know that you are in the house. The nurse you will have to confide in, I suppose. Mr. Haufmann"—he turned to the latter—"you will occupy your old room. Do not, I beg of you, go outside after dusk upon any consideration. If either of you shall hear it again—the evil whispering—come out by the front door, and keep in the shadow. Carry no light. Above all, do not come out upon the balcony!"

"Then you," I said, "will be unable to stay?"

"I shall be so unable," was the reply; "for I go to Brighton to secure the interview with Miss Greta which the poor Ottley so much required!"

"You don't suggest that she knows——"

"She knows no more than we do, Mr. Searles! But I think she holds a clue and does not know that she holds a clue! For an hour I shall slumber—I, who, like the tortoise, know that to sleep is to live—I shall slumber beside the sick man's bed. Then, we shall see!"

IV

It was a quarter to seven when Moris Klaw entered the sick-room. Ottley lay in a trance-like condition, and the eccentric investigator, of whose proceedings the nurse strongly disapproved, settled himself in a split-cane armchair by the bedside and waving his hand in dismissal to Haufmann and myself, placed a large silk handkerchief over his sparsely covered skull and composed himself for slumber.

We left him, and tiptoed from the room.

"If you hadn't told me what he's done in the past," whispered Haufmann, "I should say our old friend was mad a lot!"

The great empty house was eerily silent, and during the time that we sat smoking and awaiting the end of Moris Klaw's singular telepathic experiment, neither of us talked very much. At eight o'clock the man whose proceedings savoured so much of charlatanry, but whom I knew for one of the foremost criminologists of the world, emerged, spraying his face with verbena.

"Ah, gentlemen," he said, coming in to us, "I have recovered some slight impression"—he tapped his moist forehead—"of that agonising thought which preceded the unconsciousness of Ottley. I depart. Some time to-night will come Sir Bartram Vane from Half-Moon Street, the specialist, to confer with the physician who is attending here. Mr. Searles, remain concealed. Not even he must know of your being here; no one outside the house must know. Remember my warnings. I depart.''

Behind the thick pebbles his eyes gleamed with some excitement repressed. By singular means, he would seem to have come upon a clue.

"Good-night, Mr. Haufmann," he said. "Good-night, Mr. Searles. To the nurse I have said good-night and she only glared. She thinks I am the mad old fool!''

He departed, curtly declining company, and carrying his huge plaid rug and heavy grip. As his slouching footsteps died away along the avenue, Haufmann and I looked grimly at one another.

"Seems we're left!" said my friend. "You won't desert me, Searles?''

"Most certainly I shall not! You are tied here by the presence of poor Ottley, in any event, and you can rely upon me to keep you company.''

At about ten o'clock Sir Bartram Vane drove up bringing with him the local physician who was attending upon Ottley. I kept well out of sight, but learnt, when the medical men had left, that the course of treatment had been entirely changed.

Thus commenced our strange ordeal; how it terminated you presently shall learn.

Moris Klaw, in pursuit of whatever plan he had formed never appeared on the scene, but evidence of his active interest reached us in the form of telegraphic instructions. Once it was a wire telling Haufmann to detain the American servants in London should they arrive and to go on living as we were. Again it was a warning not to go out on the balcony after dusk, and, again, that we should not desert our posts for one single evening. On the fourth day the doctor pronounced a slight improvement in Ottley's condition, and Haufmann determined to run down to Brighton on the following morning, returning in the afternoon.

That night we again heard the voice.

The house was very still, and Haufmann and I had retired to our rooms, when I discerned above the subdued rustling whisper of the leaves, that other sound that no leaf ever made. In an instant I was crouching by the open window. A lull followed. Then, again, I heard the soft voice calling. I could not detect the words, but in obedience to the instructions of Klaw, I picked up the pistol which I had brought for the purpose, and ran to the door. The idea that the whispering menace was something that could be successfully shot at, robbed it of much of its eerie horror, and I relished the prospect of action after the dreary secret sojourn in the upper rooms of the house.

I groped my way down to the hall. As we had carefully oiled the bolts, I experienced no difficulty in silently opening the door. Inch by inch I opened it, listening intently.

Again I heard the queer call.

Now, by craning my neck, I could see the moon-bright front of the house; and looking upward, I was horrified to see Shan Haufmann, a conspicuous figure in his light pyjama suit, crouching on the balcony! The moonlight played vividly on the nickelled barrel of the pistol he carried, as he rose slowly to his feet.

Though I did not know what danger threatened, nor from whence it would proceed, I knew well that Klaw's was no idle warning. I could not imagine what madness had prompted Haufmann to neglect it, and was about to throw wide the door and call to him, when a series of strange things happened in bewildering succession.

An odd, *strumming* sound came from somewhere in the outer darkness. Haufmann dropped to his knees (I learnt, afterwards, that the loose slippers he wore had tripped him). The glass of the window behind him was shattered with a great deal of noise.

A shot!... a spurt of flame in the black darkness of the poplar avenue!... a shriek from somewhere on the west front... and I ran out on to the drive.

With a tremendous crash a bulky form rolled down the sloping roof of the coach-house, to fall with a sickening thud to the ground!

Then, out into the moonlight, Moris Klaw came running, his yet smoking pistol in his hand!

"Haufmann!" he cried, and again: "Haufmann!"

The big American peered down from the balcony hauling in something which seemed to be a line, but which I was unable to distinguish in the darkness.

"Good boy!" he panted. "I was a fool to do it! But I saw him lying behind the chimney and thought I could drop him!"

Moris Klaw ran, ungainly, across to the coach-house, and I followed him. The figure of a tall, lithe man, wearing a blue serge suit, lay face downwards on the gravel. As we turned him over, Haufmann, breathing heavily, joined us. The moonlight fell on a dark saturnine face.

"Gee!" came the cry. "It's *Corpus Chris!*"

V

"Where did I get hold upon the clue?" asked Moris Klaw, when he, Haufmann, and I sat, in the grey dawn, waiting for the police to come and take away the body of Costa. "It was from the brain of Ottley! His poor mind" (he waved long hands circularly in the air) "goes round and round about the thing that happened to him on the balcony."

"And what was that?" demanded Haufmann, eagerly. "Same as happened to me?"

"It was something—something that his knowledge of strange things tells him is venomous—which struck his wrist as he raised his revolver! What did he do? I can tell you; because he is doing it over and over again in his poor feverish mind. He clapped to the injured wrist the barrel of his revolver, and fired! Then, swooning, he toppled over and fell among the bushes. The wound that so had puzzled all becomes explained. It was self-inflicted—a precaution —a cauterising; and it saved his life. For I saw Sir Bartram Vane to-day and he had spoken with the other doctor on the telephone. The new treatment succeeds."

"I am still in the dark!" confessed Haufmann.

"Yes?" rumbled Moris Klaw. "So? Why do I go to Brighton? I go to ask Miss Greta what Ottley would have asked her."

"And that is?"

"What she feared, that made her so very anxious to get you away from your home. To me she admitted that she had received from the man Costa impassioned appeals, such as, foolish girl, she had been afraid to show to you—her father!"

"Good Heavens! the scamp!"

"The *canaille!* But no matter, he is dead *canaille!* After you got the brother hanged, this Corpus Chris (it was Fate that named him!) sent to your daughter a mad letter, swearing that if she does not fly with him, he will kill you if he has to follow you around the world! Yes, he was insane, I fancy; I think so. But he was a man of very great culture. He held a Cambridge degree! You did not know? I thought not. He tracked you to Europe and right to this house. Its history he learned in some way and used for his own ends. Probably, too, he had no opportunity of getting at you otherwise, without leaving behind a clue or being seen and pursued."

Moris Klaw picked up an Indian bow which lay upon the floor beside him.

"A bow of the Sioux pattern," he rumbled impressively.

He stooped again, picking up a small arrow to which a length of thin, black twine was attached.

"One standing on the balcony in the moonlight," he continued, "what a certain mark if the wind be not too high! And you will remember that on gently blowing nights the whispering came!"

He raised the point of the arrow. It was encrusted in some black, shining substance. Moris Klaw lowered his voice.

"*Curari!*" he said, hoarsely, "the ancient arrow-poison of the South American tribes! This small arrow would make only a tiny wound, and it could be drawn back again by means of the twine attached. Costa, of course, mistook Ottley for you, Mr. Haufmann. Ah, a clever fellow! I spent three evenings up the second tree in the avenue waiting for him. I need not have shot him if you had followed my instructions and not come out on the balcony. We could have captured him alive!"

"I'm not crying about it!" said Haufmann.

"Neither do I weep," rumbled Moris Klaw, and bathed his face with perfume. "But I loathe it, this *curari*—it smells of death. Ah! the *canaille!*"

Seventh Episode

CASE OF THE HEADLESS MUMMIES

I

The mysteries which my eccentric friend, Moris Klaw, was most successful in handling undoubtedly were those which had their origin in kinks of the human brain or in the mysterious history of some relic of ancient times.

I have seen his theory of the Cycle of Crime proven triumphantly time and time again; I have known him successfully to demonstrate how the history of a valuable gem or curio automatically repeats itself, subject, it would seem, to that obscure law of chance into which he had made particular inquiry. Then his peculiar power—assiduously cultivated by a course of obscure study—of recovering from the atmosphere, the ether, call it what you will, the thought-forms—the ideas thrown out by the scheming mind of the criminal he sought for—enabled him to succeed where any ordinary investigator must inevitably have failed.

"They destroy," he would say in his odd, rumbling voice, "the clumsy tools of their crime; they hide away the knife, the bludgeon; they sop up the blood, they throw it, the jemmy, the dead man, the suffocated poor infant, into the ditch, the pool—and they leave intact the odic negative, the photograph of their sin, the thought-thing in the air!" He would tap his high yellow brow significantly. "Here upon this sensitive plate I reproduce it, the hanging evidence! The headless child is buried in the garden, but the thought of the beheader is left to lie about. I pick it up. Poof! he swings—that child-slayer! I triumph. He is a dead man. What an art is the art of the odic photograph."

But I propose to relate here an instance of Moris Klaw's amazing knowledge in matters of archaeology—of the history of relics. In his singular emporium at Wapping, where dwelt the white rats, the singing canary, the cursing parrot, and the other stock-in-trade of this supposed dealer in oddities, was furthermore a library probably unique. It contained obscure works on criminology; it contained catalogues of every relic known to European collectors with elaborate histories of the same. What else it contained I am unable to say, for the dazzling Isis Klaw was a jealous librarian.

You who have followed these records will have made the acquaintance of Coram, the curator of the Menzies Museum; and it was through Coram that I first came to hear of the inexplicable beheading of mummies, which, commencing with that of Mr. Pettigrew's valuable mummy of the priestess Hor-ankhu, developed into a perfect epidemic. No more useless outrage could well be imagined. than the decapitation of an ancient Egyptian corpse; and if I was surprised when I heard of the first case, my surprise became stark amazement when yet other mummies began mysteriously to lose their heads. But I deal with the first instance, now, as it was brought under my notice by Coram.

He rang me up early one morning.

"I say, Searles," he said; "a very odd thing has happened. You've heard me speak of Pettigrew the collector; he lives out Wandsworth way; he's one of our trustees. Well, some demented burglar broke into his house last night, took nothing, but cut off the head of a valuable mummy!"

"Good Heavens!" I cried. "What an original idea!"

"Highly so," agreed Coram. "The police are hopelessly mystified, and as I know you are keen on this class of copy I thought you might like to run down and have a chat with Pettigrew. Shall I tell him you are coming?"

"By all means," I said, and made an arrangement forthwith.

Accordingly, about eleven o'clock I presented myself at a gloomy Georgian house standing well back from the high road, and screened by an unkempt shrubbery. Mr. Mark Pettigrew, a familiar figure at Sotheby auctions, was a little shrivelled man, clean shaven and with the complexion of a dried apricot. His big spectacles seemed to occupy a great proportion of his face, but his eyes twinkled merrily and his humour was as dry as his appearance.

"Glad to see you, Mr. Searles," he said. "You've had some experience of the *outré*, I believe, and where two constables, an imposing inspector, and a plain-clothes gentleman who looked like a horse, have merely upset my domestic arrangements, you may be able to make some intelligent suggestion."

He conducted me to a large gloomy room in which relics, principally Egyptian, were arranged and ticketed with museum-like precision. Before a wooden sarcophagus containing the swathed

figure of a mummy he stopped, pointing. He looked as though he
had come out of a sarcophagus himself.

"Hor-ankhu," he said, "a priestess of Sekhet; a very fine specimen, Mr. Searles. I was present when it was found. See—here is
her head!"

Stooping, he picked up the head of the mummy. Very cleanly
and scientifically it had been unwrapped and severed from the
trunk. It smelt strongly of bitumen, and the shrivelled features
reminded me of nothing so much as of Mr. Mark Pettigrew.

"Did you ever hear of a more senseless thing?" he asked. "Come
over and look at the window where he got in."

We crossed the dark apartment, and the collector drew my attention to a round hole which had been drilled in the glass of one of
the French windows opening on a kind of miniature prairie which
once had been a lawn.

"I am having shutters fitted," he went on. "It is so easy to cut a
hole in the glass and open the catch of these windows."

"Very easy," I agreed. "Was any one disturbed?"

"No one," he replied excitedly; "that's the insane part of the
thing. The burglar, with all the night before him and with cases
containing portable and really priceless objects about him, contented himself with decapitating the priestess. What on earth did he
want her head for? Whatever he wanted it for, why the devil didn't
he *take* it."

We stared at one another blankly.

"I fear," said Pettigrew, "I have been guilty of injustice to my
horsey visitor, the centaur. You look as stupid as the worst of us!"

"I feel stupid," I said.

"You are!" Pettigrew assured me with cheerful impertinence.
"So am I, so are the police; but the biggest fool of the lot is the fool
who came here last night and cut off the head of my mummy."

That, then, is all which I have occasion to relate regarding the
first of these mysterious outrages. I was quite unable to propound
any theory covering the facts, to Pettigrew's evident annoyance; he
assured me that I was very stupid, and insisted upon opening a
magnum of champagne. I then returned to my rooms, and since
reflection upon the subject promised to be unprofitable, had dis-
missed it from my mind, when some time during the evening
Inspector Grimsby rang me up from the Yard.

"Hullo, Mr. Searles," he said; "I hear you called on Mr. Pettigrew this morning?"

I replied in the affirmative.

"Did anything strike you'"

"No; were you on the case?"

"I wasn't on the case then, but I'm on it now."

"How's that?"

"Well, there's been another mummy beheaded in Sotheby's auction rooms!"

II

I knew quite well what was expected of me.

"Where are you speaking from?" I asked.

"The auction-rooms."

"I will meet you there in an hour," I said, "and bring Moris Klaw if I can find him."

"Good," replied Grimsby, with much satisfaction in his voice; "this case ought to be right in his line."

I chartered a taxi and proceeded without delay to the salubrious neighbourhood of Wapping Old Stairs. At the head of the blind alley which harbours the Klaw emporium I directed the man to wait. The gloom was very feebly dispelled by a wavering gaslight in the shed-like front of the shop. River noises were about me. Somewhere a drunken man was singing. An old lady who looked like a pantomime dame was critically examining a mahogany chair with only half a back, which formed one of the exhibits displayed before the establishment.

A dilapidated person whose nose chronically blushed for the excesses of its owner hovered about the prospective purchaser. This was William, whose exact position in the Klaw establishment I had never learned, but who apparently acted during his intervals of sobriety as a salesman.

"Good-evening," I said. "Is Mr. Moris Klaw at home?"

"He is, sir," husked the derelict; "but he's very busy, sir, I believe, sir."

"Tell him Mr. Searles has called."

"Yes, sir," said William; and, turning to the dame, "Was you thinking of buyin' that chair, mum, after you've done muckin' it about?"

He retired into the cavernous depths of the shop, and I followed him as far as the dimly seen counter.

"Moris Klaw, Moris Klaw! the devil's come for you!"

Thus the invisible parrot hailed my entrance. Indescribable smells, zoo-like, with the fusty odour of old books and the unclassifiable perfume of half-rotten furniture, assailed my nostrils; and mingling with it was the distinct scent of reptile life. Scufflings and scratchings sounded continuously about me, punctuated with squeals. Then came the rumbling voice of Moris Klaw.

"Ah, Mr. Searles—good-evening, Mr. Searles! It is the Pettigrew mummy, is it not?"

He advanced through the shadows, his massive figure arrayed for travelling, in the caped coat, his toneless beard untidy as ever, his pince-nez glittering, his high bald brow yellow as that of a Chinaman.

"There has been a second outrage," I said, "at Sotheby's."

"So?" said Moris Klaw, with interest; "another mummy is executed!"

"Yes, Inspector Grimsby has asked us to join him there."

Moris Klaw stooped, and from beneath the counter took out his flat-topped brown bowler. From its lining he extracted a cylindrical scent-spray and mingled with the less pleasing perfumes that of verbena.

"A cooling Roman custom, Mr. Searles," he rumbled, "so refreshing when one lives with rats. So it is Mr. Grimsby who is puzzled again? It is Mr. Grimsby who needs the poor old fool to hold the lantern for him, so that he, the clever Grimsby, can pick up the credit out of the darkness! And why not, Mr. Searles, and why not? It is his business; it is my pleasure."

He raised his voice. "Isis! Isis!"

Out into the light of the fluttering gas-lamp, out from that nightmare abode, stepped Isis Klaw—looking more grotesque than a French fashion-plate in an ironmonger's catalogue. She wore a costume of lettuce-green silk, absolutely plain and unrelieved by any ornament, which rendered it the more remarkable. It was cut low at the neck, and at the point of the V, suspended upon a thin gold chain, hung a big emerald. Her darkly beautiful face was one to inspire a painter seeking a model for the Queen of Sheba, but an ultra modern note was struck by a hat of some black, gauzy material which loudly proclaimed its Paris origin. She greeted me with her wonderful smile.

"What, then," I said. "Were you about to go out?"

"When I hear who it is," rumbled Moris Klaw, "I know that we are about to go out; and behold we are ready!"

He placed the quaint bowler on his head and passed through to the front of the shop.

"William," he admonished the ripe-nosed salesman, "there is here a smell of fourpenny ale. It will be your ruin, William. You will close at half-past nine, and be sure you do not let the cat in the cupboard with the white mice. See that the goat does not get at the Dutch bulbs. They will kill him, that goat—those bulbs; he has for them a passion."

The three of us entered the waiting cab; and within half-an-hour we arrived at the famous auction rooms. The doors were closed and barred, but a constable who was on duty there evidently had orders to admit us.

The thing we had come to see lay upon the table with an electric lamp burning directly over it. The effect was indescribably weird. All about in the shadows fantastic "lots" seemed to leer at us. A famous private collection was to be sold in the morning and a rank of mummies lined one wall, whilst, from another, stony Pharaohs, gods and goddesses, scorned us through the gloom. We were a living group in a place of long-dead things. And yellow on the table beneath the white light, with partially unwrapt coils of discoloured linen hanging gruesomely from it, lay a headless mummy!

I heard the spurt of Moris Klaw's scent-spray behind me, and a faint breath of verbena stole to my nostrils.

"Pah!" came the rumbling voice; "this air is full of deadness!"

"Good-evening, Mr. Klaw," said Grimsby, appearing from somewhere out of the gloom. "I am so glad you have come." He bowed to Isis. "How do you do, Miss Klaw?"

The bright green figure moved forward into the pool of light. I think I had never seen a more singular picture than that of Isis Klaw bending over the decapitated mummy. Indeed the whole scene had delighted Rembrandt.

"I am pleased to meet you, Mr. Klaw," said a middle-aged gentleman, stepping up to the curio dealer; "the Inspector has been telling me about you."

Moris Klaw bowed, and his daughter turned to him with a little nod of the head.

"It is the same period," she said, "as Mr. Pettigrew's mummy. Possibly this was a priest of the same temple. Certainly both are of the same dynasty."

"It is instructive," rumbled Moris Klaw, "but so confusing."

"It's amazing, Mr. Klaw," said Grimsby. "If I understand Miss Klaw rightly, this is the mummy of some one who lived at the same period as the priestess whose mummy is in Mr. Pettigrew's possession?"

"I do not trouble to look," rumbled Moris Klaw, who, in fact, was staring all about the room. "If Isis has said so, it is so."

"If I happened to be superstitious," said Grimsby, "I should think this was a sort of curse being fulfilled, or some fantastic thing of that sort."

"You should call a curse fantastic, eh, my friend?" said Moris Klaw. "Yet here in your own country you have seen a whole family that was cursed to be wiped out mysteriously. Am I with you?"

Grimsby looked very perplexed.

"There's nothing very mysterious about how the thing was done," he said. "Some madman got in here with a knife early in the evening. It's always pretty dark even during the daytime. But the mystery is his object."

"His object is a mystery, yes," agreed Klaw. "I would sleep here in order to procure a mental negative of what he hoped or what he feared, this lunatic headsman, only that I know he is a man possessed."

"Possessed!" I cried; and even Isis looked surprised.

"I said possessed," continued Klaw, impressively. "He is some madman with a one idea. His mad brain will have charged the ether"—he waved his long arms right and left—"with mad thoughts. The room of Mr. Pettigrew also will be filled with these grotesque thought-forms. Certainly he is insane, this butcher of mummies. In this case I shall rely not upon the odic photography, not upon that great science the Cycle of Crime, but upon my library."

None of us, I am sure, entirely understood his meaning; and following a brief silence, during which in a curiously muffled way the sounds of the traffic in Wellington Street came to us as we stood there around that modern bier with its 4000-year-old burden, Grimsby asked with hesitancy:

"Don't you want to make any investigations, Mr. Klaw?"

Then Moris Klaw startled us all.

"I have a thought!" he cried, loudly. "Name of a dog! I have a thought!"

Grabbing his brown bowler, which he had laid on the table beside the headless mummy, "Come, Isis!" he cried, and grasped the girl by the arm. "I have yet another thought, most disturbing! Mr. Searles, would you be so good as also to come?"

Wondering greatly whence we were bound and upon what errand, I hastened down the room after them, leaving Inspector Grimsby staring blankly. I think he was rather disappointed with the result of Moris Klaw's inquiry—if inquiry this hasty visit may be termed. He was disappointed, too, at having spent so short a time in the company of the charming Isis.

The middle-aged gentleman came running to let us out.

"Good-night, Inspector Grimsby!" called Moris Klaw.

"Good-night! good-night, Miss Klaw!"

"Good-night, Mr. Some One who has not been introduced!" said Klaw.

"My name is Welby," smiled the other.

"Good-night, Mr. Welby!" said Moris Klaw.

III

During the whole of the journey back to Wapping, Moris Klaw regaled me with anecdotes of travels in the Yucatan Peninsula. I had never met a man before who had ventured fully to explore those deadly swamps; but Moris Klaw chatted about the Izamal temples as unconcernedly as another man might chat about the Paris boulevards. Isis took no part in the conversation, from which I gathered that, although she seemed to accompany her father everywhere, she had not accompanied him into the jungles of Yucatan.

"In the heart of those forests, Mr. Searles," he whispered, "are stranger things than these headless mummies. Do you know that the secret of those great temples buried in the swamps and the jungles and guarded only by serpents and slimy, crawling things, is a door which science has yet to unlock? What people built them, and what god was worshipped in them? Suppose"—he bent to my ear—"I hold the key to that riddle; am I assured to be immortal? Yes? No?"

His conversation, although it often seemed to be studiously eccentric, was always that of a man of powerful and unusual mind, a man of vast and unique experience. I was rather sorry when we arrived at our destination.

As the cab drew up at the head of the court, I saw that the shop of Moris Klaw was in darkness; but again telling the man to wait, we walked down past the warehouse, beyond whose bulk tided muddy Thames, and, my eccentric companion producing a key from one of the bulging pockets of his caped coat, he inserted it into the lock of a door which looked less like a door than a section of a dilapidated hoarding.

The door swung open.

"Ah!" he hissed. "It was not locked!"

Klaw struck a match and peered into the odorous darkness.

"William!" he rumbled. "William!"

But there was no reply. Isis suddenly laid her hand upon my arm, and it occurred to me that for once her wonderful composure was shaken.

"Something has happened!" she whispered.

Her father lighted a gas-burner, and the yellow light flared up, reclaiming from the gloom, furniture, pictures, cages, glass cases, statuettes, heaps of cheap jewellery and false teeth, books, and a hundred-and-one other items of that weird stock-in-trade.

Then, under the littered counter we found William lying flat on his back with his arms spread widely.

"Ah! *cochon!*" muttered Klaw; "beer-swilling pig!"

He stooped to raise the head of the prostrate man, and then to to my surprise dropped upon his knees beside him, stooped yet lower, and sniffed suspiciously. Again Isis Klaw seized my arm, and her dark eyes were opened very widely as she leaned forward watching her father. He stood up, holding a glass in his hand which yet contained some drops of what was apparently beer. At this, too, he sniffed. He walked over to the gaslight and examined the fluid closely, whilst Isis and I watched him, together. Finally Moris Klaw inserted a long white forefinger into the dirty glass and applied the tip to his tongue.

"Opium!" he said. "Many drops of pure opium were put in this beer."

He turned to me with a curious expression upon his parchment-coloured face.

"Mr. Searles," he said, "my second idea was a good idea. I shall now surprise you."

He led the way through that neat and businesslike office which opened out of the unutterably dirty and untidy shop. Although within the shop and in front of it, only gaslight was used, in the office he switched on an electric lamp. But we did not delay long in Moris Klaw's sanctum, lined with its hundreds of books, its obscure works of criminology, its records of strange things: we proceeded through another door and up a thickly carpeted stair.

I had never before penetrated thus far into the habitable portion of Moris Klaw's establishment; the book-lined office hitherto had marked the limit of my explorations. But now as more electric lights were switched on, I saw that we stood upon a wide landing panelled in massive black oak. Armoured figures stood sentinel-like against the walls, and several magnificent specimens of Chinese porcelain met my gaze. I might have thought myself in some old English baronial hall. Next we entered a big, rectangular room, which I wholly despair of describing. Apparently it was used as a study, a library, a laboratory, and a warehouse for all sorts of things, from marble Buddhas to innumerable pairs of boots. Also, there was in it a French stove; and upon a Persian coffee-table stood a frying-pan containing a cooked sausage solidified in its own fat. There was clear evidence, moreover, in the form of a rolled-up hammock, that the place served as a bedroom.

Altogether there were four mummies in the apartment. One of these, partly unwrapped, lay amongst the litter on the floor... headless!

"Mon Dieu!" cried Isis, clasping her hands; "it is uncanny, this!"

She was evidently excited, for her French accent suddenly asserted itself to a marked degree. Moris Klaw, from somewhere amongst the rubbish at his feet, picked up the severed head of the mummy and stared at it intently. In the stillness I could hear the river noises very distinctly, and a sort of subterranean lapping and creaking which suggested that at high tide the cellars of the establishment became flooded. Moris Klaw dropped the head from his hands. It fell with a dull thud to the floor.

From the lining of his hat he took out the inevitable scent-spray and moistened his brow with verbena.

"I need the cool brain, Mr. Searles," he said. "I, the old cunning, the fox, the wily, am threatened with defeat. This slaughter of mummies it surpasses my experience. I am nonplussed; I am a stupid old fool. Let me think!"

Isis was looking about her in a startled way.

"It is horribly uncanny, Miss Klaw," I said. "But the drugging of the man downstairs points to very human agency. Perhaps if we could revive him—"

"He will not revive," interrupted Moris Klaw, "for twelve hours at least. In his beer was enough opium to render unconscious the rhinoceros!"

"Is there anything missing?" I asked.

"Nothing," rumbled Klaw. "He came for the mummy. Isis, will you prepare for us those cooling drinks that help the fevered mind, and from downstairs bring me the seventh volume of the *Books of the Temples.*"

Isis Klaw immediately walked forward to the door.

"And Isis, my child," added her father, "remove the tall cage to the top end of the shop. Presently that William's snores will awake the Borneo squirrel."

As the girl departed, Klaw opened an inner door and ushered me into a dainty white room, an amazing apartment indeed, a true Parisian boudoir. The air was heavy with the scent of roses for bowls of white and pink roses were everywhere. Klaw lighted a silver table-lamp with an unique silver gauze shade apparently lined with pale rose-coloured silk. Evidently this apartment belonged to Isis, and was as appropriate for her, exquisite Parisian that she seemed to be, as the weird barn through which we had come was an appropriate abode for her father.

When presently Isis returned I saw her for the first time in her proper setting, a dainty green figure in a white frame. Moris Klaw opened the bulky leather-bound volume which she had handed to him, and whilst I sat sipping my wine and watching him, he busily turned over the pages (apparently French MS.) in quest of the reference he sought.

Ah!'' he cried in sudden triumph; ''vaguely I had it in my memory, but here it is, the clue. I will translate for you, Mr. Searles, what is written here: 'The *Book of the Lamps*, which was revealed to the priest, Pankhaur, and by him revealed only to the Queen' (it was the ancient Egyptian Queen, Hatshepsu, Mr. Searles), 'was kept locked in the secret place beneath the altar and each high priest of the temple—all of whom were of the family of Pankhaur—held the key and alone might consult the magic writing. In the 14th dynasty, Seteb was high priest, and was the last of the family of Pankhaur. At his death the newly appointed priest, receiving the key of the secret place, complained to Pharaoh that the *Book of the Lamps* was missing.' ''

He closed the volume, and placed it on a little table beside him.

''Isis,'' he rumbled, looking across at his daughter, ''does the mystery become clear to you? Am I not an old fool? Mr. Searles, there is only one other copy of this work''—he laid a long white hand upon the book—''known to European collectors. Do I know where that copy is? Yes? No? I think so!''

There was triumph in his hoarse voice. Personally I was quite unable to see in what way the history of the *Book of the Lamps* bore upon the case of the headless mummies; but Moris Klaw evidently considered that it afforded a clue. He stood up.

''Isis,'' he said, ''bring me my catalogue of the mummies of the Bubastite priests.''

That imperious beauty departed in meek obedience.

''Mr. Searles,'' said Moris Klaw, ''this will be for Inspector Grimsby another triumph; but without these records of a poor old fool, who shall say if the one that beheads mummies had ever been detected? I neglected to secure the odic negative because I thought I had to deal with a madman; but I was more stupid than an owl. This decapitating of mummies is no madman's work, but is done with a purpose, my friend—with a wonderful purpose."

IV

The Menzies Museum (scene of my first meeting with Moris Klaw) was not yet opened to the public when Coram (the curator), Moris Klaw, Grimsby and I stood in the Egyptian Room before a case containing mummies. The room adjoining—the Greek Room—had been the scene of the dreadful tragedies which first had acquainted me with the wonderful methods of the eccentric investigator.

"Whoever broke into Sotheby's last night, Mr. Klaw," said Grimsby, "knew the ins and outs of the place; knew it backwards. It's my idea that he was known to the people there. After having cut off the head of the mummy he probably walked out openly. Then, again, it must have been somebody who knew the habits of Mr. Pettigrew's household that got at *his* mummy. Of course"— his eyes twinkled with a satisfaction which he could not conceal— "I'm very sorry to hear that our man has proved too clever for *you!* Think of a burglar breaking into Mr. Moris Klaw's house!"

"Think of it, my friend," rumbled the other; "if it makes you laugh go on thinking of it, and you will grow fat!"

Grimsby openly winked at me. He was out of his depth himself, and was not displeased to find the omniscient Moris Klaw apparently in a similar position.

"I am not resentful," continued Klaw, "and I will capture for you the mummy man."

"What?" cried Grimsby. "Are you on the track?"

"I will tell you something, my laughing friend. You will secretly watch this Egyptian Room like the cat at the mouse-hole, and presently—I expect it will be at night—he will come here, this hunter of mummies!"

Grimsby stared incredulously.

"I don't doubt your word, Mr. Klaw," he said; "but I don't see how you can possibly know that. Why should he go for the mummies here rather than for those in one of the other museums or in private collections?"

"Why do you order a bottle of Bass," rasped Klaw, "in a saloon, rather than a bottle of water or a bottle of vinegar? It is because what you want is a bottle of Bass. Am I a damn fool? There are others. I am not alone in my foolishness!''

The group broke up: Grimsby, very puzzled, going off to make arrangements to have the Egyptian Room watched night and day, and Coram, Klaw, and I walking along in the direction of the Greek Room.

''I have no occasion to remind you, Mr. Klaw,'' said Coram, ''that the Menzies Museum is a hard nut for any burglar to crack. We have a night watchman, you will remember, who hourly patrols every apartment. For any one to break into the Egyptian Room, force one of the cases and take out a mummy, would be a task extremely difficult to perform undetected.''

''This mummy hunter,'' replied Klaw, ''can perform it with ease; but because we shall all be waiting for him he cannot perform it undetected.''

''I shouldn't think there is much likelihood of any attempt during the day?'' I said.

''There is no likelihood,'' agreed Klaw; ''but I like to see that Grimsby busy! The man with the knife to decapitate mummies will come to-night. Without fear he will come, for how is he to know that an old fool from Wapping anticipates his arrival?''

We quitted the Museum together. The affair brought back to my mind the gruesome business of the Greek Room murders, and for the second time in my life I made arrangements to watch in the Menzies Museum at night.

On several occasions during the day I found myself thinking of this most singular affair and wondering in what way the *Book of the Lamps,* mentioned by Moris Klaw, could be associated with it. I was quite unable to surmise, too, how Klaw had divined that the Menzies Museum would become the scene of the next outrage.

We had arranged to dine with Coram in his apartments, which adjoined the Museum buildings, and an oddly mixed party we were, comprising Coram, his daughter, Moris Klaw, Isis Klaw, Grimsby and myself.

A man had gone on duty in the Egyptian Room directly the doors were closed to the public, and we had secretly arranged to watch the place from night-fall onward. The construction of the room greatly facilitated our plan; for there was a long glass skylight in the centre of its roof, and by having the blinds drawn back we could look down into the room from a landing window of a higher floor—a portion of the curator's house.

Dinner over, Isis Klaw departed.

"You will not remain, Isis," said her father. "It is so unnecessary. Good-night, my child!"

Accordingly, the deferential and very admiring Grimsby descended with Coram to see Isis off in a taxi. I marvelled to think of her returning to that tumble-down, water-logged ruin in Wapping.

"Now, Mr. Grimsby," said Moris Klaw, when we four investigators had gathered together again, "you will hide in the case with the mummies!"

"But I may find myself helpless! How do we know that any particular case is going to be opened? Besides I don't know what to expect!"

"Blessed is he that expecteth little, my friend. It is quite possible that no attempt will be made to-night. In that event you will have to be locked in again to-morrow night!"

Grimsby accordingly set out. He held a key to the curator's private door, which opened upon the Greek Room, and also the key of a wall-case. Moris Klaw had especially warned him against making the slightest noise. In fact he had us all agog with curiosity and expectation. As he and Coram and I, having opened, very carefully, the landing window, looked down through the skylight into the Egyptian Room, Grimsby appeared beneath us. He was carrying an electric pocket torch.

Opening the wall-case nearest to the lower end of the room, he glanced up rapidly, then stepped within, reclosing the glass door. As Klaw had pointed out earlier in the evening, an ideal hiding-place existed between the side of the last sarcophagus and the angle of the wall.

"I hope he has refastened the catch," said our eccentric companion; "but not with noisiness."

"Why do you fear his making a noise?" asked Coram, curiously.

"Outside, upon the landing," replied Moris Klaw, "is a tall piece of a bas-relief; it leans back against the wall. You know it?"

"Certainly."

"To-night, you did not look behind it, in the triangular space so formed."

"There's no occasion. A man could not get in there."

"He could not, you say? No? That exploits to me, Mr. Coram, that you have no eye for capacity! But if you are wrong, what then?"

"Any one hiding there would have to remain in hiding until the morning. He could not gain access to any of the rooms; all are locked, and he could not go downstairs, because of the night attendant in the hall-way."

"No? Yes? You are two times wrong! First—some one is concealed there!"

"Mr. Klaw!" began Coram, excitedly.

"Ssh!" Moris Klaw raised his hand. "No excitement. It is noisy and a tax upon the nerves. Second—you are wrong, because presently that hidden one will come into the Egyptian Room!"

"How? How in Heaven's name is he going to *get* in?"

"We shall see."

Utterly mystified, Coram and I stared at Moris Klaw, for we stood one on either side of him; but he merely wagged his finger enjoining us to silence, and silent perforce we became.

The view was a cramped one, and standing there looking out at the clear summer night, I for one grew very weary of the business. But I was sustained by the anticipation that the mystery of the headless mummies was about to come to a climax. I felt very sorry for poor Grimsby, cramped in the corner of the Egyptian room, for I knew him to be even more hopelessly in the dark respecting the purpose of these manoeuvres than I was myself. In vain I racked my brain in quest of the link which united the ancient *Book of the Lamps* with the singular case which had brought us there that night.

Coram began to fidget, and I knew intuitively that he was about to speak.

"Ssh!" whispered Moris Klaw.

A beam of light shone out beneath us, across the Egyptian Room!

I concluded that something had attracted the attention of Grimsby. I leaned forward in tense expectancy, and Coram was keenly excited.

The beam of light moved; it shone upon the door of the very case in the corner of which Grimsby was hiding, but upon the nearer end, fully upon the face of a mummy.

A small figure was dimly discernible, now, the figure of the man who carried the light. Cautiously he crossed the room. Evidently he held the key of the wall-case, for in an instant he had swung the door back and was hauling the mummy on to the floor.

Then out upon the midnight visitor leapt Grimsby. The light was extinguished—and Moris Klaw, drawing back from the window, seized Coram by the arm, crying, "The key of the door! The key of the door!"

We were down and into the Egyptian Room in less than half a minute. Coram switched on all the lights; and there with his back

to the open door of the wall-case, handcuffed and wild-eyed, was...
Mr. Mark Pettigrew!

Coram's face was a study—for the famous archaeologist whom
we now saw manacled before us was a trustee of the Menzies
Museum!

"Mr. Pettigrew!" he said hoarsely. "Mr. Pettigrew! there must
be some mistake——"

"There is no mistake, my good sir," rumbled Moris Klaw.
"Look, he has with him a sharp knife to cut off the head of the
priest!"

It was true. An open knife lay upon the floor beside the fallen
mummy!

Grimsby was breathing very heavily and looking in rather a
startled way at his captive, who seemed unable to realise what had
happened. Coram cleared his throat nervously. It was one of the
strangest scenes in which I had ever anticipated.

"Mr. Pettigrew," he began, "it is incomprehensible to me——"

"I will make you to comprehend," interrupted Moris Klaw.
"You ask"—he raised a long finger—"why should Mr. Pettigrew
cut off the head of his own mummy? I answer for the same reason
that he cut off the head of the one at Sotheby's. You ask why did
he cut off the head of the one at Sotheby's? I answer for the same
reason that he cut off the head of the one at my house, and for the
same reason that he came to cut off the head of this one! What is
he looking for? He is looking for the *Book of the Lamps!*" He
paused, gazing around upon us. Probably, excepting the prisoner, I
alone amongst his listeners understood what he meant.

"I have related to Mr. Searles," he continued, "some of the history of that book. It contained the ritual of the ancient Egyptian
ceremonial magic. It was priceless; it gave its possessors a power
above the power of kings! And when the line of Pankhaur became
extinct it vanished. Where did it go? According to a very rare
record—of which there are only two copies in existence—one of
them in my possession and one in Mr. Pettigrew's!—it was hidden
in the skull of the mummy of a priest or a priestess of the temple!"

Pettigrew was staring at him like a man fascinated.

"Mr. Pettigrew had only recently acquired that valuable manuscript work in which the fact is recorded; and being an enthusiast,
gentlemen—" (he spread wide his hands continentally), "all we
poor collectors are enthusiasts—he set to work upon the first available mummy of a priest of that temple. It was his own. The skull
did not contain the priceless papyrus! But all these mummies are
historic; there are only five in Europe."

"*Five?*" blurted Pettigrew.

"Five," replied Klaw; "you thought there were only four, eh? But as a blind you called in the police and showed them how your mummy had been mutilated. It was good. It was clever. No one suspected you of the outrages after that—no one but the old fool who knew that you had secured the second copy of that valuable work of guidance!

"So you did not hesitate to use the keys you had procured in your capacity as trustee, to gain access to this fourth mummy here." He turned to Grimsby and Coram. "Gentlemen," he said, "there will be no prosecution. The fever of research is a disease; never a crime."

"I agree," said Coram; "most certainly there must be no prosecution; no scandal. Mr. Pettigrew, I am very, very sorry for this."

Grimsby, with a rather wry face, removed the handcuffs. A singular expression proclaimed itself upon Pettigrew's shrivelled countenance.

"The thing I'm most sorry for," he said, dryly, but with the true fever of research burning in his eyes, "if you will excuse me saying it, Coram, for I'm very deeply indebted to you—is that I can't cut off the head of this fourth mummy!"

Mr. Mark Pettigrew was a singularly purposeful and rudely truculent man.

"It would be useless," rumbled Moris Klaw. "I found the fifth mummy in Egypt two years ago! And behold"—he swept his hand picturesquely through the air—"I beheaded him!"

"What!" screamed Pettigrew, and leapt upon Klaw with blazing eyes.

"Ah," rumbled Klaw, massive and unruffled, "that is the question—*what?* And I shall not tell you!"

From his pocket he took out the scent-spray and squirted verbena into the face of Mr. Pettigrew.

Eighth Episode

CASE OF THE HAUNTING
OF GRANGE

I

A large lamp burned in the centre of the table; a red-shaded candle stood close by each diner; and the soft light made a brave enough show upon the snowy napery and spotless silver, but dispersed nothing of the gloom about us. The table was a lighted oasis in the desert of the huge apartment. One could barely pick out the suits of armour and trophies which hung from distant panelled walls, and I started repeatedly when the butler appeared, silent, at my elbow.

Of the party of five, four were men—three of them (for I venture to include myself) neatly groomed and dressed with care in conventional dinner fashion. The fourth was a heavy figure in a dress-coat with broad satin lapels such as I have seen, I think, in pictures of Victorian celebrities. I have no doubt, judging from its shiny appearance, that it was the workmanship of a Victorian tailor. The vest was cut high and also boasted lapels; the trousers, though at present they were concealed beneath the table, belonged to a different suit, possibly a mourning suit, and to a different sartorial epoch.

The woman, young, dark and exceedingly pretty, wore a gown of shimmering amber, cut with Parisian daring. Her beautiful eyes were more often lowered than raised, for Sir James Leyland, our host, was unable to conceal his admiration; his face, tanned by his life in the Bush, was often turned to her. Clement Leyland, the baronet's cousin, bore a striking resemblance to Sir James, but entirely lacked the latter's breezy manner. I set him down for a man who thought much and said little.

However, conversation could not well flag at a board boasting the presence of such a genial colonial as Sir James, and such a storehouse of anecdotal oddities as Moris Klaw. Mr. Leyland and

myself, then, for the most part practised the difficult art of listening; for Isis Klaw, I learned, could talk almost as entertainingly as
her father.

"I am so glad," said Moris Klaw, and his voice rumbled thun-
derously about the room, "that I have this opportunity to visit
Grange."

"It certainly has great historic interest," agreed Sir James. "I
had never anticipated inheriting the grand old place, much less the
title. My uncle's early death, unmarried, very considerably altered
my prospects; I became a landed proprietor who might otherwise
have become a 'Murrumbidgee whaler!' "

He laughed, light-heartedly, glancing at Isis Klaw, and from her
to his cousin.

"Clem had everything in apple-pie order for me," he added,
"including the family goblin!"

"Ah! that family goblin!" rumbled Moris Klaw. "It is him I am
after, that goblin!"

The history of Grange, in fact, was directly responsible for Moris
Klaw's presence that night. An odd little book, *Psychic Angles,* had
recently attracted considerable attention amongst students of the
occult, and had proved equally interesting to the general public. It
dealt with the subject of ghosts from quite a new standpoint, and
incidentally revealed its anonymous author as one conversant
apparently with the history of every haunted house in Europe. Few
knew that the curio-dealer of Wapping was the author, but as
Grange was dealt with in *Psychic Angles,* amongst a number of
other haunted homes of England, a letter from Sir James Leyland,
forwarded by the publisher, had invited the author to investigate
the latest developments of the Leyland family ghost.

I had had the privilege to be associated with Moris Klaw, in another case of apparent haunting—that which I have dealt with in an
earlier paper; the haunting of The Grove. He had courteously
invited me, then, to assist him (his own expression) in the inquiry
at Grange. I welcomed the opportunity; for I was anxious to
include in my annals at least one other case of the apparent
occult.

"We shall without delay," continued the eccentric investigator,
"endeavour to meet him face to face—this disturber of the peace.
Sir James, it is with the phenomena you call ghosts the same as with
valuable relics, with jewels, with mummies—ah, those mummies!
—with beautiful women!"

"To liken a beautiful woman to a relic," said Sir James, "would
be—well——" he glanced at Isis, "hardly complimentary!"

"It would be true!" Moris Klaw assured him impressively. "Nature, that mystic process of reproduction, wastes not its models. Sir James, all beauty is duplicated. Look at my daughter, Isis." (Sir James readily obeyed.) "You see her, yes? And what do you see?"

Isis lowered her eyes, but, frankly, I was unable to perceive any evidence of embarrassment in this singularly self-possessed girl.

"Perhaps," resumed her father, "I could tell you what you see; but I will only tell you what it is you *may* see. You may see a beauty of your Regency or a favourite of your Charles; the daughter of a Viking, an ancient British princess; the slave of a Caesar, the dancer of a Pharaoh!"

"You believe in reincarnation?" suggested Clement Leyland, quietly.

"Yes, certainly, why not, of course!" rumbled Moris Klaw. "But I do not speak of it now, not I; I speak of Nature's reproduction; I tell you how Nature wastes nothing which is beautiful. What has the soul to do with the body? I tell you how the reproduction goes on and on until the mould, the plate, the die, has perished! So is it with ghosts. You write me that your goblin has learned some new tricks. I answer, your goblin can never learn new tricks; I answer this is not he, it is another goblin! Nature is conservative with her goblins as with her beautiful women; she does not disfigure the old model with alterations. What! Chop them about! Never! she makes new ones."

Clement Leyland smiled discreetly, but Sir James was evidently interested.

"Of course I've read *Psychic Angles,* Mr. Klaw," he said, "consequently your novel theories do not altogether surprise me. I gather your meaning to be this: a haunted house is haunted in exactly the same way generation after generation? Any new development points to the presence of a new force or intelligence?"

"It is exactly quite so," Moris Klaw nodded sympathetically. "You have the receptive mind, Sir James; you should take up ghosts; they would like you. There is a scientific future for the sympathetic ghost-hunter—for I will whisper it—these poor ghosts are sometimes so glad to be hunted! It is a lonely life, that of a ghost!"

"The Grange ghost," Sir James assured him, "is a most gregarious animal. He doesn't go in for lonely groanings in the chapel or anything of that kind; he drops into the billiard-room frequently, he's often to be met with right here in the dining-room, and of late he's been sleeping with me regularly!"

"So I hear," rumbled Moris Klaw; "so I hear. It is quaint, yes, proceed, my friend."

Isis Klaw sat with her big eyes fixed upon Sir James as he continued:

"The traditional ghost of Grange was a grey monk who on certain nights—I forget the exact dates—came out from the chapel beyond the orchard carrying a long staff, walked up to a buttress of the west wall and disappeared at the point where formerly there was a private entrance. In fact there used to be a secret stair opening at that point and communicating with a room built by a remote Leyland of the eighth Henry's time—a notorious *roué*. The last Leyland to use the room was Sir Francis, an intimate of Charles II. The next heir had the wing rebuilt, and the ancient door walled up."

"Yes, yes," said Moris Klaw. "I know it all, but you tell it well. This is a most interesting house, this Grange. I have recorded him, the grey monk, and I learn with surprise how another spook comes poaching on his preserves! Tell us now of these new developments, Sir James."

Sir James cleared his throat and glanced about the table.

"Please smoke," said Isis; "because I should like to smoke, too!"

"Yes, yes!" agreed Moris Klaw. "Remain, my child, we will all remain; do not let us move an inch. This banqueting-hall is loaded with psychic impressions. Let us smoke and concentrate our minds upon the problem."

Coffee and liqueurs were placed upon the table and cigarettes lighted. In deference to the presence of Isis, I suppose, no cigars were smoked; but the girl lighted an Egyptian cigarette proffered by Sir James with the insouciance of an old devotee of my Lady Nicotine. The butler having made his final departure, we were left—a lonely company in our lighted oasis—amid the shadow desert of that huge and ghostly apartment.

"All sorts of singular things have happened," began Sir James, "since my return from Australia. Of course I cannot say if these are recent developments, because my uncle, for seven or eight years before his death, resided entirely in London, and Grange was in charge of the housekeeper. It is notorious, is it not, that housekeepers and such worthy ladies never by any chance detect anything unseemly in family establishments with which they are associated? Anyway, when I was dug up out of the Bush, and all the formalities were through, good old Clement here set about putting things to rights for me and I arrived to find Grange a perfect picture from floor to roof. New servants engaged, too, though the housekeeper and the butler, who have been in the family for years, remained, of course, with some other old servants. As I have said, everything was in apple-pie order.''

"Including the ghost!" interpolated his cousin, laughing.

"That's the trouble," said Sir James, banging his fist upon the table; "the very first night I dined in this room there was a most uncanny manifestation. Clement and I were sitting here at this very table; we had dined—not unwisely, don't think that—and were just smoking and chatting, when——"

He ceased abruptly; in fact the effect was similar to that which would have resulted had a solid door suddenly been closed upon the speaker. But the stark silence which ensued was instantly interrupted. My blood seemed to freeze in my veins; a horrid, supernatural dread held me fast in my chair.

For, echoing hollowly around and about the huge, ancient apartment, rolled, booming, a peal of demoniacal laughter! From whence it proceeded I was wholly unable to imagine. It seemed to be all about, above us, and beneath us. It was mad, devilish, a hell-sound impossible to describe. It rose, it fell, it rose again—and ceased abruptly.

"My God!" I whispered. "What was it?"

II

In the silence that followed the ghostly disturbance we sat around the table listening. Sir James was the first to speak.

"A demonstration, Mr. Klaw!" he said. "This sort of thing happens every night!"

"Ah!" rumbled Moris Klaw, "every night, eh? That laughing? You have investigated—yes—no?"

"I tried to investigate," explained the baronet, "but quite frankly I didn't know where to begin."

We were all recovering our composure somewhat, I think.

"You hear that laughter nowhere but in this room?" asked Klaw.

"I have always heard it when we have been seated at this table," was the reply; "at no other time, but it can be heard clearly beyond the room. The servants have heard it. Excepting the housekeeper and the butler, they are leaving almost immediately."

"Ah! *canaille!*" grunted Moris Klaw, "fear-pigs! It is always so, these servants. So you have not located the one that laughs, no?"

"No," answered Sir James; "and he doesn't stop at laughing—does he, Clem?"

Clement Leyland shook his head. He looked even paler than usual, I thought, and the uncanny incident seemed to have disturbed him greatly.

"What else?" rumbled Moris Klaw. "The grey monk is forgetting his manners. He becomes rude, eh—that grey monk?"

"The house has practically become uninhabitable," said the baronet, bitterly. "None of the unusual phenomena are missing. We have slamming doors, phantom footsteps, and, if the servants are to be believed, half the forces of hell loose here at night!"

"But your *own* experiences?" interrupted Klaw.

"My own experiences in brief amount to this: I rarely sit at this table at night without hearing that beastly laughter, at least once. I never go into the billiard-room, which opens out under the gallery yonder, without feeling a cold wind blowing upon my face or head, even in perfectly still weather, or with all the windows closed. To the left of the billiard-room, and opening out of it, is a third centre of these disturbances. It's the gun-room, and guns have been fired there in the night with the door locked, on no fewer than five occasions!"

Moris Klaw, from a tail pocket of his coat, produced a cylindrical scent-spray and squirted verbena upon his high, yellow forehead.

"It grows exciting, this," he said. "I require the cool brain."

"Finally," added Sir James, "the only other point worth mentioning is the ghostly voice which regularly wakes me from my sleep at night."

"A voice," rumbled Klaw, "what voice and what does it say, that voice?"

"I won't repeat what it says!" replied the baronet, glancing at Isis; "but it offers obscene suggestions, or that is the impression I have of it—a low filthy mumbling; if you can follow me, the voice of something dead and infinitely evil."

Moris Klaw stood up.

"This intelligence," he rumbled, "a living or a dead one, has thoughts then, and thoughts, Sir James, are things. I shall sleep in one of the centres of its activity to-night, perhaps here, perhaps in the billiard-room or the gun-room. Isis, my child, bring for me my odically sterilised pillows. This is a charming case and worthy of the subtle method."

He placed his hands upon the shoulders of Sir James Leyland, who stood facing him.

"Evil thoughts live, Sir James," he said. "I cannot explain to you how hard it is to slay them. Few good thoughts survive; but such an ancient abode as this"—he waved his long hands characteristically about him—"is peopled with thought-forms surviving from the dark ages. I have opened the inner eye, my friend. Mercifully, perhaps, the inner eye is closed in most of us; in some it is blind. But I have opened that eye and trained it. As I sleep"—he lowered his voice oddly—"those thought-things come to me. It is an uncomfortable gift, yes; for here in Grange I shall find myself to-night in evil company. Murders long forgotten will be accomplished again before that inner eye of mine! I shall swim in blood! Assassins will come stealing to me, murdered ones will scream in my ears, the secret knife will flash, the honest axe do its deadly work; for in the moment of such deeds two imperishable thought-forms are created: the thought-form of the slayer, strong to survive, because a blood-lustful thought, a revengeful thought; and the thought of the slain, likewise a long-surviving thought because a thought of wildest despair, a final massing of the mental forces greater than any generally possible in life, upon that last awful grievance."

He paused, looking around him.

"From the phantom company," he said, "I must pick out that one whose thought is of laughter, of firing guns, and of evil whisperings. What a task! Wondrous is the science of the mental negative!"

The meeting broke up, then, and Isis Klaw, having brought from a large case, which formed part of her father's luggage, two huge red cushions, bade us good-night and retired to her own room. Moris Klaw, with a cushion swinging in each hand, went shuffling ungainly from room to room like some strange animal seeking a lair.

"Do I understand," Clement Leyland whispered to me, "that your friend proposes to sleep down here?"

"Yes," I replied, smiling at his evident wonderment; "such is his method of investigation, eccentric, but effective."

"It is really effective, then? The experiences given in *Psychic Angles* are not fabulous?"

"In no way. Moris Klaw is a very remarkable man. I have yet to meet the mystery which is beyond him."

Moris Klaw's rumbling voice, which frequently reminded me of the rolling of casks in a distant cellar, broke in upon our conversation—

"Here is the ideal spot; here upon this settee by the door of the gun-room I am in the centre of these psychic storms which nightly arise in Grange."

"If you are determined to remain here, Mr. Klaw," said Sir James, "I shall not endevour to dissuade you, of course; but I should prefer to see you turn into more comfortable quarters."

"No, no," was the reply; "it is here I shall lay down my old head, it is here I shall lie and wait for him, the one who laughs."

Accordingly, since the hour grew late, we left this novel ghost-hunter stretched out upon the settee in the billiard-room; and as I knew his objection to any disturbance, I suggested to Sir James that we should retire out of earshot for a final smoke ere seeking our separate apartments.

We sat chatting for close upon an hour, I suppose. Then Clement Leyland left us, saying that he had had a heavy day.

"Clement's been working real hard," the baronet confided to me. "In the circumstances, as I think I told you, I have decided to abandon Grange, and we are having the old Friars House, a mile from here, but on part of the estate, restored. It hasn't been inhabited for about three generations, and it's very much older than Grange; part of it dates back to King John. Perhaps I can get servants to stop there, though, and it's quite impossible to keep up Grange without a staff. Clement has been superintending the work over there all day; he's one of the best."

A few moments later we parted for the night. I left Sir James at the door of his room, which had formerly opened off the balcony overlooking the banqueting-hall. That door was now walled up, however, and the entrance was from the corridor beyond. The room allotted to me was upon the opposite side of the same corridor and farther to the north.

I felt particularly unlike sleep. The extremely modern furniture of my room could not rob the walls, with their small square paneling, of the air of hoary antiquity which was theirs. The one window, deep set, and overlooking an extensive orchard, was such as might have formed the focus for cavalierly glance, was such as might have framed the head of a romantic maid of Stuart days. And with it all was that gloomy air that had a more remote antiquity, that harked back to darker times than those of the Merry Monarch: the air of ghostly evil, the cloud from which proceeded the devilish laughter, the obscene whisperings.

Where the shadows of the trees lay beneath me on the turf, I could fancy a grey cowled figure flitting across the lighted patches and lurking, evilly watching, amid the pools of darkness. Sleep was impossible. Moris Klaw, to whom such fears as mine were utterly unknown, might repose, nay, was actually reposing, in the very vortex of this psychical storm; but I was otherwise constituted. I had been with him in many cases of dark enough evil-doing, but this purely ghostly menace was something that sapped my courage.

Grange stood upon rather high ground, and in a north-easterly direction, peeping out from the trees of a wooded slope, showed a grey tower almost like a giant monkish figure under the moon. I watched it with a vague interest. It was Friars House, to which the baronet projected retreat from the haunted Grange. Lighting my pipe, I leaned from the window, idly watching that ancient tower and wondering if more evil deeds had taken place within it—long as it had stood there amid the trees—than those which had left their mark ghostly upon Grange.

The night was very beautiful and very still. Not the slightest sound could I detect within or without the house. How long I had lounged there in this half-dreamy, but vaguely fearful, mood I cannot say, but I was aroused by a tremendous outcry. Loud it broke in upon the silence of the night, broke in on my mood with nerve-racking effect. My pipe dropped upon the floor, and taking one step across the room I stood there, rooted to the spot with indefinable horror.

"Father!" it came in a piercing scream, and again: "Father! O God! save him! save him!"

III

The voice was that of Isis Klaw!

Whenever I accompanied her father upon any of his inquiries I came armed, and now with a magazine pistol held in my hand I leapt out into the corridor and turned toward the stair. A door slammed open in front of me and Sir James Leyland also came running out, pulling on his dressing-gown as he ran. One quick glance he gave me; his face was very pale; and together we went racing down the stairs into the hall patched with ghostly moonlight.

"You heard it?" he breathed, hoarsely. "It was Miss Klaw! What in God's Name has happened? Where is she?"

But even as he asked the question, and as we pressed on into the billiard-room, it was answered. For Isis Klaw, with a dressing-gown thrown over her night apparel, was kneeling beside the settee upon which her father lay!

"What has happened? What has happened?" groaned Sir

James. Then, as we approached together: "Mr. Klaw! Mr. Klaw!" he cried.

"All right, my friend!" came the rumbling voice, and to my inestimable relief, Moris Klaw sat up and looked around upon us, adjusting his pince-nez to the bridge of his massive nose: "I live! It has saved me, the Science of the Mind!"

Isis Klaw bowed her head upon the red cushion, and I saw that she was trembling violently. It was the first time I had known her to lose her regal composure, and, utterly mystified, I wondered what awful danger had threatened Moris Klaw.

"Thank Heaven for that!" said the baronet, earnestly.

Approaching footsteps sounded now, and a group of frightened servants, headed by the butler, appeared at the door of the billiard-room. Through them came pressing Mr. Clement Leyland. His face was ghastly, showing a startling white against the dull red of the dressing-gown he wore.

"James!" he said, huskily. "James! that awful screaming! What was it? What has occurred?"

I knew that he slept in the west wing and that he must have been unable to distinguish the words which Isis had cried. Thus heard, the shrill scream must have sounded even more terrifying.

Moris Klaw raised his hand protestingly.

"No fuss, dear friends," he implored, in rumbling accents, "no wonderings and botherings. They so disturb the nerves. Let us be calm, let us be peaceful." He laid his hand upon the head of the girl who knelt beside him. "Isis, my child, what a delicate instrument is the psychic perception! You knew it, the danger to your poor old father, to the poor old fool who lies here waiting to be slaughtered! Almost you knew it before I knew it myself!"

"For God's sake, Mr. Klaw," said Clement Leyland, shakily, "what has happened? Who, or what, came to you here? What occasioned Miss Klaw's terror?"

"My friend," replied Klaw, "you ask me conundrum-riddles. Some dreadful thing haunts this Grange, some deadly thing. The man has not lived who has not tasted fear, and I, the old foolish, have lived indeed to-night! I fail, my friend. There is some evil intelligence ruling this Grange, which I cannot capture upon my negative"—he tapped his brow characteristically—"to attempt it would be to die. It is too powerful for me. Grange is unclean, Sir James. You will leave Grange without delay; it is I, the old experienced who knows, that warns you. Fly from Grange. Take up your residence, to-morrow, at Friars House!"

No further explanation would he vouchsafe.

"I am defeated, my friends!" he declared, shrugging resignedly.

Accordingly, Isis, her beautiful face deathly pale and her great eyes feverishly bright, returned to her room. She covered her face with her hands as she passed to the door. Moris Klaw accepted the use of an apartment next to mine, and we all sought our couches again in states of varying perturbation.

That there was some profound mystery underlying these happenings of the night was evident to me. Moris Klaw and Isis Klaw were keeping something back. They shared some dark secret and guarded it jealously; but with what motive they acted in this fashion was a problem that defied my efforts at solution.

The morning came, and brought a haggard company to the breakfast table. Few, if any, beneath the roof of Grange, had known sleep that night, although, so far as I could gather, there had been no manifestations of any kind.

Moris Klaw talked incessantly about the fauna of the Sahara Desert, and so monopolised the conversation with his queer anecdotes of snakes and scorpions, that no other topic found entrance.

After breakfast the whole party, in Sir James's car, drove over to Friars House; and despite the up-to-date furniture and upholstery, I found it a very gloomy residence. Stripped of its ghostly atmosphere, Grange had been quite a charming seat for any man; but this dungeonesque place, with its lichened tower that had dominated the valley when John signed Magna Charta, with its massive walls and arrow-slit windows, its eccentrically designed apartments and crypt-like smell, was altogether too archaic to be comfortable.

Moris Klaw, standing in the room which had been fitted up as a library, removed his flat-topped brown bowler and fumbled for his scent-spray.

"This place," he said, "smells abominably of dead abbots!"

He squirted verbena upon himself and upon Isis. He replaced the scent-spray in the lining of the hat, and was about to replace the hat on his head, when he paused, staring straight up at the ceiling reflectively.

"My notes!" he said abruptly; "I have left those notes in my valise. I must have them. Curse me, for an old foolish! Sir James, you will show Isis this charming old tower in my absence? Do I intrude? But I would borrow the car and return to Grange for my notes!"

"Not a bit!" replied the baronet readily. "Clement can go with you!"

"No, no! Certainly no! I could not think of it! My old friend, Mr. Searles, may come if he so likes; if not, I go alone."

Naturally I agreed to accompany him; and leaving the others at the ancient gateway, we set off in Sir James's car back to Grange. Down into the valley we swept and up the slope to Grange, Moris Klaw sitting muttering in his beard, but offering no remark and patently desirous to avoid conversation.

"Come, my friend," he said, as the car drew up before the house, "and I will show you what my mental negative recorded to me last night, just before the great danger came."

He led the way into the billiard-room, curtly directing the butler to leave us. When we were alone—

"You will note something," he rumbled, swinging his arm vaguely around in the direction of the banqueting-hall. "What you will note is this: the laughter—where is it heard? It is heard here, in the gun-room on my right, in the banquet-room before me. Great is the science of the mind! I will now test my negative."

I followed him with wondering gaze as he stepped into the deep old-fashioned fireplace which formed one of the quaintest features of the room. He bent his tall figure to avoid striking his head upon the stonework, and placed the historic brown bowler upon one of the settles.

"Perhaps I cannot find it," came his rumbling voice; "my negative was fogged by assassinations, murderous sieges, candle-light duels, and other thought-forms of the troubled past; but I may triumph—I may triumph!"

He was standing on a settle with his head far up the chimney, and presently a faint grating sound proceeded from that sooty darkness.

"I have it!" he rumbled, triumphantly. "And in my pocket reposes the electric lamp. I ascend; you, my good friend, will follow."

True enough he scrambled upwards, and to my unspeakable amazement disappeared in the chimney. Filled with great wonder I followed and saw him standing in a recess high above my head, a recess which he must have opened in some way unknown to me. He extended a long arm and grasped my hand in his.

"Up!" he cried, exerted his surprising strength, and jerked me up beside him with as little effort as though I had been a child.

He pressed the button of a torch which he held and I saw that we stood upon an exceedingly steep and narrow wooden stair.

"It is in the thickness of the wall between the panellings," he whispered, solemnly; "a Jacobite hiding-place. Sir James knows nothing of it, for has he not spent his life in the Bush."

He mounted the stair.

"On the right," his voice came back to me, "the gun-room, the billiard-room! On the left the banquet-room. From here comes the laughter—from here comes the danger."

Still he ascended and I followed. The narrow stair terminated in a dusty box-like apartment no more than six feet high by six feet square. Moris Klaw, ducking his head grotesquely, stood there shining the light about him. From the floor he took up a square wooden case, and waved to me to descend again.

"No exit," he said; "no exit. Sir James's bedroom is upon the further side, but, as I had anticipated, there is no exit."

We returned the way we had come; clearly there was no other. Beneath his caped coat Moris Klaw jealously concealed the case which he had discovered in the secret chamber. I was filled with intense curiosity; but Moris Klaw, having gone to his room, asking me to await him outside in the drive, returned ultimately, without the case, but carrying a huge notebook, and intimated that he was prepared to re-enter the waiting car.

Behind the pebbles of his pince-nez, his strange eyes gleamed triumphantly.

"We triumph," he said. "The haunting of Grange succumbs to the Science of the Mind!"

IV

We all had lunch at Friars House, but were by no means a jovial party. Sir James seemed worried and preoccupied, and Clement Leyland even more reticent than usual. Moris Klaw talked, certainly, but his conversation turned entirely upon the subject of the Borgias, concerning which notorious family he was possessed of a stock of most unsavoury anecdote. So realistic were his gruesome stories, delivered in that rumbling whisper, wholly impossible to describe or imitate, that every mouthful of food which I swallowed threatened to choke me.

Afterwards we wandered idly about the beautiful old grounds, which bore ineffaceable marks of monkish cultivation. Sir James, who was walking ahead with Moris Klaw and Isis, suddenly turned and waited for me. I had been examining a sundial with much interest, but I now walked on and joined our host.

"Mr. Searles," he said, "may I press you to remain here over the week-end?"

"That's very good of you," I replied. "I think I could manage it, and I should enjoy the stay immensely."

I concluded that Moris Klaw also was remaining, and consequently was surprised when a short time later he drew me aside into a rose-covered arbour, and announced that he was leaving by the four o'clock train.

"But I shall be back in the morning, Mr. Searles," he assured me, wagging his finger mysteriously, "I shall be back in the morning!"

"And Miss Klaw?"

"She, too, goes by the four o'clock train and will not be returning—for the present."

"I understand that Sir James is taking up his residence here at Friars House from now onward?"

"It is so, my friend; he deserts Grange. The servants come over here to-day. Is he not well advised? Mr. Clement has all along recommended that this shall be his residence. He was against it, the idea of inhabiting Grange, from the first. He is wise, that Mr. Clement. He has lived in these parts so long. He knows that Grange is haunted, is uninhabitable."

Later, then, Moris Klaw and Isis took their departure; and just as the car was about to drive off my eccentric friend removed his brown bowler, and sprayed his bald brow with verbena. He bent to me:

"Day and night," he whispered, huskily, "do not lose sight of him, Sir James! Above all, allow him not to *explore!*"

With that the car drove off, and I stood looking after it, wondering, utterly mystified. On the steps behind me stood Clement Leyland and his cousin. The latter's gaze followed the course of the car along the picturesque winding road until it became lost from view. I thought I heard him sigh.

Ensued an uneventful day and night. Life was pleasant enough at Friars House, if a trifle dull; and Sir James seemed unsettled, whilst his disquietude was reflected in his cousin. The latter, now that his active labours in preparing this new residence for the baronet were checked, seemed a man at a loss what to do with himself. His was one of those quietly ardent temperaments, I divined, and idleness palled upon him. Apparently he had no profession, and although I presumed that he had some residence of his own in the neighbour-hood, he, apparently, was prepared indefinitely to prolong his stay at Friars House. I think his companionship was welcome to Sir James, for the latter was yet strange to the new duties of a landed gentleman.

The next morning brought Moris Klaw, and I learned with ever-growing surprise that he had made arrangements to spend the following week beneath the hospitable roof of Friars House.

I have nothing to record of interest up to the time I left; but often during the ensuing six days the problem of the haunting of Grange, and the mystery of Moris Klaw's protracted visit to Friars House came between me and my work. Then on the Saturday morning arrived a telegram—

"Can you join us for week-end—car will meet 2.30. Wire reply. Best wishes.—LEYLAND."

I determined to accept the invitation; for respecting the nature of Moris Klaw's business at Friars House—and that he had some other motive than ordinary in sojourning there I was persuaded—my curiosity knew no bounds. Accordingly I packed my grip, and at about five o'clock on a delightful afternoon found myself taking tea in a cloister-like apartment of the former Friary.

"Grange," said Sir James, in answer to a question of mine, "is shut up."

"It is shut, yes," rumbled Moris Klaw. "What a pity! What a pity!"

In the course of the day occurred incidents which I have since perceived to have been significant. I will pass over them, however, and hasten to what I may term the catastrophe of this very singular case.

Four of us sat down to dinner in an apartment which clearly had been the ancient refectory of the monks. Clement Leyland, who had arrived barely in time to dress, looked haggard and wor-ried. I determined that he had some private troubles of his own, and beneath his quiet geniality I thought I could detect a sort of brooding gloom. His pale, clean-shaven face, so like, yet so unlike, that of his cousin, was a mask that ill repaid study; yet I knew that the real Clement Leyland was a stranger to me, perhaps to all of us.

I was most anxious to learn if Moris Klaw had divulged the secret of the hidden chamber at Grange to Sir James; and I was unspeakably curious concerning the box of which I had had but a glimpse—the box that he had found there. But he baffled my curiosity at every point.

Have you experienced that sense of impending calamity which sometimes heralds tragic things? It was with me that night, throughout dinner; and afterwards, when we entered the library and sat over our cigars, it grew portentously. I felt that I stood upon the brink of a precipice. And literally I was not in great error. Moris Klaw, to the evident discomfort of Sir James, brought the conversation around to the subject of the haunting. I observed him to glance at his watch, with a rather odd expression upon his vellum-hued face.

"Is it not singular," he said, "how poor spectres are confined, like linnets, to their cages? They seem, these spooks, never to roam. That laughing demon of Grange—look at him. He remains in that empty, desolate house; he——"

There was a dreadful interruption.

Commencing with a sort of guttural rattle, out upon the cloisteresque stillness burst a peal of wicked laughter!

It rang throughout the room; it poured fear into my every fibre. It died away—and was gone.

Sir James, clutching the leather-covered chair-arms, looked like a man of stone. I was frankly terrorised. Moris Klaw stood behind me, by a bookcase; him I could not see. But Clement Leyland's face I can never forget. It was positively deathlike. His eyes seemed starting from their sockets, and his teeth chattered horribly.

"God in Heaven!" he whispered, brokenly. "What is it? O God! What is it! Take it away—take it away!"

Then Moris Klaw spoke, slowly—

"It is for *you* to take it away, Mr. Leyland!"

Clement Leyland rose from his seat; he swayed like a drunken man, and there was madness in the glaring eyes that he turned in Klaw's direction.

"You—you——" he gasped.

"I—I——" rumbled Moris Klaw sternly, and took a step forward—"I have entered the Jacobite hiding-place at Grange, and there I found a box! Ah! you glare! glare on, my friend! I returned that box to where I found it; but first I examined its contents! What! that demon laughter frightens you! Then descend, Mr. Leyland, descend and bring him out—the one who laughs!"

Rigidly, Sir James sat in his chair; I, too, seemed to be palsied.

But at sight of the next happening we both stood up. Moris Klaw stamped heavily upon the oaken floor in a deep recess; then applied his weight to a section of the seemingly solid stone wall.

It turned, as on a pivot, revealing a dark cavity.

He stood there, a bizarre figure, pointing down into the blackness.

"Descend, my friend!" he cried. "The one who laughs is upon the seventh step!"

"The seventh step!"

In a whisper the words came from Clement Leyland. A draft of damp, cavernous air blew into the library out of the opening.

"Descend, my friend!"

Remorselessly, Moris Klaw repeated the words. In the centre of the room, Clement Leyland, a pitiable sight, stood staring—and hesitating. Suddenly his cousin spoke.

"Don't go, Clement!" he whispered.

The other turned to him, dazedly.

"Don't go—down that place. But—O God! I understand at last, or partly....*Quit!* I give you half an hour!"

Sir James sank back into his chair and buried his face in his hands; Moris Klaw never moved from where he stood by the cavity. But Clement Leyland with bowed head, walked from the room.

In the silence that followed his going—

"Await me, gentlemen," rumbled Klaw; "I descend for the laughter!"

He stepped into the opening.

"One," he counted, "two—three—four—five——" his voice came up to us from the depths, *"six!"*

We heard him ascending. Walking into the library he placed upon the table beside Sir James a very large and up-to-date gramophone!

"The laughter!" he explained, simply. "That night, my friends, when first I slept at Grange, I secured, among a host of other dreadful negatives, the negative of one who lurked in a secret hiding-place. I saw him come creeping from the chimney-corner, bearing a great mace which I recognised for one that had hung in the hall! Almost, the Science of the Mind betrayed me; for I mistook him for a thought-form! But the mind of Isis is *en rapport* with the mind of her poor old father. In her dreams she saw my peril, and she it was who, screaming, saved me!—saved me from the murderer with the mace!"

Sir James made no sign. Moris Klaw continued—

"I gathered, then, that the one who sometimes lurked in the Jacobite hiding-place and who, somehow, made the demon laughter, and the other phenomena, sought *one* end. It was to cause you to leave Grange and to live in Friars House! Beyond so far, my science could not show me. I assisted, therefore, the project of the lurker; and came myself, too, in order to watch, my friend, to guard and to spy!

"His gramophone I found, examined, and replaced. It had a clockwork attachment, very ingenious, which both started and stopped it; there was little or no scraping. To-night, from his room, unknown to him, I removed the instrument from its case which lay hidden at the bottom of his trunk. Yes! I stole his key! I am the old fox! Why did he bring it here? I cannot reply. Perhaps he meant again to use it; his future projects are dark to me, but their object is all too light."

Sir James groaned.

"Old Clem!" he whispered, "and how I trusted him!"

"He did not quite believe in my science," resumed Moris Klaw, "but he did not know that, hidden, I slept almost beside him as he sat, planning, in this very room! From his own bad mind I secured my second negative; and it showed me the death-trap of some bad old son of Mother Church! At Grange there was but the Jacobite hiding-place, but here was the devilry of feudal times! I returned to London. Why? To learn if my suspicions were well founded. Yes! You may, or may not, be aware; but if you die childless, the wicked Clement inherits Grange!"

"I knew that," whispered Sir James.

"Ah! you knew? *So.* I returned to here, for, even at that time, I suspected that your *accidental* death was the object of removal! Then I secured it, my second negative. Biding my time, I explored that death-smelling place. Its wicked machinery had been *freshly oiled!* Ah! he knew its secrets well, the old house that he hoped to inherit!

"One night, all innocent, as you sat here, with other guests, he would have blundered upon that doorway! And *you,* the host, would have led the search-party! But I saw that he feared to move whilst I remained, and so I played the ghost upon him with his own spook!"

Sir James Leyland looked up. His bronzed face was transformed with emotion.

"Mr. Klaw," he said, huskily, "why did you lay so much emphasis upon the words, 'the seventh step'?"

Moris Klaw shrugged, replying simply:

"Because *there is no seventh step—only the mouth of a well!*"

Episode IX

CASE OF THE VEIL OF ISIS

I

I have made no attempt, in these chronicles, to arrange the cases of my remarkable friend, Moris Klaw, in sections. Yet, as has recently been pointed out to me, they seem naturally to fall into two orders. There were those in which he appeared in the role of criminal investigator, and in which he was usually associated with Inspector Grimsby. There was another class of inquiry in which the criminal element was lacking; mysteries which never came under the notice of New Scotland Yard.

Since Moris Klaw's methods were, if not supernatural, at any rate supernormal, I have been asked if he ever, to my knowledge, inquired into a case which proved insusceptible of a natural explanation—which fell strictly within the province of the occult.

To that I answer that I am aware of several; but I have refrained from including them because readers of these papers would be unlikely to appreciate the nature of Klaw's investigations outside the sphere of ordinary natural laws. Those who are curious upon the point cannot do better than consult the remarkable work by Moris Klaw entitled *Psychic Angles*.

But there was one case with which I found myself concerned that I am disposed to include, for it fell between the provinces of the natural and supernatural in such a way that it might, with equal legitimacy, be included under either head. On the whole, I am disposed to bracket it with the case of the headless mummies.

I will take leave to introduce you, then, to the company which met at Otter Brearley's house one night in August.

"This is most truly amazing," Moris Klaw was saying; "and I am indebted to my good friend Searles"—he inclined his sparsely covered head in my direction—"for the opportunity to be one of you. It is a séance? Yes and no. But there is a mummy in it—and those mummies are so instructive!"

He extracted the scent-spray from his pocket and refreshed his yellow brow with verbena.

"How to be regretted that my daughter is in Paris," he continued, his rumbling voice echoing queerly about the room. "She loves them like a mother—those mummies! Ah, Mr. Brearley, this will cement your great reputation!"

Otter Brearley shook his head.

"I am not yet prepared to make it public property," he declared, slowly. "No one, outside the present circle, knows of my discovery. I do not wish it to go further—at present."

He glanced around the table, his prominent blue eyes passing from myself to Moris Klaw and from Klaw to the clean-cut, dark face of Dr. Fairbank. The latter, scarce heeding his host's last words, sat watching how the shaded light played, tenderly, amid the soft billows of Ailsa Brearley's wonderful hair.

"Shall you make it the subject of a paper?" he asked suddenly.

"My dear Dr. Fairbank!" rumbled Moris Klaw, solemnly, "if you had been paying attention to our good friend you would have heard him say that he was not prepared, at present, to make public his wonderful discovery."

"Sorry!" said Fairbank, turning to Brearley. "But if it is not to be made public I don't altogether follow the idea. What *do* you intend, Brearley?"

"In what way?" I asked.

"In every way possible!"

Dr. Fairbank sat back in his chair and looked thoughtful.

"Rather a comprehensive scheme?"

Brearley toyed with the bundle of notes under his hand.

"I have already," he said, "exhaustively examined seven of the possibilities; the eighth, and—I believe, the last—remains to be considered."

"Listen now to me, Mr. Brearley," said Moris Klaw, wagging a long finger. "I am here, the old curious, and find myself in delightful company. But until this evening I know nothing of your work except that I have read all your books. For me you will be so good as to outline all the points—yes?"

Otter Brearley mutely sought permission of the company, and turned the leaves of his manuscript. All men have an innate love of "talking shop," but few can make such talk of general interest. Brearley was an exception in this respect. He loved to talk of Egypt, of the Pharaohs, of the temples, of the priesthood and its mysteries; but others loved to hear him. That made all the difference.

"The discovery," he now began, "upon which I have blundered —for pure accident, alone, led me to it—assumes its great importance by reason of the absolute mystery surrounding certain phases of Egyptian worship. In the old days, Fairbank, you will recall that it was my supreme ambition to learn the secrets of Isis-worship as practised in early Egyptian times. Save for impostors, and legitimate imaginative writers, no one has yet lifted the veil of Isis. That mystical ceremony by which a priest was consecrated to the goddess, or made an arch adept, was thought to be hopelessly lost, or, by others, to be a myth devised by the priesthood to awe the ignorant masses. In fact, we know little of the entire religion but its outward form. Of that occult lore so widely attributed to its votaries we know nothing—absolutely nothing! By we, I mean students in general. I, individually, have made a step, if not a stride, into that holy of holies!"

"Mind you don't lose yourself!" said Fairbank, lightly.

But, professionally, he was displeased with Brearley's drawn face and with the feverish brightness of his eyes. So much was plain for all to see. In the eyes of Ailsa Brearley, so like, yet so unlike, her brother's, he read understanding of his displeasure, I think, together with a pathetic appeal.

Brearley waved his long, white hand carelessly.

"Rest assured of that, doctor!" he replied. "The labyrinth in which I find myself is intricate, I readily admit; but all my steps have been well considered. To return, Mr. Klaw"—addressing the latter—"I have secured the mummy of one of those arch adepts! That he was one is proved by the papyrus, presumably in his own writing, which lay upon his breast! I unwrapped the mummy in Egypt, where it now reposes; but the writing I brought back with me, and have recently deciphered. A glance had showed me that it was not the usual excerpts from the Book of the Dead. Six months' labour has proved it to be a detailed account of his initiation into the inner mysteries!"

"Is such a papyrus unique?" I asked.

"Unique!" cried Moris Klaw. "Name of a little blue man! It is priceless!"

"But why," I pursued, "should this priest, alone amongst the many who must have been so initiated, have left an account of the ceremony?"

"It was forbidden to divulge any part, any word, of it, Searles!" said Brearley. "Departure from this law was visited with fearful punishments in this world and dire penalties in the next. Khamus, for so this priest was named, well knew this. But some reason which, I fear, can never be known, prompted him to write the papyrus. It is probable, if not certain, that no eye but his, and mine, has read what is written there."

A silence of a few seconds followed his words.

"Yes," rumbled Klaw presently; "it is undoubtedly a discovery of extraordinary importance, this. You agree, my friend?"

I nodded.

"That's evident," I replied. "But I cannot altogether get the hang of the ceremony itself, Brearley. That is the point upon which I am particularly hazy."

"To read you the entire account in detail," Brearley resumed, "would occupy too long, and would almost certainly confuse you. But the singular thing is this: Khamus distinctly asserts that the goddess appeared to him. His writing is eminently sane and reserved, and his account of the ceremony, up to that point, highly interesting. Now, I have tested the papyrus itself—though no possibility of fraud is really admissible, and I have been able to confirm many of the statements made therein. There is only one point, it seems to me, remaining to be settled."

"What is that?" I asked.

"Whether, as a result of the ceremony described, Khamus did see Isis, or whether he merely imagined he did!"

No one spoke for a moment. Then—

"My friend," said Moris Klaw, "I have a daughter whom I have named Isis. Why did I name her Isis? Mr. Brearley, you must know that that name has a mystic and beautiful significance. But I will say something—I am glad that my daughter is not here! Mr. Brearley—beware! Beware, I say: you play with burning fires; my friend—beware!"

His words impressed us all immensely; for there was something underlying them more portentous than appeared upon the surface.

Fairbank stared at Brearley, hard.

"Do I understand," he began, quietly, "that you admit the first possibility?"

"Certainly!" replied Brearley, with conviction.

"You are prepared to admit the existence, as an entity, of Isis?"

"I am prepared to admit the existence of *anything* until it can be proved not to exist!"

"Then, admitting the existence of Isis, what should you assume it, or her, to be?"

"That is not a matter for presumption; it is a matter for inquiry!"

The doctor glanced quickly toward Ailsa Brearley, and her beautiful face was troubled.

"And this inquiry—how should you propose to conduct it?"

"In surroundings as nearly as possible identical with those described in the papyrus," replied Brearley, with growing excitement. "I should follow the ceremony, word by word, as Khamus did!"

His eyes gleamed with pent-up enthusiasm. We four listeners, again stricken silent, watched him; and again it was the doctor who broke the silence.

"Is the ceremony spoken?"

"In the first half there is a long prayer, which is chanted."

"But Egyptian, as a *spoken* language, is lost, surely?"

"The exact pronunciation, or accent, is lost, of course; but there are many who can speak it. I can, for instance."

"And I," rumbled Moris Klaw, gloomily. "But these special surroundings? Eh, my friend?"

"I have spent a year in searching for the necessary things, as specified in the writing. At last, my collection is complete. Some of the things I have had made, in the proper materials mentioned. These materials, in some cases, have been exceedingly difficult to procure. But now I have a complete shrine of Isis fitted up! Khamus's initiation took place in a small chamber of which he gives a concise and detailed account. It is because my duplicate of this chamber is ready that I have asked you to meet me here to-night."

"How long have you been at work upon this inquiry?" said Fairbank.

He put the question as he might have put one relating to a patient's symptoms; and this Brearley detected in his tone, with sudden resentment.

"Fairbank," he said, huskily, "I believe you think me insane!"

With his pale, drawn face and long, fair hair, he certainly looked anything but normal, as he sat with bright, staring eyes fixed upon the other across the table.

"My dear chap," replied the doctor, soothingly, "what a strange idea! My question was prompted by a professional spirit, I will admit, for I thought you had been sticking to this business too closely. You are the last man in the world I should expect to go mad, Brearley, but I should not care to answer for your nerves if you don't give this Isis affair a rest."

Brearley smiled, and waved his hand characteristically. "Excuse me, Fairbank," he said, "but to the average person my ideas do seem fantastic, I know. That is what makes me so touchy on the point, I suppose."

"You are hoping for too much from what is at most only a wild conjecture, Brearley. Your translation of the manuscript, alone, is a sufficiently notable achievement. If I were in your place, I should leave the occult business to the psychical societies. 'Let the cobbler,' you know."

"It has gone too far for that," returned Brearley, "and I must see it through, now."

"You are putting too much into it," said the doctor, severely. "I want you to promise me that if nothing results from your final experiment, you will drop the whole inquiry."

Brearley frowned thoughtfully.

"Do you really think I am overdoing it?" he asked.

"Sure," was the answer. "Drop the whole thing for a month or two."

"That is impossible."

"Why?"

"Because the ceremony must take place upon the first night of *Panoi,* the tenth month of the Sacred Sothic year. This we take to correspond to the April of the Julian year."

"Yes," rumbled Moris Klaw, "it is to-night!"

"Why!" I cried, "of course it is! Do you mean, Brearley, that you are going to conduct your experiment *now?*"

"Exactly," was the calm reply; "and I have asked you all—Mr. Moris Klaw in particular—in order that it may take place in the presence of competent witnesses!"

Moris Klaw shook his massive head and pulled at his scanty, toneless beard, in a very significant manner. All of us were vaguely startled, I think, and through my mind the idea flashed that the first of April was a date pathetically appropriate for such an undertaking. Frankly, I was beginning to entertain serious doubts regarding Brearley's sanity.

"I have given the servants a holiday," said the latter. "They are at a theatre in town; so there is no possibility of the experiment being interrupted."

Something of his enthusiasm, unnatural though it seemed, strangely enough began to communicate itself to me.

"Come upstairs," he continued, "and I will explain what we all have to do."

Moris Klaw squirted verbena upon his brow.

II

"Doctor Fairbank!"

Fairbank, startled by the touch on his arm, stopped. It was Ailsa Brearley who had dropped behind her brother and now stood confronting us. In the dense shadows of the corridor one could barely distinguish her figure, but a stray beam of light touched one side of her pure oval face and burnished her fair hair.

She wanted help, guidance. I had read it in her eyes before. I was sorry that her sweet lips should have that pathetic little droop.

"Doctor Fairbank! I have wanted to ask you all night—do you think he——"

She could not speak the words, and stood biting her lips, with eyes averted.

"Miss Brearley," he replied, "I do, certainly, fear that your brother is liable to a nervous breakdown at any moment. He has applied his mind too closely to this inquiry, and has studiously surrounded himself with a morbid atmosphere."

Ailsa Brearley was now watching him, anxiously.

"Should we allow him to go on with it?"

"I fear any attempt to prevent him would prove most detrimental, in his present condition."

"But——" There was clearly something else which she wanted to say. "But, apart from that—" she suddenly turned to Moris Klaw, instinctively it almost seemed—"Mr. Klaw—is this—ceremony *right?*"

He peered at her through his pince-nez.

"In what way, my dear Miss Brearley—how right?"

"Well—what I mean is—it amounts to idolatry, does it not!"

I started. It was a point of view which had not, hitherto, occurred to me.

"You probably understand the nature of the thing better than we do, Miss Brearley," said Fairbank. "Do you mean that it involves worship of Isis?"

"He has always avoided a direct answer when I have asked him that," she said. "But it is only reasonable to suppose that it does. His translation of the writing I have never seen. But he has been dieting in a most extraordinary manner for nearly a year! Since the workmen completed it, no one but himself has been inside the chamber which he has had constructed at the end of his study; and he spends hours and hours there every day—and every night!"

Her anxiety became more evident with each word.

"You saw that he ate nothing at dinner," she continued, and taxed him with faddism. "But it is something more than that. Why has he sent the servants away to-night? Oh, Dr. Fairbank! I have a dreadful foreboding! I am so afraid!"

The light in her eyes, suddenly upturned to him in the vague half-light, the tone in her voice, the appeal in her attitude—were unmistakable. Fairbank had been abroad for three years, and I could see that between these two was an undeclared love, and almost I felt that I intruded. Moris Klaw looked away for a moment, too. Then—

"My dear young lady," he rumbled, paternally, "do not be afraid. I, the old know-all, so fortunately am here! Perhaps there is danger—yes, I admit it; there may be danger. But it is such danger as dwells here"—he tapped his yellow brow—"it is a danger of the mind. For thoughts are things, Miss Brearley—that is where it lies, the peril—and thought-things can kill!"

"Ailsa! Fairbank! Mr. Klaw!" came Brearley's voice. "We have none too much time!"

"Proceed, my friends," rumbled Moris Klaw; "I am with you." And, oddly enough, I was comforted by his presence; so, it was evident, were the girl and the doctor; for Moris Klaw, beneath that shabby, ramshackle exterior, Moris Klaw, the Wapping curio-dealer was a man of power — an intellectual ark of refuge.

In the Egyptologist's study all appeared much the same as when last I had set foot there. The cases filled with vases, scarabs, tablets, weapons, and the hundred-and-one relics of the great, dead age with which the student had surrounded himself; the sarcophagi; the frames of papyri: all seemed familiar.

"We must begin almost immediately!" he said, as we entered.

A danger-spot burned lividly upon either pale cheek. His eyes gleamed brilliantly. The prolonged excitement of his strange experiment was burning the man up. His nerve-centres must be taxed abnormally I knew.

Brearley glanced at his watch.

"I must be very brief," he explained hurriedly, "as it is vitally important that I commence in time. Beyond the book-case, there, you will see that a part of the room has been walled off."

We looked in the direction indicated. Although it was not noticeable at first glance I now saw that the apartment was, indeed, smaller than formerly. The usual books covered the new wall, giving it much the same aspect as the old; but, where hitherto there had been nothing but shelves, a small, narrow door of black wood now broke the imposing expanse of faded volumes.

"In there," Brearley resumed, "is the Secret Place described by Khamus!"

He placed his long, thin hand upon a yellow roll that lay partly opened on the table.

"No one but myself may enter there—until after to-night, at any rate!" with a glance at Moris Klaw. "To the most minute particular"—patting the papyrus—"it is equipped as Khamus describes. For many months I have prepared myself, by fasting and meditation, as *he* prepared! There was, as no doubt you know, a widespread belief in ancient times that for any but the chosen to look upon the goddess was death. As I admit the possibility of Isis existing I must also admit the possibility of this belief being true—the more so as it is confirmed by Khamus! Therefore none may enter with me."

"One moment, Mr. Brearley," interrupted Klaw; "in what form does Khamus relate that the goddess appeared?"

A cloud crossed Brearley's face.

"It is the one point upon which he is not clear," was the reply. "I do not know, in the least, *what* to expect!"

"Go on!" I said, quickly. Although I seriously doubted my poor friend's sanity, I began to find the affair weirdly, uncannily fascinating.

Brearley continued—

"The ritual opens with a chant, which I may broadly translate as 'The Hymn of Dedication.' Its exact purport is not very clear to me. This hymn is the only part of the ceremony in which I am assisted. It is to be 'sung by a virgin beyond the door.' That is, directly I have entered yonder it must be sung out here. Ailsa has composed a sort of chant to the words, which, I think, is the proper kind of setting. Have you not, Ailsa?"

She bowed her graceful head, glancing, under her lashes, towards Fairbank.

"She has learned the words—for, of course, it must be sung in Egyptian——"

"But have no idea of their meaning," said his sister, softly.

"That is unnecessary," he went on, quickly. "After this, I want you all just to remain here in this room. I am afraid you will have to sit in the dark! Any sounds which you detect, please note. I will not tell you what to expect, then imagination cannot deceive you. I will be back in a moment."

With another hasty glance at his watch, he went out in high excitement.

"Please," began Ailsa Brearley, the moment he was gone, "do not think that because I assist him I approve of this attempt! I think it is horrible! But what am I to do? He is wrapped up in it! I *dare* not try to check him!"

"We understand that," said Fairbank; "all of us. Do as he desires. When he has made the attempt, and failed—as, of course, he must do—the folly of the whole thing will become apparent to him. Do not let it worry you, Miss Brearley. Your brother is not the first man to succumb, temporarily, to the glamour of the Unknown."

She shook her head sadly.

"It is an unpleasant farce," she said. "But there is something more in it than that."

Her blue eyes were full of trouble.

"What do you mean, Miss Brearley?" asked Moris Klaw.

"I hardly know, myself!" was the reply; "but for the past two months an indefinable horror of some kind has been growing upon me."

With a deep sigh, she turned to a tall case and took from it a kind of slender harp. The instrument, of which the frame, at any rate, was evidently ancient Egyptian work, rested upon a claw-shaped pedestal.

"Do you play this? Yes? No?" inquired Moris Klaw, with interest.

"Yes," she said, wearily. "It comes from the tomb of a priestess of Isis and was played by her in the temple. It is scaled differently from the modern harp, but any one with a slight knowledge of the ordinary harp, or even of the piano, can perform upon it with ease. It is sweet toned, but—creepy!"

She smiled slightly at her own expression, and I was glad to see it.

Brearley returned.

He wore a single, loose garment of white linen, and thin sandals were upon his feet. Save for his long, fair hair, he looked a true pagan priest, his eyes bright with the fire of research that consumed him, his features gaunt, ascetic.

Some ghost of his old humorous expression played, momentarily, about his lips as he observed the astonishment depicted upon our faces. But it was gone almost in the moment of its coming.

"You wonder at me, no doubt," he said; "and at times I have wondered at myself! Do not think me fanatic. I scarcely hope for any result. But remembering that the writing is authentic and that there prevails, to this day, a wide-spread belief in the occult wisdom of the Egyptians, *why* should not this problem in psychics receive the same attention from me that one in physics would receive from you, Fairbank?''

There was reason in his argument and in his manner of advancing it. Fairbank glanced from Brearley to the girl sitting with her white hands listlessly caressing the harp-strings. The silence of the great, empty house grew oppressive. Suppose the ancients indeed possessed the strange lore attributed to them? Suppose in those Dark Continents, the Past and the Future, somewhere in the vast unknown, there existed a power, a being, a spirit, named by the Egyptians, Isis?

Those were my thoughts, when Moris Klaw said suddenly—

"Mr. Brearley, it is not yet too late to turn back! This sensitive plate''—he tapped his forehead—"warns me that some evil thought-thing hovers about us! You are about to give form to that thought-being. Be wise, Mr. Brearley—abandon your experiment!''

His tone surprised every one. Otter Brearley looked at him, with an odd expression, and then glanced at the watch upon the writing-table.

"Mr. Klaw,'' he said, quietly, "I had hoped for a different attitude in you; but if you really disapprove of what I am about to attempt, I can only ask you to withdraw; it is too late for further arguments——''

"I remain, my friend! I spoke not for myself—my life has been passed in this coping with evil things; I spoke for others.''

None of us entirely understood his words, but Brearley went on, impatiently—

"Listen, please. I rely upon your co-operation. From now onward I require absolute silence. Whatever happens make no noise.''

"I shall not be noisy, I, my friend!'' rumbled Moris Klaw. "I am the old silent; I watch and wait—until I am wanted.''

He shrugged his shoulders and nodded, significantly.

"Good!'' said Brearley and his voice quivered with excitement; "then the experiment, the final experiment, has begun!''

III

He suddenly extinguished the light.

Passing to a window, he looked up to the moon, and, a moment later, lowered the blind. Dimly visible, in his white garment, he crossed the room. He might be heard unfastening the door of the inner chamber, and a faint, church-like smell crept to our nostrils. The door closed.

Immediately the harp sounded.

Its tone was peculiar—uncomfortable. The strain which Ailsa played was a mere repetition of three notes. Then she began to sing.

Our eyes becoming more accustomed to the gloom, we could vaguely discern her, now; the soft outlines of her figure; the white, ghost-like fingers straying over the strings of the instrument. The music of the chant was very monotonous, and weird to a marked degree. The sound of that ancient tongue, dead for many ages, chanted softly by Ailsa Brearley's beautiful voice, was almost incredibly eerie. I found myself gripped hard by a powerful sense of the uncanny.

No other sound was audible. Throughout the rambling old house intense silence prevailed. A slight breeze stirred the cedars, outside. Every now and again it came—like a series of broken sighs.

How long the chant lasted, I cannot pretend to state. It seemed interminable. I became aware of a curious sense of physical loss. I found myself drawn to high tension, as though the continuance of the chant demanded a vast effort on my part. Though I told myself that imagination was tricking me, the music seemed to be draining my nerve force!

Ailsa's voice grew louder and clearer, until the queer words, of unknown purport, rang out passionately, imperatively.

She ceased.

In the ensuing silence, I could hear distinctly Moris Klaw's heavy breathing. A compelling atmosphere of mystery had grown up about us. Repel it how we might, it was there—commanding acknowledgment.

Fairbank, who sat nearest, was the first to see Ailsa Brearley rise, unsteadily, and move in the direction of the study door.

Something in her manner alarmed us all, and the doctor quietly left his seat and followed her. As she quitted the room, he came out behind her; and in the better light on the landing, as he told us later, saw that she was deathly pale.

"Miss Brearley!" he said.

She turned.

"*Ssh!*" she whispered, anxiously, "it is nothing—Dr. Fairbank. The excitement has made me rather faint, that is all. I shall go to my room and lie down. Believe me, I am quite well!"

"But there is no servant in the house," he whispered, "if you should become worse——"

"If I need anything I shall not hesitate to ring," she answered. "It is so still, you will hear the bell. Please go back! He has hoped so much from this."

Fairbank was nonplussed. But the appeal was so obviously sincere, and the situation so difficult, that he saw no alternative. Ailsa Brearley passed along the corridor. Fairbank slipped back into the study, where Moris Klaw and I anxiously awaited him.

From the inner room came Brearley's voice, muffled.

The long vigil began.

I found myself claimed by the all-pervading spirit of mystery. For some little time I listened in expectation of hearing Ailsa Brearley returning. But soon the strange business of the night claimed my mind, to the exclusion of every other idea. I found myself listening only for Brearley's muffled voice. Although the half-audible words were meaningless, their sound assumed, as time wore on, a curious significance. They seemed potent with a strange power proceeding not *from* them, but *to* them.

Then I heard a new sound.

Fairbank heard it—for I saw him start, and Moris Klaw muttered something.

It did not come from the trees outside, nor from the inner room. It was somewhere in the house.

A faint rattling it was, bell-like but toneless.

Brearley's voice had ceased.

Again the sound arose—nearer.

I turned my head toward Fairbank, and seemed to perceive him more clearly. I had less difficulty in distinguishing the objects about.

Again it came—the shivering, bell-like sound.

Even the strings of the harp were visible, now.

"Curse me!" came Moris Klaw's hoarse whisper; "it seems to grow light! That is a delusion of the mind, my friends—repel it—repel it!"

Fairbank drew a quick, sibilant breath. A half-suppressed exclamation from Klaw followed; for the high-pitched rattle came from close at hand! The sense of the supernormal had grown unbearable. Fairbank's science, and my own semi-scepticism, were but weapons of sand against it.

The door opened silently, admitting a flood of the soft moon-like radiance. And Ailsa Brearley entered!

Her slim figure was bathed in light; her fair hair, unbound, swept like a gleaming torrent about her shoulders. She looked magnificently, unnaturally beautiful. A diaphanous veil was draped over her face. From her radiant figure I turned away my head in sudden, stark *fear!*

Fairbank, clutching the arms of his chair, seemed to strive to look away, too.

Her widely opened eyes, visible even through the veil, were awful in their supernormal, significant beauty. *Was* it Ailsa Brearley? I clenched my fists convulsively; I felt my reason tottering. As the luminous figure, so terrible in its perfect loveliness, moved slowly towards the inner door, with set gaze that was not for any about her, Dr. Fairbank wrenched himself from his chair and leapt forward.

"Ailsa!"

His voice came in a hoarse shriek. But it was drowned by a rumbling roar from Moris Klaw.

"Look away! look away!" he shouted. "The good God! do not look at her! *Look away!*"

The warning came too late. Fairbank had all but reached her side, when she turned her eyes upon him—looking fully in his face.

With no sound or cry he went down as though felled with a mighty blow!

She passed to the door of the inner room. It swung open noiselessly. A stifling cloud of some pungent perfume swept into the study; and the door reclosed.

"Fairbank!" I whispered, huskily. "My God! he's dead!"

Moris Klaw sprang forward to where Fairbank, clearly visible in the soft light, lay huddled upon the floor.

"Lift him!" he hissed. "We must get him out—before she returns—you understand?—before she returns!"

Bending together, we raised the doctor's inanimate body and half dragged, half carried him from the room. On the landing we laid him down, and stood panting. A voice, clear and sweet, was speaking. I recognised neither the language nor the voice. But each liquid syllable thrilled me like an icy shock. I met Moris Klaw's gaze, set upon me through the pince-nez.

"Do not listen, my friend!" he said.

Raising Fairbank, we dragged him into the first room we came to—and Klaw locked the door.

"Here we remain," he rumbled, "until something has gone back where it came from!"

Fairbank lay motionless at our feet.

Presently came the rattling.

"It is the *sistrum,*" whispered Moris Klaw, "the sacred instrument of the Isis temples."

The sound passed—and faded.

"Searles! Fairbank!" It was Brearley's voice, sobbingly intense—"do not *touch* her! Do not *look* at her!"

The study door crashed open and I heard his sandals pattering on the landing.

"Fairbank! Mr. Klaw! Good God! answer me! Tell me you are safe!"

Moris Klaw unlocked the door.

Brearley, his face white as death and bathed in perspiration, stood outside. As Klaw appeared, he leapt forward, wild eyed.

"Quick! Did any one——"

"Fairbank!" I said huskily.

Brearley pushed into the room and turned on the light. Fairbank, very pale, lay propped against an armchair. Moris Klaw immediately dropped on his knee beside him and felt his heart.

"Ah, the good God! he is alive!" he whispered. "Get some water—no brandy, my friend—water. Then look to your sister!"

Brearley plunged his trembling hands into his hair, and tugged at it distractedly.

"How was I to know!" he moaned, "how was I to know! There is water in the bottle, Mr. Klaw. Searles will come with me. I must look for Ailsa!"

A bizarre figure, in his linen robe, he ran off. Moris Klaw waved me to follow him.

The door of his sister's room was closed.

He knocked, but there was no reply. He turned the knob and went in, whilst I waited in the corridor.

"Ailsa!" I heard him call, and again: "Ailsa!" then, following an interval, "Are you all right, dear?" he whispered.

"Oh, thank Heaven it is finished!" came a murmur in Ailsa Brearley's soft voice. "It *is* finished, is it not?"

"Quite finished," he answered.

"Just look at my hair!" she went on, with returning animation. "My head was so bad—I think that was why I took it down. Then I must have dropped off to sleep."

"All right, dear," said Brearley. "I want you to come downstairs; be as quick as you can."

He rejoined me in the corridor.

"She was lying with her hair strewn all over the pillow!" he whispered, "and she had been burning something—ashes in the hearth——"

Ailsa came out. She seemed suddenly to observe her brother's haggard face.

"Is there anything the matter?" she said, quickly. "Oh! has something dreadful happened?"

"No, dear," he answered, reassuringly. "Only Dr. Fairbank was overcome——"

She turned very pale.

"He is not ill?"

"No. He became faint. You can come and see for yourself."

Very quickly, we all hurried downstairs. Moris Klaw, on his knees beside the doctor, was trying to force something between his clenched teeth. Ailsa, with a little cry, ran forward and knelt upon the other side of him.

"Ralph!" she whispered; "Ralph!"—and smoothed the hair back from his forehead.

He sighed deeply, and with an effort swallowed the draught which Klaw held to his lips. A moment later he opened his eyes, glaring wildly in Ailsa's face.

"Ralph!" she said, brokenly.

Then, realising how tenderly she had spoken—using his Christian name—she hung her graceful head in hot confusion. But he had heard her. And the wild light died from his eyes. He took both her hands in his own and held them fast; then, rather unsteadily, he stood up.

As his features came more fully into the light, we all saw that a small bruise discoloured his forehead, squarely between the brows.

Then Brearley, who had been back into the study, came running, crying—

"The papyrus! And my translation! Gone!"

I thought of the ashes in Ailsa Brearley's room.

IV

"My friends," rumbled Moris Klaw, impressively, "we are fortunate. We have passed through scorching fires unscathed!"

He applied himself with vigour to the operating of the scent-spray.

"God forgive me!" said Brearley. "What did I do?"

"I will tell you, my friend," replied Klaw; "you clothed a thought in the beautiful form which you knew as your sister! Ah! you stare! Ritual, my friends, is the soul of what the ignorant call magic. With the sacred incense, *kyphi* (yes, I detected it!), you invoked secret powers. Those powers, Mr. Brearley, were but *thoughts.* All such forces are thoughts.

"Thoughts are things—and you gathered together in this house, by that ancient formula, a thought-thing created by generations of worshippers who have worshipped the moon!

"The light that we saw was only the moonlight, the sounds that we heard were thought-sounds. But so powerful was this mighty thought-force, this centuries-old power which you loosed upon us, that it drove out Miss Ailsa's own thoughts from her mind, bringing what she mistook for sleep; and it implanted itself there!

"She was transformed by that mighty power which for a time dwelled within her. She was as powerful, as awful, as a goddess! None might look upon her and be sane. Hypnotism has similarities with the ancient science of thought—yes! *Suggestion* is the secret of all so-called occult phenomena!"

With his eyes gleaming oddly, he stepped forward, resting his long white hands upon Fairbank's shoulders."

"Doctor," he rumbled, "you have a bruise on your forehead."

"Have I!" said Fairbank, in surprise. "I hadn't noticed it."

"Because it is not a physical bruise; it is a mental bruise, physically reflected! Nearly were you slain, my friend—oh, so nearly! But another force—as great as the force of ancient thought— weakened the blow. Dr. Fairbank, it is fortunate that Miss Ailsa loves you!"

His frank words startled us all.

"Look well at the shape of this little bruise, my friends," continued Moris Klaw. "Mr. Brearley—it is a shape that will be familiar to you. See! it is thus:" (He drew an imaginary outline with his long forefinger)—

"And that is the sign of Isis!"

A CATALOGUE OF SELECTED DOVER BOOKS
IN ALL FIELDS OF INTEREST

A CATALOGUE OF SELECTED DOVER BOOKS
IN ALL FIELDS OF INTEREST

LEATHER TOOLING AND CARVING, Chris H. Groneman. One of few books concentrating on tooling and carving, with complete instructions and grid designs for 39 projects ranging from bookmarks to bags. 148 illustrations. 111pp. 7⅞ x 10.
23061-9 Pa. $2.50

THE CODEX NUTTALL, A PICTURE MANUSCRIPT FROM ANCIENT MEXICO, as first edited by Zelia Nuttall. Only inexpensive edition, in full color, of a pre-Columbian Mexican (Mixtec) book. 88 color plates show kings, gods, heroes, temples, sacrifices. New explanatory, historical introduction by Arthur G. Miller. 96pp. 11⅜ x 8½.
23168-2 Pa. $7.50

AMERICAN PRIMITIVE PAINTING, Jean Lipman. Classic collection of an enduring American tradition. 109 plates, 8 in full color—portraits, landscapes, Biblical and historical scenes, etc., showing family groups, farm life, and so on. 80pp. of lucid text. 8⅜ x 11¼.
22815-0 Pa. $4.00

WILL BRADLEY: HIS GRAPHIC ART, edited by Clarence P. Hornung. Striking collection of work by foremost practitioner of Art Nouveau in America: posters, cover designs, sample pages, advertisements, other illustrations. 97 plates, including 8 in full color and 19 in two colors. 97pp. 9⅜ x 12¼.
20701-3 Pa. $4.00
22120-2 Clothbd. $10.00

THE UNDERGROUND SKETCHBOOK OF JAN FAUST, Jan Faust. 101 bitter, horrifying, black-humorous, penetrating sketches on sex, war, greed, various liberations, etc. Sometimes sexual, but not pornographic. Not for prudish. 101pp. 6½ x 9¼.
22740-5 Pa. $1.50

THE GIBSON GIRL AND HER AMERICA, Charles Dana Gibson. 155 finest drawings of effervescent world of 1900-1910: the Gibson Girl and her loves, amusements, adventures, Mr. Pipp, etc. Selected by E. Gillon; introduction by Henry Pitz. 144pp. 8¼ x 11⅜.
21986-0 Pa. $3.50

STAINED GLASS CRAFT, J.A.F. Divine, G. Blachford. One of the very few books that tell the beginner exactly what he needs to know: planning cuts, making shapes, avoiding design weaknesses, fitting glass, etc. 93 illustrations. 115pp.
22812-6 Pa. $1.50

CREATIVE LITHOGRAPHY AND HOW TO DO IT, Grant Arnold. Lithography as art form: working directly on stone, transfer of drawings, lithotint, mezzotint, color printing; also metal plates. Detailed, thorough. 27 illustrations. 214pp.
21208-4 Pa. $3.00

DESIGN MOTIFS OF ANCIENT MEXICO, Jorge Enciso. Vigorous, powerful ceramic stamp impressions — Maya, Aztec, Toltec, Olmec. Serpents, gods, priests, dancers, etc. 153pp. 6⅛ x 9¼.
20084-1 Pa. $2.50

AMERICAN INDIAN DESIGN AND DECORATION, Leroy Appleton. Full text, plus more than 700 precise drawings of Inca, Maya, Aztec, Pueblo, Plains, NW Coast basketry, sculpture, painting, pottery, sand paintings, metal, etc. 4 plates in color. 279pp. 8⅜ x 11¼.
22704-9 Pa. $4.50

CHINESE LATTICE DESIGNS, Daniel S. Dye. Incredibly beautiful geometric designs: circles, voluted, simple dissections, etc. Inexhaustible source of ideas, motifs. 1239 illustrations. 469pp. 6⅛ x 9¼.
23096-1 Pa. $5.00

JAPANESE DESIGN MOTIFS, Matsuya Co. Mon, or heraldic designs. Over 4000 typical, beautiful designs: birds, animals, flowers, swords, fans, geometric; all beautifully stylized. 213pp. 11⅜ x 8¼.
22874-6 Pa. $5.00

PERSPECTIVE, Jan Vredeman de Vries. 73 perspective plates from 1604 edition; buildings, townscapes, stairways, fantastic scenes. Remarkable for beauty, surrealistic atmosphere; real eye-catchers. Introduction by Adolf Placzek. 74pp. 11⅜ x 8¼.
20186-4 Pa. $2.75

EARLY AMERICAN DESIGN MOTIFS, Suzanne E. Chapman. 497 motifs, designs, from painting on wood, ceramics, appliqué, glassware, samplers, metal work, etc. Florals, landscapes, birds and animals, geometrics, letters, etc. Inexhaustible. Enlarged edition. 138pp. 8⅜ x 11¼.
22985-8 Pa. $3.50
23084-8 Clothbd. $7.95

VICTORIAN STENCILS FOR DESIGN AND DECORATION, edited by E.V. Gillon, Jr. 113 wonderful ornate Victorian pieces from German sources; florals, geometrics; borders, corner pieces; bird motifs, etc. 64pp. 9⅜ x 12¼.
21995-X Pa. $2.75

ART NOUVEAU: AN ANTHOLOGY OF DESIGN AND ILLUSTRATION FROM THE STUDIO, edited by E.V. Gillon, Jr. Graphic arts: book jackets, posters, engravings, illustrations, decorations; Crane, Beardsley, Bradley and many others. Inexhaustible. 92pp. 8⅛ x 11.
22388-4 Pa. $2.50

ORIGINAL ART DECO DESIGNS, William Rowe. First-rate, highly imaginative modern Art Deco frames, borders, compositions, alphabets, florals, insectals, Wurlitzer-types, etc. Much finest modern Art Deco. 80 plates, 8 in color. 8⅜ x 11¼.
22567-4 Pa. $3.00

HANDBOOK OF DESIGNS AND DEVICES, Clarence P. Hornung. Over 1800 basic geometric designs based on circle, triangle, square, scroll, cross, etc. Largest such collection in existence. 261pp.
20125-2 Pa. $2.50

150 MASTERPIECES OF DRAWING, edited by Anthony Toney. 150 plates, early 15th century to end of 18th century; Rembrandt, Michelangelo, Dürer, Fragonard, Watteau, Wouwerman, many others. 150pp. 8⅜ x 11¼. 21032-4 Pa. $3.50

THE GOLDEN AGE OF THE POSTER, Hayward and Blanche Cirker. 70 extraordinary posters in full colors, from Maîtres de l'Affiche, Mucha, Lautrec, Bradley, Cheret, Beardsley, many others. 9⅜ x 12¼. 22753-7 Pa. $4.95
21718-3 Clothbd. $7.95

SIMPLICISSIMUS, selection, translations and text by Stanley Appelbaum. 180 satirical drawings, 16 in full color, from the famous German weekly magazine in the years 1896 to 1926. 24 artists included: Grosz, Kley, Pascin, Kubin, Kollwitz, plus Heine, Thöny, Bruno Paul, others. 172pp. 8½ x 12¼. 23098-8 Pa. $5.00
23099-6 Clothbd. $10.00

THE EARLY WORK OF AUBREY BEARDSLEY, Aubrey Beardsley. 157 plates, 2 in color: Manon Lescaut, Madame Bovary, Morte d'Arthur, Salome, other. Introduction by H. Marillier. 175pp. 8½ x 11. 21816-3 Pa. $3.50

THE LATER WORK OF AUBREY BEARDSLEY, Aubrey Beardsley. Exotic masterpieces of full maturity: Venus and Tannhäuser, Lysistrata, Rape of the Lock, Volpone, Savoy material, etc. 174 plates, 2 in color. 176pp. 8½ x 11. 21817-1 Pa. $4.00

DRAWINGS OF WILLIAM BLAKE, William Blake. 92 plates from Book of Job, Divine Comedy, Paradise Lost, visionary heads, mythological figures, Laocoön, etc. Selection, introduction, commentary by Sir Geoffrey Keynes. 178pp. 8½ x 11. 22303-5 Pa. $3.50

LONDON: A PILGRIMAGE, Gustave Doré, Blanchard Jerrold. Squalor, riches, misery, beauty of mid-Victorian metropolis; 55 wonderful plates, 125 other illustrations, full social, cultural text by Jerrold. 191pp. of text. 8⅛ x 11. 22306-X Pa. $5.00

THE COMPLETE WOODCUTS OF ALBRECHT DÜRER, edited by Dr. W. Kurth. 346 in all: Old Testament, St. Jerome, Passion, Life of Virgin, Apocalypse, many others. Introduction by Campbell Dodgson. 285pp. 8½ x 12¼. 21097-9 Pa. $6.00

THE DISASTERS OF WAR, Francisco Goya. 83 etchings record horrors of Napoleonic wars in Spain and war in general. Reprint of 1st edition, plus 3 additional plates. Introduction by Philip Hofer. 97pp. 9⅜ x 8¼. 21872-4 Pa. $3.00

ENGRAVINGS OF HOGARTH, William Hogarth. 101 of Hogarth's greatest works: Rake's Progress, Harlot's Progress, Illustrations for Hudibras, Midnight Modern Conversation, Before and After, Beer Street and Gin Lane, many more. Full commentary. 256pp. 11 x 14. 22479-1 Pa. $7.00
23023-6 Clothbd. $13.50

PRIMITIVE ART, Franz Boas. Great anthropologist on ceramics, textiles, wood, stone, metal, etc.; patterns, technology, symbols, styles. All areas, but fullest on Northwest Coast Indians. 350 illustrations. 378pp. 20025-6 Pa. $3.50

MOTHER GOOSE'S MELODIES. Facsimile of fabulously rare Munroe and Francis "copyright 1833" Boston edition. Familiar and unusual rhymes, wonderful old woodcut illustrations. Edited by E.F. Bleiler. 128pp. 4½ x 6⅜. 22577-1 Pa. $1.00

MOTHER GOOSE IN HIEROGLYPHICS. Favorite nursery rhymes presented in rebus form for children. Fascinating 1849 edition reproduced in toto, with key. Introduction by E.F. Bleiler. About 400 woodcuts. 64pp. 6⅞ x 5¼. 20745-5 Pa. $1.00

PETER PIPER'S PRACTICAL PRINCIPLES OF PLAIN & PERFECT PRONUNCIATION. Alliterative jingles and tongue-twisters. Reproduction in full of 1830 first American edition. 25 spirited woodcuts. 32pp. 4½ x 6⅜. 22560-7 Pa. $1.00

MARMADUKE MULTIPLY'S MERRY METHOD OF MAKING MINOR MATHEMATICIANS. Fellow to Peter Piper, it teaches multiplication table by catchy rhymes and woodcuts. 1841 Munroe & Francis edition. Edited by E.F. Bleiler. 103pp. 4⅝ x 6.
22773-1 Pa. $1.25
20171-6 Clothbd. $3.00

THE NIGHT BEFORE CHRISTMAS, Clement Moore. Full text, and woodcuts from original 1848 book. Also critical, historical material. 19 illustrations. 40pp. 4⅝ x 6. 22797-9 Pa. $1.00

THE KING OF THE GOLDEN RIVER, John Ruskin. Victorian children's classic of three brothers, their attempts to reach the Golden River, what becomes of them. Facsimile of original 1889 edition. 22 illustrations. 56pp. 4⅝ x 6⅜.
20066-3 Pa. $1.25

DREAMS OF THE RAREBIT FIEND, Winsor McCay. Pioneer cartoon strip, unexcelled for beauty, imagination, in 60 full sequences. Incredible technical virtuosity, wonderful visual wit. Historical introduction. 62pp. 8⅜ x 11¼. 21347-1 Pa. $2.50

THE KATZENJAMMER KIDS, Rudolf Dirks. In full color, 14 strips from 1906-7; full of imagination, characteristic humor. Classic of great historical importance. Introduction by August Derleth. 32pp. 9¼ x 12¼. 23005-8 Pa. $2.00

LITTLE ORPHAN ANNIE AND LITTLE ORPHAN ANNIE IN COSMIC CITY, Harold Gray. Two great sequences from the early strips: our curly-haired heroine defends the Warbucks' financial empire and, then, takes on meanie Phineas P. Pinchpenny. Leapin' lizards! 178pp. 6⅛ x 8⅜. 23107-0 Pa. $2.00

WHEN A FELLER NEEDS A FRIEND, Clare Briggs. 122 cartoons by one of the greatest newspaper cartoonists of the early 20th century — about growing up, making a living, family life, daily frustrations and occasional triumphs. 121pp. 8½ x 9½.
23148-8 Pa. $2.50

THE BEST OF GLUYAS WILLIAMS. 100 drawings by one of America's finest cartoonists: The Day a Cake of Ivory Soap Sank at Proctor & Gamble's, At the Life Insurance Agents' Banquet, and many other gems from the 20's and 30's. 118pp. 8⅜ x 11¼. 22737-5 Pa. $2.50

THE BEST DR. THORNDYKE DETECTIVE STORIES, R. Austin Freeman. The Case of Oscar Brodski, The Moabite Cipher, and 5 other favorites featuring the great scientific detective, plus his long-believed-lost first adventure — 31 New Inn — reprinted here for the first time. Edited by E.F. Bleiler. USO 20388-3 Pa. $3.00

BEST "THINKING MACHINE" DETECTIVE STORIES, Jacques Futrelle. The Problem of Cell 13 and 11 other stories about Prof. Augustus S.F.X. Van Dusen, including two "lost" stories. First reprinting of several. Edited by E.F. Bleiler. 241pp. 20537-1 Pa. $3.00

UNCLE SILAS, J. Sheridan LeFanu. Victorian Gothic mystery novel, considered by many best of period, even better than Collins or Dickens. Wonderful psychological terror. Introduction by Frederick Shroyer. 436pp. 21715-9 Pa. $4.00

BEST DR. POGGIOLI DETECTIVE STORIES, T.S. Stribling. 15 best stories from EQMM and The Saint offer new adventures in Mexico, Florida, Tennessee hills as Poggioli unravels mysteries and combats Count Jalacki. 217pp. 23227-1 Pa. $3.00

EIGHT DIME NOVELS, selected with an introduction by E.F. Bleiler. Adventures of Old King Brady, Frank James, Nick Carter, Deadwood Dick, Buffalo Bill, The Steam Man, Frank Merriwell, and Horatio Alger — 1877 to 1905. Important, entertaining popular literature in facsimile reprint, with original covers. 190pp. 9 x 12. 22975-0 Pa. $3.50

ALICE'S ADVENTURES UNDER GROUND, Lewis Carroll. Facsimile of ms. Carroll gave Alice Liddell in 1864. Different in many ways from final Alice. Handlettered, illustrated by Carroll. Introduction by Martin Gardner. 128pp. 21482-6 Pa. $1.50

ALICE IN WONDERLAND COLORING BOOK, Lewis Carroll. Pictures by John Tenniel. Large-size versions of the famous illustrations of Alice, Cheshire Cat, Mad Hatter and all the others, waiting for your crayons. Abridged text. 36 illustrations. 64pp. 8¼ x 11. 22853-3 Pa. $1.50

AVENTURES D'ALICE AU PAYS DES MERVEILLES, Lewis Carroll. Bué's translation of "Alice" into French, supervised by Carroll himself. Novel way to learn language. (No English text.) 42 Tenniel illustrations. 196pp. 22836-3 Pa. $2.50

MYTHS AND FOLK TALES OF IRELAND, Jeremiah Curtin. 11 stories that are Irish versions of European fairy tales and 9 stories from the Fenian cycle — 20 tales of legend and magic that comprise an essential work in the history of folklore. 256pp. 22430-9 Pa. $3.00

EAST O' THE SUN AND WEST O' THE MOON, George W. Dasent. Only full edition of favorite, wonderful Norwegian fairytales — Why the Sea is Salt, Boots and the Troll, etc. — with 77 illustrations by Kittelsen & Werenskiöld. 418pp. 22521-6 Pa. $4.00

PERRAULT'S FAIRY TALES, Charles Perrault and Gustave Doré. Original versions of Cinderella, Sleeping Beauty, Little Red Riding Hood, etc. in best translation, with 34 wonderful illustrations by Gustave Doré. 117pp. 8⅛ x 11. 22311-6 Pa. $2.50

EARLY NEW ENGLAND GRAVESTONE RUBBINGS, Edmund V. Gillon, Jr. 43 photographs, 226 rubbings show heavily symbolic, macabre, sometimes humorous primitive American art. Up to early 19th century. 207pp. 8⅜ x 11¼.
21380-3 Pa. $4.00

L.J.M. DAGUERRE: THE HISTORY OF THE DIORAMA AND THE DAGUERREOTYPE, Helmut and Alison Gernsheim. Definitive account. Early history, life and work of Daguerre; discovery of daguerreotype process; diffusion abroad; other early photography. 124 illustrations. 226pp. 6⅙ x 9¼.
22290-X Pa. $4.00

PHOTOGRAPHY AND THE AMERICAN SCENE, Robert Taft. The basic book on American photography as art, recording form, 1839-1889. Development, influence on society, great photographers, types (portraits, war, frontier, etc.), whatever else needed. Inexhaustible. Illustrated with 322 early photos, daguerreotypes, tintypes, stereo slides, etc. 546pp. 6⅛ x 9¼.
21201-7 Pa. $5.95

PHOTOGRAPHIC SKETCHBOOK OF THE CIVIL WAR, Alexander Gardner. Reproduction of 1866 volume with 100 on-the-field photographs: Manassas, Lincoln on battlefield, slave pens, etc. Introduction by E.F. Bleiler. 224pp. 10¾ x 9.
22731-6 Pa. $5.00

THE MOVIES: A PICTURE QUIZ BOOK, Stanley Appelbaum & Hayward Cirker. Match stars with their movies, name actors and actresses, test your movie skill with 241 stills from 236 great movies, 1902-1959. Indexes of performers and films. 128pp. 8⅜ x 9¼.
20222-4 Pa. $2.50

THE TALKIES, Richard Griffith. Anthology of features, articles from Photoplay, 1928-1940, reproduced complete. Stars, famous movies, technical features, fabulous ads, etc.; Garbo, Chaplin, King Kong, Lubitsch, etc. 4 color plates, scores of illustrations. 327pp. 8⅜ x 11¼.
22762-6 Pa. $6.95

THE MOVIE MUSICAL FROM VITAPHONE TO "42ND STREET," edited by Miles Kreuger. Relive the rise of the movie musical as reported in the pages of Photoplay magazine (1926-1933): every movie review, cast list, ad, and record review; every significant feature article, production still, biography, forecast, and gossip story. Profusely illustrated. 367pp. 8⅜ x 11¼.
23154-2 Pa. $6.95

JOHANN SEBASTIAN BACH, Philipp Spitta. Great classic of biography, musical commentary, with hundreds of pieces analyzed. Also good for Bach's contemporaries. 450 musical examples. Total of 1799pp.
EUK 22278-0, 22279-9 Clothbd., Two vol. set $25.00

BEETHOVEN AND HIS NINE SYMPHONIES, Sir George Grove. Thorough history, analysis, commentary on symphonies and some related pieces. For either beginner or advanced student. 436 musical passages. 407pp.
20334-4 Pa. $4.00

MOZART AND HIS PIANO CONCERTOS, Cuthbert Girdlestone. The only full-length study. Detailed analyses of all 21 concertos, sources; 417 musical examples. 509pp.
21271-8 Pa. $4.50

THE FITZWILLIAM VIRGINAL BOOK, edited by J. Fuller Maitland, W.B. Squire. Famous early 17th century collection of keyboard music, 300 works by Morley, Byrd, Bull, Gibbons, etc. Modern notation. Total of 938pp. 8⅜ x 11.

ECE 21068-5, 21069-3 Pa., Two vol. set $14.00

COMPLETE STRING QUARTETS, Wolfgang A. Mozart. Breitkopf and Härtel edition. All 23 string quartets plus alternate slow movement to K156. Study score. 277pp. 9⅜ x 12¼.

22372-8 Pa. $6.00

COMPLETE SONG CYCLES, Franz Schubert. Complete piano, vocal music of Die Schöne Müllerin, Die Winterreise, Schwanengesang. Also Drinker English singing translations. Breitkopf and Härtel edition. 217pp. 9⅜ x 12¼.

22649-2 Pa. $4.50

THE COMPLETE PRELUDES AND ETUDES FOR PIANOFORTE SOLO, Alexander Scriabin. All the preludes and etudes including many perfectly spun miniatures. Edited by K.N. Igumnov and Y.I. Mil'shteyn. 250pp. 9 x 12.

22919-X Pa. $5.00

TRISTAN UND ISOLDE, Richard Wagner. Full orchestral score with complete instrumentation. Do not confuse with piano reduction. Commentary by Felix Mottl, great Wagnerian conductor and scholar. Study score. 655pp. 8⅛ x 11.

22915-7 Pa. $10.00

FAVORITE SONGS OF THE NINETIES, ed. Robert Fremont. Full reproduction, including covers, of 88 favorites: Ta-Ra-Ra-Boom-De-Aye, The Band Played On, Bird in a Gilded Cage, Under the Bamboo Tree, After the Ball, etc. 401pp. 9 x 12.

EBE 21536-9 Pa. $6.95

SOUSA'S GREAT MARCHES IN PIANO TRANSCRIPTION: ORIGINAL SHEET MUSIC OF 23 WORKS, John Philip Sousa. Selected by Lester S. Levy. Playing edition includes: The Stars and Stripes Forever, The Thunderer, The Gladiator, King Cotton, Washington Post, much more. 24 illustrations. 111pp. 9 x 12.

USO 23132-1 Pa. $3.50

CLASSIC PIANO RAGS, selected with an introduction by Rudi Blesh. Best ragtime music (1897-1922) by Scott Joplin, James Scott, Joseph F. Lamb, Tom Turpin, 9 others. Printed from best original sheet music, plus covers. 364pp. 9 x 12.

EBE 20469-3 Pa. $6.95

ANALYSIS OF CHINESE CHARACTERS, C.D. Wilder, J.H. Ingram. 1000 most important characters analyzed according to primitives, phonetics, historical development. Traditional method offers mnemonic aid to beginner, intermediate student of Chinese, Japanese. 365pp.

23045-7 Pa. $4.00

MODERN CHINESE: A BASIC COURSE, Faculty of Peking University. Self study, classroom course in modern Mandarin. Records contain phonetics, vocabulary, sentences, lessons. 249 page book contains all recorded text, translations, grammar, vocabulary, exercises. Best course on market. 3 12" 33⅓ monaural records, book, album.

98832-5 Set $12.50

MANUAL OF THE TREES OF NORTH AMERICA, Charles S. Sargent. The basic survey of every native tree and tree-like shrub, 717 species in all. Extremely full descriptions, information on habitat, growth, locales, economics, etc. Necessary to every serious tree lover. Over 100 finding keys. 783 illustrations. Total of 986pp.
20277-1, 20278-X Pa., Two vol. set $8.00

BIRDS OF THE NEW YORK AREA, John Bull. Indispensable guide to more than 400 species within a hundred-mile radius of Manhattan. Information on range, status, breeding, migration, distribution trends, etc. Foreword by Roger Tory Peterson. 17 drawings; maps. 540pp.
23222-0 Pa. $6.00

THE SEA-BEACH AT EBB-TIDE, Augusta Foote Arnold. Identify hundreds of marine plants and animals: algae, seaweeds, squids, crabs, corals, etc. Descriptions cover food, life cycle, size, shape, habitat. Over 600 drawings. 490pp.
21949-6 Pa.$5.00

THE MOTH BOOK, William J. Holland. Identify more than 2,000 moths of North America. General information, precise species descriptions. 623 illustrations plus 48 color plates show almost all species, full size. 1968 edition. Still the basic book. Total of 551pp. 6½ x 9¼.
21948-8 Pa. $6.00

AN INTRODUCTION TO THE REPTILES AND AMPHIBIANS OF THE UNITED STATES, Percy A. Morris. All lizards, crocodiles, turtles, snakes, toads, frogs; life history, identification, habits, suitability as pets, etc. Non-technical, but sound and broad. 130 photos. 253pp.
22982-3 Pa. $3.00

OLD NEW YORK IN EARLY PHOTOGRAPHS, edited by Mary Black. Your only chance to see New York City as it was 1853-1906, through 196 wonderful photographs from N.Y. Historical Society. Great Blizzard, Lincoln's funeral procession, great buildings. 228pp. 9 x 12.
22907-6 Pa. $6.00

THE AMERICAN REVOLUTION, A PICTURE SOURCEBOOK, John Grafton. Wonderful Bicentennial picture source, with 411 illustrations (contemporary and 19th century) showing battles, personalities, maps, events, flags, posters, soldier's life, ships, etc. all captioned and explained. A wonderful browsing book, supplement to other historical reading. 160pp. 9 x 12.
23226-3 Pa. $4.00

PERSONAL NARRATIVE OF A PILGRIMAGE TO AL-MADINAH AND MECCAH, Richard Burton. Great travel classic by remarkably colorful personality. Burton, disguised as a Moroccan, visited sacred shrines of Islam, narrowly escaping death. Wonderful observations of Islamic life, customs, personalities. 47 illustrations. Total of 959pp.
21217-3, 21218-1 Pa., Two vol. set$10.00

INCIDENTS OF TRAVEL IN CENTRAL AMERICA, CHIAPAS, AND YUCATAN, John L. Stephens. Almost single-handed discovery of Maya culture; exploration of ruined cities, monuments, temples; customs of Indians. 115 drawings. 892pp.
22404-X, 22405-8 Pa., Two vol. set $8.00

CONSTRUCTION OF AMERICAN FURNITURE TREASURES, Lester Margon. 344 detail drawings, complete text on constructing exact reproductions of 38 early American masterpieces: Hepplewhite sideboard, Duncan Phyfe drop-leaf table, mantel clock, gate-leg dining table, Pa. German cupboard, more. 38 plates. 54 photographs. 168pp. 8⅜ x 11¼. 23056-2 Pa. $4.00

JEWELRY MAKING AND DESIGN, Augustus F. Rose, Antonio Cirino. Professional secrets revealed in thorough, practical guide: tools, materials, processes; rings, brooches, chains, cast pieces, enamelling, setting stones, etc. Do not confuse with skimpy introductions: beginner can use, professional can learn from it. Over 200 illustrations. 306pp. 21750-7 Pa. $3.00

METALWORK AND ENAMELLING, Herbert Maryon. Generally conceded best all-around book. Countless trade secrets: materials, tools, soldering, filigree, setting, inlay, niello, repoussé, casting, polishing, etc. For beginner or expert. Author was foremost British expert. 330 illustrations. 335pp. 22702-2 Pa. $3.50

WEAVING WITH FOOT-POWER LOOMS, Edward F. Worst. Setting up a loom, beginning to weave, constructing equipment, using dyes, more, plus over 285 drafts of traditional patterns including Colonial and Swedish weaves. More than 200 other figures. For beginning and advanced. 275pp. 8¾ x 6⅜. 23064-3 Pa. $4.00

WEAVING A NAVAJO BLANKET, Gladys A. Reichard. Foremost anthropologist studied under Navajo women, reveals every step in process from wool, dyeing, spinning, setting up loom, designing, weaving. Much history, symbolism. With this book you could make one yourself. 97 illustrations. 222pp. 22992-0 Pa. $3.00

NATURAL DYES AND HOME DYEING, Rita J. Adrosko. Use natural ingredients: bark, flowers, leaves, lichens, insects etc. Over 135 specific recipes from historical sources for cotton, wool, other fabrics. Genuine premodern handicrafts. 12 illustrations. 160pp. 22688-3 Pa. $2.00

THE HAND DECORATION OF FABRICS, Francis J. Kafka. Outstanding, profusely illustrated guide to stenciling, batik, block printing, tie dyeing, freehand painting, silk screen printing, and novelty decoration. 356 illustrations. 198pp. 6 x 9. 21401-X Pa. $3.00

THOMAS NAST: CARTOONS AND ILLUSTRATIONS, with text by Thomas Nast St. Hill. Father of American political cartooning. Cartoons that destroyed Tweed Ring; inflation, free love, church and state; original Republican elephant and Democratic donkey; Santa Claus; more. 117 illustrations. 146pp. 9 x 12. 22983-1 Pa. $4.00
23067-8 Clothbd. $8.50

FREDERIC REMINGTON: 173 DRAWINGS AND ILLUSTRATIONS. Most famous of the Western artists, most responsible for our myths about the American West in its untamed days. Complete reprinting of *Drawings of Frederic Remington* (1897), plus other selections. 4 additional drawings in color on covers. 140pp. 9 x 12. 20714-5 Pa. $3.95

How to Solve Chess Problems, Kenneth S. Howard. Practical suggestions on problem solving for very beginners. 58 two-move problems, 46 3-movers, 8 4-movers for practice, plus hints. 171pp. 20748-X Pa. $2.00

A Guide to Fairy Chess, Anthony Dickins. 3-D chess, 4-D chess, chess on a cylindrical board, reflecting pieces that bounce off edges, cooperative chess, retrograde chess, maximummers, much more. Most based on work of great Dawson. Full handbook, 100 problems. 66pp. 7⅞ x 10¾. 22687-5 Pa. $2.00

Win at Backgammon, Millard Hopper. Best opening moves, running game, blocking game, back game, tables of odds, etc. Hopper makes the game clear enough for anyone to play, and win. 43 diagrams. 111pp. 22894-0 Pa. $1.50

Bidding a Bridge Hand, Terence Reese. Master player "thinks out loud" the binding of 75 hands that defy point count systems. Organized by bidding problem—no-fit situations, overbidding, underbidding, cueing your defense, etc. 254pp. EBE 22830-4 Pa. $2.50

The Precision Bidding System in Bridge, C.C. Wei, edited by Alan Truscott. Inventor of precision bidding presents average hands and hands from actual play, including games from 1969 Bermuda Bowl where system emerged. 114 exercises. 116pp. 21171-1 Pa. $1.75

Learn Magic, Henry Hay. 20 simple, easy-to-follow lessons on magic for the new magician: illusions, card tricks, silks, sleights of hand, coin manipulations, escapes, and more —all with a minimum amount of equipment. Final chapter explains the great stage illusions. 92 illustrations. 285pp. 21238-6 Pa. $2.95

The New Magician's Manual, Walter B. Gibson. Step-by-step instructions and clear illustrations guide the novice in mastering 36 tricks; much equipment supplied on 16 pages of cut-out materials. 36 additional tricks. 64 illustrations. 159pp. 6⅝ x 10. 23113-5 Pa. $3.00

Professional Magic for Amateurs, Walter B. Gibson. 50 easy, effective tricks used by professionals —cards, string, tumblers, handkerchiefs, mental magic, etc. 63 illustrations. 223pp. 23012-0 Pa. $2.50

Card Manipulations, Jean Hugard. Very rich collection of manipulations; has taught thousands of fine magicians tricks that are really workable, eye-catching. Easily followed, serious work. Over 200 illustrations. 163pp. 20539-8 Pa. $2.00

Abbott's Encyclopedia of Rope Tricks for Magicians, Stewart James. Complete reference book for amateur and professional magicians containing more than 150 tricks involving knots, penetrations, cut and restored rope, etc. 510 illustrations. Reprint of 3rd edition. 400pp. 23206-9 Pa. $3.50

The Secrets of Houdini, J.C. Cannell. Classic study of Houdini's incredible magic, exposing closely-kept professional secrets and revealing, in general terms, the whole art of stage magic. 67 illustrations. 279pp. 22913-0 Pa. $2.50

THE MAGIC MOVING PICTURE BOOK, Bliss, Sands & Co. The pictures in this book move! Volcanoes erupt, a house burns, a serpentine dancer wiggles her way through a number. By using a specially ruled acetate screen provided, you can obtain these and 15 other startling effects. Originally "The Motograph Moving Picture Book." 32pp. 8¼ x 11.   23224-7 Pa. $1.75

STRING FIGURES AND HOW TO MAKE THEM, Caroline F. Jayne. Fullest, clearest instructions on string figures from around world: Eskimo, Navajo, Lapp, Europe, more. Cats cradle, moving spear, lightning, stars. Introduction by A.C. Haddon. 950 illustrations. 407pp.   20152-X Pa. $3.00

PAPER FOLDING FOR BEGINNERS, William D. Murray and Francis J. Rigney. Clearest book on market for making origami sail boats, roosters, frogs that move legs, cups, bonbon boxes. 40 projects. More than 275 illustrations. Photographs. 94pp.
20713-7 Pa. $1.25

INDIAN SIGN LANGUAGE, William Tomkins. Over 525 signs developed by Sioux, Blackfoot, Cheyenne, Arapahoe and other tribes. Written instructions and diagrams: how to make words, construct sentences. Also 290 pictographs of Sioux and Ojibway tribes. 111pp. 6⅛ x 9¼.   22029-X Pa. $1.50

BOOMERANGS: HOW TO MAKE AND THROW THEM, Bernard S. Mason. Easy to make and throw, dozens of designs: cross-stick, pinwheel, boomabird, tumblestick, Australian curved stick boomerang. Complete throwing instructions. All safe. 99pp.   23028-7 Pa. $1.50

25 KITES THAT FLY, Leslie Hunt. Full, easy to follow instructions for kites made from inexpensive materials. Many novelties. Reeling, raising, designing your own. 70 illustrations. 110pp.   22550-X Pa. $1.25

TRICKS AND GAMES ON THE POOL TABLE, Fred Herrmann. 79 tricks and games, some solitaires, some for 2 or more players, some competitive; mystifying shots and throws, unusual carom, tricks involving cork, coins, a hat, more. 77 figures. 95pp.   21814-7 Pa. $1.25

WOODCRAFT AND CAMPING, Bernard S. Mason. How to make a quick emergency shelter, select woods that will burn immediately, make do with limited supplies, etc. Also making many things out of wood, rawhide, bark, at camp. Formerly titled Woodcraft. 295 illustrations. 580pp.   21951-8 Pa. $4.00

AN INTRODUCTION TO CHESS MOVES AND TACTICS SIMPLY EXPLAINED, Leonard Barden. Informal intermediate introduction: reasons for moves, tactics, openings, traps, positional play, endgame. Isolates patterns. 102pp. USO 21210-6 Pa. $1.35

LASKER'S MANUAL OF CHESS, Dr. Emanuel Lasker. Great world champion offers very thorough coverage of all aspects of chess. Combinations, position play, openings, endgame, aesthetics of chess, philosophy of struggle, much more. Filled with analyzed games. 390pp.   20640-8 Pa. $3.50

SLEEPING BEAUTY, illustrated by Arthur Rackham. Perhaps the fullest, most delightful version ever, told by C.S. Evans. Rackham's best work. 49 illustrations. 110pp. 7⅞ x 10¾.   22756-1 Pa. $2.00

THE WONDERFUL WIZARD OF OZ, L. Frank Baum. Facsimile in full color of America's finest children's classic. Introduction by Martin Gardner. 143 illustrations by W.W. Denslow. 267pp.   20691-2 Pa. $2.50

GOOPS AND HOW TO BE THEM, Gelett Burgess. Classic tongue-in-cheek masquerading as etiquette book. 87 verses, 170 cartoons as Goops demonstrate virtues of table manners, neatness, courtesy, more. 88pp. 6½ x 9¼.
                                                   22233-0 Pa. $1.50

THE BROWNIES, THEIR BOOK, Palmer Cox. Small as mice, cunning as foxes, exuberant, mischievous, Brownies go to zoo, toy shop, seashore, circus, more. 24 verse adventures. 266 illustrations. 144pp. 6⅝ x 9¼.   21265-3 Pa. $1.75

BILLY WHISKERS: THE AUTOBIOGRAPHY OF A GOAT, Frances Trego Montgomery. Escapades of that rambunctious goat. Favorite from turn of the century America. 24 illustrations. 259pp.   22345-0 Pa. $2.75

THE ROCKET BOOK, Peter Newell. Fritz, janitor's kid, sets off rocket in basement of apartment house; an ingenious hole punched through every page traces course of rocket. 22 duotone drawings, verses. 48pp. 6⅞ x 8⅜.   22044-3 Pa. $1.50

PECK'S BAD BOY AND HIS PA, George W. Peck. Complete double-volume of great American childhood classic. Hennery's ingenious pranks against outraged pomposity of pa and the grocery man. 97 illustrations. Introduction by E.F. Bleiler. 347pp.   20497-9 Pa. $2.50

THE TALE OF PETER RABBIT, Beatrix Potter. The inimitable Peter's terrifying adventure in Mr. McGregor's garden, with all 27 wonderful, full-color Potter illustrations. 55pp. 4¼ x 5½.   USO 22827-4 Pa. $1.00

THE TALE OF MRS. TIGGY-WINKLE, Beatrix Potter. Your child will love this story about a very special hedgehog and all 27 wonderful, full-color Potter illustrations. 57pp. 4¼ x 5½.   USO 20546-0 Pa. $1.00

THE TALE OF BENJAMIN BUNNY, Beatrix Potter. Peter Rabbit's cousin coaxes him back into Mr. McGregor's garden for a whole new set of adventures. A favorite with children. All 27 full-color illustrations. 59pp. 4¼ x 5½.
                                               USO 21102-9 Pa. $1.00

THE MERRY ADVENTURES OF ROBIN HOOD, Howard Pyle. Facsimile of original (1883) edition, finest modern version of English outlaw's adventures. 23 illustrations by Pyle. 296pp. 6½ x 9¼.   22043-5 Pa. $2.75

TWO LITTLE SAVAGES, Ernest Thompson Seton. Adventures of two boys who lived as Indians; explaining Indian ways, woodlore, pioneer methods. 293 illustrations. 286pp.   20985-7 Pa. $3.00

HOUDINI ON MAGIC, Harold Houdini. Edited by Walter Gibson, Morris N. Young. How he escaped; exposés of fake spiritualists; instructions for eye-catching tricks; other fascinating material by and about greatest magician. 155 illustrations. 280pp.   20384-0 Pa. $2.50

HANDBOOK OF THE NUTRITIONAL CONTENTS OF FOOD, U.S. Dept. of Agriculture. Largest, most detailed source of food nutrition information ever prepared. Two mammoth tables: one measuring nutrients in 100 grams of edible portion; the other, in edible portion of 1 pound as purchased. Originally titled Composition of Foods. 190pp. 9 x 12.   21342-0 Pa. $4.00

COMPLETE GUIDE TO HOME CANNING, PRESERVING AND FREEZING, U.S. Dept. of Agriculture. Seven basic manuals with full instructions for jams and jellies; pickles and relishes; canning fruits, vegetables, meat; freezing anything. Really good recipes, exact instructions for optimal results. Save a fortune in food. 156 illustrations. 214pp. 6⅛ x 9¼.   22911-4 Pa. $2.50

THE BREAD TRAY, Louis P. De Gouy. Nearly every bread the cook could buy or make: bread sticks of Italy, fruit breads of Greece, glazed rolls of Vienna, everything from corn pone to croissants. Over 500 recipes altogether. including buns, rolls, muffins, scones, and more. 463pp.   23000-7 Pa. $3.50

CREATIVE HAMBURGER COOKERY, Louis P. De Gouy. 182 unusual recipes for casseroles, meat loaves and hamburgers that turn inexpensive ground meat into memorable main dishes: Arizona chili burgers, burger tamale pie, burger stew, burger corn loaf, burger wine loaf, and more. 120pp.   23001-5 Pa. $1.75

LONG ISLAND SEAFOOD COOKBOOK, J. George Frederick and Jean Joyce. Probably the best American seafood cookbook. Hundreds of recipes. 40 gourmet sauces, 123 recipes using oysters alone! All varieties of fish and seafood amply represented. 324pp.   22677-8 Pa. $3.00

THE EPICUREAN: A COMPLETE TREATISE OF ANALYTICAL AND PRACTICAL STUDIES IN THE CULINARY ART, Charles Ranhofer. Great modern classic. 3,500 recipes from master chef of Delmonico's, turn-of-the-century America's best restaurant. Also explained, many techniques known only to professional chefs. 775 illustrations. 1183pp. 6⅝ x 10.   22680-8 Clothbd. $17.50

THE AMERICAN WINE COOK BOOK, Ted Hatch. Over 700 recipes: old favorites livened up with wine plus many more: Czech fish soup, quince soup, sauce Perigueux, shrimp shortcake, filets Stroganoff, cordon bleu goulash, jambonneau, wine fruit cake, more. 314pp.   22796-0 Pa. $2.50

DELICIOUS VEGETARIAN COOKING, Ivan Baker. Close to 500 delicious and varied recipes: soups, main course dishes (pea, bean, lentil, cheese, vegetable, pasta, and egg dishes), savories, stews, whole-wheat breads and cakes, more. 168pp.
                                                        USO 22834-7 Pa. $1.75

COOKIES FROM MANY LANDS, Josephine Perry. Crullers, oatmeal cookies, chaux au chocolate, English tea cakes, mandel kuchen, Sacher torte, Danish puff pastry, Swedish cookies —a mouth-watering collection of 223 recipes. 157pp.
22832-0 Pa. $2.00

ROSE RECIPES, Eleanour S. Rohde. How to make sauces, jellies, tarts, salads, pot-pourris, sweet bags, pomanders, perfumes from garden roses; all exact recipes. Century old favorites. 95pp.
22957-2 Pa. $1.25

"OSCAR" OF THE WALDORF'S COOKBOOK, Oscar Tschirky. Famous American chef reveals 3455 recipes that made Waldorf great; cream of French, German, American cooking, in all categories. Full instructions, easy home use. 1896 edition. 907pp. 6⅝ x 9⅜.
20790-0 Clothbd. $15.00

JAMS AND JELLIES, May Byron. Over 500 old-time recipes for delicious jams, jellies, marmalades, preserves, and many other items. Probably the largest jam and jelly book in print. Originally titled May Byron's Jam Book. 276pp.
USO 23130-5 Pa. $3.00

MUSHROOM RECIPES, André L. Simon. 110 recipes for everyday and special cooking. Champignons à la grecque, sole bonne femme, chicken liver croustades, more; 9 basic sauces, 13 ways of cooking mushrooms. 54pp.
USO 20913-X Pa. $1.25

FAVORITE SWEDISH RECIPES, edited by Sam Widenfelt. Prepared in Sweden, offers wonderful, clearly explained Swedish dishes: appetizers, meats, pastry and cookies, other categories. Suitable for American kitchen. 90 photos. 157pp.
23156-9 Pa. $2.00

THE BUCKEYE COOKBOOK, Buckeye Publishing Company. Over 1,000 easy-to-follow, traditional recipes from the American Midwest: bread (100 recipes alone), meat, game, jam, candy, cake, ice cream, and many other categories of cooking. 64 illustrations. From 1883 enlarged edition. 416pp.
23218-2 Pa. $4.00

TWENTY-TWO AUTHENTIC BANQUETS FROM INDIA, Robert H. Christie. Complete, easy-to-do recipes for almost 200 authentic Indian dishes assembled in 22 banquets. Arranged by region. Selected from Banquets of the Nations. 192pp.
23200-X Pa. $2.50

Prices subject to change without notice.
Available at your book dealer or write for free catalogue to Dept. GI, Dover Publications, Inc., 180 Varick St., N.Y., N.Y. 10014. Dover publishes more than 150 books each year on science, elementary and advanced mathematics, biology, music, art, literary history, social sciences and other areas.